# A Summons to New Orleans

*a novel*

## Barbara Hall

**Simon & Schuster**
New York London Toronto Sydney Singapore

SIMON & SCHUSTER
Rockefeller Center
1230 Avenue of the Americas
New York, NY 10020

SIMON & SCHUSTER and colophon are registered
trademarks of Simon & Schuster, Inc.

Designed by Elina D. Nudelman
Manufactured in the United States of America

1   3   5   7   9   10   8   6   4   2

Library of Congress Cataloging-in-Publication Data
Hall, Barbara.
A summons to New Orleans : a novel / Barbara Hall.
p.   cm.
1. New Orleans (La.)—Fiction. 2. Female friendship—Fiction.
3. Trials (Rape)—Fiction. 4. Rape victims—Fiction. I. Title.
PS3558.A3585 S86 2000
813'.54—dc21          00-032199
ISBN 0-684-86319-7

For Paul

"Don't you just love those long afternoons in New Orleans when an hour isn't just an hour— but a little piece of eternity dropped into your hands—and who knows what to do with it?"

—Tennessee Williams, *A Streetcar Named Desire*

# A Summons *to* New Orleans

# 1

Nora sat on the four-poster bed, cradling the phone in her lap as if it were a cat. She was trying to think of someone in New Orleans to call. She had to go out, and she didn't think she could do it alone.

Her room was nice enough, with a high ceiling and ornate molding, hardwood floors and antique rugs and mirrors, an armoire, a high-backed sofa with Queen Anne legs, or at least what her mother would call Queen Anne. To her, everything curved was Queen Anne. Maybe this was more like Regency, or one of the Louis, Nora thought, lamenting the fact that she knew so little about antiques, or history, or anything, for that matter. All Nora knew was raising children, and she wasn't even particularly good at that. Or maybe she was just feeling that way because her thirteen-year-old son, Michael, had announced his intention to move in with his father when the school year was over. He did not give her a good reason, but thirteen-year-olds never had reasons for anything, good or bad. They lived deeply rooted in the moment, completely wedded to the now, in a way that would put Buddhist monks to shame.

Her daughter, Annette, was six, and she found her brother's actions to be highly repulsive. Annette put a premium on logic. She was the most literal-minded child Nora had ever encountered. Even though that was age-appropriate, Annette seemed particularly afflicted with linear thinking. Obsessed with fairness, intent on making the numbers add up at every turn, needing answers to the most unanswerable questions. She was a rule-follower, an easy child who never had to be told anything twice. As pleasant as that was to deal with, Nora worried. She worried that Annette was unimaginative, not creative, incapable of feeling joy.

Or maybe Nora was thinking of herself.

New Orleans was supposed to be an antidote to that. As usual, it was Simone who had talked her into doing something so out of character as making this trip. She had called Nora at work one day, and launched immediately into this great vacation she had dreamed up, in New Orleans, right after Jazz Fest, she said, when the hotel rates would be down. She knew all the chefs in town, of course, so they would eat like royalty. There were a lot of single men in New Orleans, and she knew most of them, if Nora was ready for that kind of thing. She'd pay Nora's airfare if she would just please, please, please do an old friend a favor—come spend a week in New Orleans.

At the time, Nora had had a client in her office, a woman, six months' pregnant, whose boyfriend was reluctantly giving in to marriage. She was there with her mother, who was insisting on a proper wedding despite the circumstances. The bride-to-be looked miserable. She was not the least bit interested in the calligraphed invitation that Nora had to offer. This was a business Nora had started after Annette entered the first grade. At home with nothing to do, and trained to do nothing in particular, she taught herself calligraphy and then set up shop doing handwritten invitations and announcements. She was surprised, even now, at how many people were actually interested in this service. She was making money at it. And even as she did it, she couldn't help wondering, who would want to spend that kind of money on fancy, pretentious writing? It was strange, being successful at something that meant nothing to her.

In any event, it was hard for her to respond to Simone's demand, though a generous one, with these miserable people sitting right there across from her, looking as if they were about to be led to their execution.

"Can we talk about this later, Simone? I'm interested, but I'm busy."

"Just say yes," Simone insisted. "That's all you have to do. Say yes."

"The kids are still in school . . ."

"Leave 'em with your mama."

Even though Simone was not the least bit Southern, having been born and raised in Los Angeles, she had developed a strong accent during the time spent at the University of Virginia, despite having moved back to California immediately after her four years were up. Sometimes Nora wondered exactly what those four years had been about. Simone was the daughter of a successful movie executive, and she had been offered modeling contracts right out of high school. There was no need for her to spend four years in Charlottesville, Virginia, hanging out with people like Nora and all her other friends in oxford-cloth button-downs, Top-Siders, khakis, add-a-pearl necklaces, kelly green and navy skirts, and tortoiseshell hair bands, shagging to beach music and pretending to care about basketball and the honor code and Thomas Jefferson. But that was what Simone had done, unapologetically, and during her time there she never even hinted at her life in California. She tried to pass for a Virginian.

"Nora Kay? Are you listening? Leave the kids with your mama and meet me in New Orleans. When are you going to get a chance like this again?"

"But what's it for?" Nora asked. She always needed a reason to get on a plane.

"For fun. Think about having some before you die."

"But why New Orleans?"

"Only a person who's never been there could ask that question. God's sake, Nora. How many things have I ever asked you for in my life? I need this. I need you to help me."

This gave Nora pause. Simone often demanded, but Nora could not remember the last time she really needed anything.

"Well, okay, let me think about it," Nora had said, but she knew that meant yes. She knew she was going. Out of curiosity, if nothing else.

Now here she was, alone in the Collier House, a charming nineteenth-century town house with wrought-iron railings and open courtyards and fountains and cats and ferns and black men in starched white jackets hurrying around, their keys jangling. She could hear distant laughter and the occasional sound of a horse and carriage clopping down Chartres Street. The air was thick and humid, even more humid than back home, and bugs as big as mice crawled around on the bricks outside, and there was a faint sweet-and-sour stench to the place, an amalgam of stale water and garlic and smoke and pungent flowers. It was getting close to seven o'clock and the sky was washed with that sad, retreating light, enhancing the general atmosphere of romantic decay, and music was starting to drift up from somewhere. Probably from Bourbon Street, she imagined, though she couldn't really imagine what Bourbon Street was. She had heard it was a big deal, always lively, a favorite area for pickpockets, but basically safe. "Generally safe." This was what she was told about the Quarter. When she checked in, the clerk had taken a map and blacked out the streets of the Quarter where she should not go—nothing beyond Dauphine, he said, and blacked out that area with a pen.

"Beyond here, thar be dragons?" Nora questioned.

The clerk had smiled but did not answer. It was hard for her to imagine living in a place where streets had to be struck from a map, places declared off limits, like a haunted forest.

Still, lovely as this setting was, and as exciting and historic and educational as the city seemed from a distance, Nora did not feel festive. She felt icky, as Annette might say. She had a low-level sense of unease. She knew it might be coming from the fact that she never really went anywhere alone, hardly ever to a strange city, and she certainly never left her children with her mother. Her mother, who had stoically (if not, in fact, proudly) submitted to the nickname Boo years before Nora was born, was walking that fine line between mean and crazy. Everyone knew she was mean, there was no disputing it. There was only a question of when she would no longer be able to control that meanness, thus rendering her unpredictable, mentally unstable enough to be put away. Michael and Annette found her amusing, and harmless enough. She was not mean to them, ever. Instead, she entertained them by informing them of just what a troublemaking hellion their mother had been in her day, and by regaling them with all the bad choices Nora had made in her life, including marrying that Braxton man, "your father, sorry to speak against him, but look how he's behaved, y'all deserved better than that, and I tried to tell her, I tried as God is my witness, but her head has always been hard as a rock and she's never been scared of the devil. . . ."

Nora pictured it, her children eating bologna sandwiches and bruising each other with their knees under the Formica kitchen table, while Grandma Boo rattled on. Michael was probably not going to be so tolerant of criticism of his father, and it would serve Boo right to get an earful from him. *But God help Michael,* Nora thought, *if he dares to talk back. Then again, that might do* him *some good.*

Her life felt completely out of control.

The phone in her lap rang and she jumped and threw it to the ground, as if it had burned her.

She scrambled for the receiver and said, "I'm sorry about that."

"Mrs. Braxton?" It was a man's voice, sweet and slow and Southern. "This is Jerome at the front desk."

"Oh, yes. What can I do for you?" she said. She realized that she had started to talk to everyone as if they were potential clients.

Jerome laughed and said, "Well, I was going to ask you the same thing, Mrs. Braxton. Just wanted to let you know that you did receive a message from a Mr. Simon Gray. That was at six thirty-five, by way of a facsimile."

"Simone," Nora said. "I think that's Simone Gray. It's a she."

"Okay," Jerome said, as if he had no objection. "And the message is, Mrs. Gray will not be arriving today."

"Miss," Nora said, flustered, then corrected herself. "I mean, Ms., Ms. Gray."

"Yes, ma'am."

"And you're supposed to know her. She's supposed to be well known by the owners of the hotel."

"Well, maybe she is. I just work here on occasion. Is there anything we can do for you, Mrs. Braxton? Any dinner reservations you'd like us to make?"

"Wait a minute. What do you mean, she's not coming?"

"Would you like me to read the fax to you?"

"Yes, please."

"'Dear Nora, Sorry, but I won't make it in today. See you tomorrow. Explain later.'"

"That's it?"

"Yes, ma'am."

"I came here for her. She talked me into it. She paid my airfare."

"Yes, ma'am."

"And she's not coming? What am I going to do in New Orleans? I don't know anyone in New Orleans."

"I could help you with dinner reservations. We recommend Nola's in the Quarter. It's a short walk, but you do need reservations."

"I don't want to go out to eat."

"All right."

"Did she leave a number?"

"Just a fax number, ma'am. Would you like to send a fax?"

"No," Nora said. She felt petulant and hopeless, and now she understood why Michael got into these moods, where every suggestion she made to him was answered by an irascible "No." When a situation got irritating enough, all solutions were annoying, simply by being solutions. Seeing your way out of the fix was a form of defeat, because it was the fix you didn't want to begin with. Nora wanted Simone to arrive and show her around New Orleans, and take her mind off her kids back in Virginia, sitting at the kitchen table with her crazy mother. But this was not going to happen. Not tonight, anyway.

She did not want to hate Simone. Could not, in fact, hate Simone. Never could. She loved her the way she loved men who were bad for her. Loved her shortcomings as much if not more than her virtues. After all, if Simone were a different sort of person, she would not have found herself in New Orleans, about to embark on an adventure. That was the good news and the bad news.

"No," Nora said, "no fax. Just . . . I don't know. Just give me . . . give me room service."

"We don't have room service, ma'am. There is an honor bar outside your door. And, of course, I'd be happy to help you with reservations . . ."

"No, thank you, I'll figure something out."

She placed the phone on the bedside table and continued to sit, staring at the coffee stain on her black sundress, a mishap during turbulence on the plane, which made her feel a little depressed about herself, remembering that no matter how many frivolous trips she embarked on, and how hard she tried to be sophisticated and adventurous, she was basically a spiller of things. A mess-maker. This tendency had caused her, in recent years, to start dressing in black almost exclusively. She was tired of trying to get mustard and tea and wine out of pastel-colored blouses, and anyway, she just felt like wearing black. It suited her these days, and in a perverse way she enjoyed going against the grain. If she lived in New York, it would be one thing. But in Charlottesville, Virginia, no one wore black unless they were going to a funeral. Michael didn't pay much attention to her dressing habits, didn't pay much attention to her, period, but Annette was supremely embarrassed by her mother's recent fashion trend.

"Other mothers don't go around wearing black," she often accused.

Nora wanted to say, "Other mothers didn't have their husbands leave them for a twenty-eight-year-old waitress, and then run away to Florida to escape paying back taxes in Virginia, and ruin their credit and leave them liable for his debts and make them take up an odd occupation like calligraphed invitations, now, did they?" How she longed to say some inappropriate thing like that to her children, who still blamed her for the breakup, and suspected her of infidelity or of being a bad homemaker or just a persistent nag—some shortcoming that had caused their perfect father to up and disappear.

"You're a fool to protect them from the truth," Boo often said to her. Hissed at her, actually. "Cliff Braxton is no better than a common criminal, and they deserve to know it."

"They'll know it soon enough, Mama, and what's the point of breaking their hearts now?"

"All right, then," Boo said, sneering. "You'll learn your lesson the hard way, but don't come crying to me, sister."

All her life, Nora had been warned against crying to her mother, and she never had and never would. Still, Boo warned against it on an almost daily basis. She was seventy-five now, and determined to see some satisfaction before she went to her grave.

She crossed the room and parted her curtains. It was barely light outside, and the crickets and cicadas were making their crazy death sounds beneath her window, and the doleful sound of the music from Bourbon Street was getting louder. Nora thought, *What the hell, I'm in New Orleans.* She went to the mirror in the big marble bathroom and brushed her hair and put on some makeup. Her hair was short and an expensive blond color. When it caught the light, it looked natural.

Ray, her gay hairdresser, had promised her it would change her life. "Nobody will know the truth but you and your sweet Jesus." And it was true that her hair looked good, but it didn't seem to belong on her. She felt she should look more depressed. Cutting her hair had made her look younger and thinner and generally more together. It was not in keeping with how her insides felt, all churned up and perpetually queasy with dread. She did not care that Cliff was sleeping with June Ann or anybody else, but it was embarrassing to have your marriage fail in such a way that it made the papers. Most people could crawl off and lick their wounds in private. Irreconcilable differences, she could have said to people, letting them wonder. But no, there the story was on page 3 of the local paper—"Town Council Member Pursued by IRS." The article went on to say that he had last been spotted outside Montgomery, Alabama. People knowing of his whereabouts were asked to notify the local authorities or the FBI.

Nora knew where he was. He was in Miami, but she wasn't about to surrender that information. Extraditing Cliff would only mean more embarrassment for her and her children. She just decided to let him stay put. He occasionally sent child-support checks, and she was afraid that if he were brought to justice, those might stop. Was that wrong, she asked herself, to protect him from the law so she could put food in her children's mouths? If it was, she'd just have to live with it. He owed her more than he owed the government.

She had not told Simone why she and Cliff broke up. Simone might know anyway—she seemed to know everything—but she was nice enough to let it go as a simple divorce. She was even nice enough to say that Cliff had never been good enough for her, that now she could find herself a real man. Simone had never been married. Lately, Nora wondered if she might be gay, but she knew that was stupid be-

cause Simone had dated nearly every man who mattered at
UVA. Tall, skinny, with Cher-like black hair (the Sonny era),
and full of that great aloof quality—indifference mixed with a
sheltered intelligence—Simone never had any trouble attract-
ing either men or women. She had a great sense of humility,
either real or convincingly affected, which made her impossible to dislike. She was a listener, a quizzer. She liked to know
about other people's problems and rarely volunteered her
own. She was the person Nora always turned to when life
seemed bleak and unimaginative. Simone could make her
laugh. Simone could make her own life seem exciting, just by
commenting on it. Like when she told her about her
breakup.

"Oh, my God!" she exclaimed. "Nora Kay, imagine you,
out there for two seconds, a single woman. You'll have men
breaking in your windows. With your brains, and that figure,
and those adorable babies, who wouldn't want you? This is
going to be the most exciting time of your life. What an opportunity, to get back out there, knowing what you know.
Now you can really start to live."

It was a nice enough thing to say, but so far from the truth
that Nora didn't even feel obligated to point out that fact. It
was true that she still looked pretty good. Her face was apple-
shaped, and all that acne in high school really had paid off
(oily skin, no wrinkles, as her mother had promised). Now
from a distance she looked like someone in her twenties. And
her children were beautiful, and she did have some life experience stored up, but no man would break her windows or
anything else. They wouldn't because she wouldn't let them.
She was, and always had been, mildly afraid of men. Not
afraid that they would hurt her, but afraid that she would
hurt them, with her quick tongue and impatient nature. She
had a history of being mean to men, and she had no real idea

why. Except for the fact that her mother had hated her father with a special intensity usually found only in skinheads or sociopaths. They had stayed married, though, letting their hatred breed unrestrained, multiplying until it finally had killed her father. *The angrier of the species survives,* Nora thought.

Cliff was the first man who had ever left her. He left her for a woman with no scars, visible or otherwise.

*Hell, I'm going out,* Nora decided. *I'm in New Orleans, and I never get to go anywhere, and it's generally safe. Tomorrow I'll figure out what I'm going to do.*

# 2

People were coming out onto the streets of the city like bugs after dark. They were tourists mostly, in khaki shorts and T-shirts, with cameras and fanny packs and shopping bags. Knots of young people moved along clutching plastic cups of alcohol, moving without much purpose. The horse-and-buggies moved through the streets, and the drivers intoned to their passengers about this or that being the oldest city in the Mississippi Valley. As Nora looked about her, everyone seemed anonymous, yet she could feel people looking at her as if she didn't belong. She walked with her purse swinging and bumping against her hip, her arms crossed over her stomach. Simone had once told her in college that she walked as if she were always leaving an argument. But in a strange city, this did not seem like a bad way to walk.

As she approached Jackson Square, it occurred to her that she had friends who lived in New Orleans, people she had known at UVA whom she now barely remembered. Some big guy, desperately overweight even then, probably more so now, who was always having Sazerac parties in his dorm room. They called him "Gentle Ben," but she couldn't remember his last name. Then there was Frankie, the gay black cheerleader who would tap-dance on command and do an Amos 'n' Andy impersonation, and generally insist on humiliating himself with the Southern stereotype. His last name was Harris, wasn't it? But she couldn't call him. He wouldn't remember her.

Then there was Poppy Marchand. Well, Poppy. Of course, there was always Poppy. She had been one of Nora's and Simone's best friends. They had all lived in a house together in their fourth year, along with a few other floaters, people who claimed to live there but who were rarely seen. Nora, Simone and Poppy had been the only constants there in that house near Vinegar Hill. They made the cooking and cleaning charts and stuck to them. They studied together and went to parties together and discussed their futures late at night while drinking or getting stoned. Poppy was from one of the oldest families in New Orleans, and her parents were rich—this they knew without ever being told it. Yet Poppy was reticent about her past, volunteering nothing except how much she hated her hometown, and how she never intended to return there. Poppy had been one of those girls whose father was the head of a krewe, and her mother had been a Mardi Gras princess or queen or whatever, and Poppy had been expected to move back home and carry on the tradition. She never said exactly why this whole business seemed so abhorrent to her, but she insisted that she would head north after graduation, and indeed she had. In fact, the last Nora had heard of Poppy, she was living in England, an artist, and had gotten a few paintings in the Tate Gallery. The truth was, she had lost touch with Poppy even before they graduated. In the last days at UVA, Poppy had withdrawn, seemingly into her studies, but really into herself. She no longer joined them for taco dinners in front of *Charlie's Angels* reruns; she didn't go with them to parties, and she dropped out of the intramural tennis team they all had played on.

"Poppy has begun her retreat," Simone used to say whenever Poppy decided to disappear. She did that a lot, but she always came out of it, except at the end.

Poppy seemed like a delicate creature: small and thin, with shiny brown hair that curled under like in old movies. She wore headbands and knee-length skirts and white blouses with a pearl necklace always nestled at her throat. She spoke several languages and had been all over the world and was a great athlete, despite her small build. She was a cox on the women's eights rowing crew, and she could have made the tennis team if she had wanted to. But Poppy always seemed to have some distant goal in mind. She was an artist, no doubt about it, and she pursued that above all else. Her paintings took up the whole apartment, and the others stepped around them, giving them a perfect right to be there.

Nora had been afraid of Poppy. Afraid to engage her in any kind of debate or meaningful conversation, afraid she would be defeated, afraid that Poppy might suddenly tell her something she didn't want to know about herself. But she had loved Poppy, too. Every now and then they had gone out drinking together, and Poppy would get a loose tongue after a few light beers and start talking about how meaningless it all was, this crazy, careless life they led at college, this notion that they all had achieved something by stumbling along the grounds that Thomas Jefferson had built, as if they had anything to gain from it. Mr. Jefferson had not envisioned keg parties or Easters or fraternities. He believed in liberty through knowledge, education, enlightenment. Poppy was the only person Nora knew who took Thomas Jefferson seriously. Poppy was the only person she knew who had ever turned anyone in under the honor code. She had witnessed someone cheating on a final English exam, and she had told. The student was expelled. Poppy had no regrets.

Nora wondered if that kind of vigilance was a virtue. Had it served anyone? Everyone cheated in college. Maybe because they knew that everyone cheated in the real world as well. Nora had never had to cheat because she found English to be such an easy major—speculating on Jane Austen or Shakespeare or James Joyce while the rest of the college slaved away at math equations or historic analysis seemed unfair to her. Her major was open to interpretation, certainly, and it relied in large part on the ability to bullshit during an essay.

Nora knew she would not try to call Poppy Marchand. There was almost no chance she had settled in New Orleans, and even if she had, Nora would not know what to say to her. They had not spoken since graduation.

Nora paused to listen to the street musicians in Jackson Square, but they weren't very impressive. They played rattly old guitars and squeaky trumpets, and one guy rubbed sticks up and down a washboard. Tourists paid attention, however, gathering around them as if they were eating fire. They took pictures. She moved past the spectacle, her arms still crossed, making her way to the more commercial end of the street.

She turned right just past the square and walked the two blocks up to Bourbon Street. As she walked, it occurred to her that New Orleans was a city that seemed always closed, despite its activity. It had that desolate, hollow feeling of a sleepy town on a Sunday afternoon. Or perhaps the scary feeling of a place on the verge of a revolution, a hushed sort of danger settling in the stale air.

Once she arrived at Bourbon Street, of course, everything changed. The city unfolded around her, full of noise and chaos and drunken activity. Tourists were everywhere, stumbling against each other and laughing much louder than they would have in any other setting. So much music, and it all merged, creating a nerve-jangling racket. There were hustlers outside all the clubs, men dressed in white shirts and black pants, waving people into the places with halfhearted enthusiasm. She continued to walk with her arms crossed, her purse now actually starting to hurt her as it hit against her thigh. Her breath came fast, and she was glad she was there, amazed she was there, and at the same time she wanted to be back in her hotel room, or, better yet, back at home watching *America's Most Wanted* with her children sleeping down the hall. Had her mother put them to bed yet? Why hadn't she called home? she thought suddenly. She was out of her league, out of control.

She noticed some men staring at her. A few of them actually attempted to talk to her, but she just kept walking. Whenever men noticed her, Nora felt something akin to rage bubbling up inside her. It had been years since she had been comfortable with that kind of attention, if ever. She had married Cliff right out of college, and had dated him for a year before graduating. So it had been about fifteen years since she had had any tolerance for flirtation. Was it harmless? It was hard to remember. Those men who lurched in her direction or winked or called her "baby"—did they have any kind of decent intention? Was that how it all began, or did serious, respectful attention occur in some other mutated form? She could distantly recall, like something she had daydreamed as a child, a time when turning a man's head was a goal, a thing to aspire to. But even back then, did she think those men were worthy or pathetic? After all, she had met Cliff at a keg party at UVA, when she was starting her fourth year and he was starting his last year in grad school. But he hadn't winked or lurched. He had offered her a beer and asked if she was in the business school, and things had just evolved from there. He seemed so serious; it took her a long time to figure out that he was interested in her.

But that, too, was just a trap. He had led her down a very circuitous path to humiliation. He had respected her, wooed her conventionally, married her in a proper ceremony at the Boar's Head Inn, moved her into a beautiful home just outside the city, impregnated her twice. Then, when she was beyond being much use to anyone, he abandoned her for a waitress.

All in all, she told herself, a one-night stand would have been better.

*I have to get over this,* she thought, making her way down Bourbon Street, being bumped by all the people who had left their manners back home, who had given themselves permission to be assholes in public. This was New Orleans, for God's sake, the birthplace of jazz, reportedly home to every vice imaginable, a place where no one was expected to behave. People were just here to have a good time, and Nora was conscious of her own puritanical nature, dressed in black, sneering at everyone, and feeling superior and angry and righteously alone.

*I have to stop hating men,* she reminded herself. It was not going to get her anywhere she wanted to be. God knows she did not want to be a man-hating feminist, or even one of those temporary man-haters, claiming to despise them all until one of them stepped up, someone with a six-figure salary and a willingness to fuck her and take her children out to dinner on Sunday evenings. Hadn't she always frowned on those people, the women she saw at the gym or her poetry-writing extension courses or her book club? Women in stretch pants and oversized denim shirts and espadrilles, defending Hillary Clinton and Janet Reno while hurling invectives at Jennifer Flowers and Monica Lewinsky, as if there were any significant difference between those types? Women always looking for other angry female authority figures to define their own misguided sense of individuality. She thought they were sad back then. Sad, and funny, and completely worthy of her disdain. She was married then. She could afford to sneer.

"Are you having an affair?" she had asked Cliff, straight out, the night he came home late, reeking of perfume. There already had been other clues. Hang-up calls, and strange numbers on the phone bill, and a lack of interest in sex, and a persistent crankiness, a constant, low-level needling about her housekeeping habits and her appearance. ("Do you have anything besides sweat pants? Do you ever think about buying new lingerie? When was the last time you put on a bathing suit?") She had ignored all the signs, the way she had ignored certain things about her children, hoping it would all go away. Like how she had allowed her son to sleep in their bed until he was seven, and she was still in denial about her daughter's compulsive chewing. She knew her son was smoking cigarettes in the bathroom, and she prayed they were only regular cigarettes. (But what could she say to her son about pot, when she had smoked an entire plantation's worth during her senior year in college?) She kept waiting for her children to grow out of these dangerous desires. And she had waited for her husband to do the same.

"I can't believe you just said that" was Cliff's response to her accusation.

"Why? Why can't you believe it? I smelled your shirt. You're home late every night. People have told me things."

"You believe everything you hear? You listen to your mother, for God's sake?"

Her mother, in fact, had come up with no concrete evidence over the years, though she had suspected Cliff of everything from mail fraud to murder since the day she met him.

"Just tell me. Are you having an affair?" she had insisted. And while she was thinking of some other approach, some stinging kind of question that might leave him breathless, he just sighed and said, "Yeah, okay, what do you want to do?"

She had not known how to answer him. She didn't know what to do. She fully expected to spend a few more months accusing him and collecting his denials like weapons to use against him. But there it was, out in the open, and she stood holding his honesty in her hands like a grenade.

Though it seemed like a lifetime away, that was only four months ago. She had felt so smug in her isolation for a while, expecting to be rewarded for being left. At first she expected Cliff to come back, but then he fled the state, and all the nastiness surrounding his illegal activities surfaced, and she knew she couldn't want him anymore, so she began to hope for his demise. It didn't come. Even though he broke the law every day, simply by getting out of bed and breathing, he was living a fairly contented life in Miami with June Ann, the waitress from the Red Lobster.

Nora remembered, with a shudder, the time she and Cliff had gone to the Red Lobster on their anniversary, and June Ann had waited on them. She hadn't a clue at the time, but she now realized the two of them were deep into their affair by then, and for some reason she could recall all the metaphors they engaged in while placing their order.

"I'll have the spicy clams," Cliff had said. "My wife will have the cold seafood plate."

"The clams are very spicy now," June Ann had said. "They could burn your mouth. They are hard to digest, some people say."

"I'll take my chances," Cliff had said. "But my wife likes hers cold. Very cold."

"I'll make sure it's chilled," June Ann had said.

Confused, Nora had said, "It doesn't have to be chilled. I just want the cold shrimp platter."

"With lemon?" June Ann had asked.

"Yes," Cliff had said. "She likes it sour, too."

June Ann had smiled down at her order pad, unable to look at Nora.

How could she have been so stupid, so naïve?

Of course, she wasn't naïve. She had always known but had not wanted to know, would have done anything to avoid facing what was heading toward her at the pace and height of a tidal wave.

But a waitress? A *waitress*? Okay, a graduate student at UVA, but that didn't make it any better. When she had learned the truth, the cliché of it had bothered her more than anything.

"You're more creative than that, aren't you?" she had asked Cliff. "Fucking a student? Jesus, aren't you even embarrassed? Don't you have a shred of dignity left?"

Apparently not.

*I must not let this whole thing bring me down to his level,* Nora thought as she continued to meander along Bourbon Street. She should see this outing as an awakening, a new part of her journey. Trouble was, she hated her journey. She had always hated journeys and until four months ago had figured she was through with hers. She disliked emotional growth. She didn't want to do this anymore, didn't want to discover anything else about herself. Her new therapist said she should see this change as an opportunity.

"You don't understand," Nora had told her. "I saw my later years as a freedom from opportunity. I thought I was through with all that. I was looking forward to the resolution. I hated my youth. I hated all that soul-searching. I wanted to find the good parking space in life. I wanted to be settled."

"Life isn't like that," her therapist had assured her. "You are constantly evolving, or should be."

"Then, when the hell do you rest?"

"When you're dead, I suppose," her terminally cheerful therapist had replied.

"But you can't enjoy it then."

"Well, Nora, you've never really seemed to enjoy your life. Isn't that true?"

It was true. Nora didn't think life was something to be enjoyed. It was something to be endured. But she didn't think this really set her apart much from the rest of the human race.

But now, as she made her way down Bourbon Street, deflecting the glances of strange men, men of all ages and sizes and degrees of inebriation, she wondered if she could even contemplate dating. What would that look like? A guy would call her up and ask her to dinner, and she'd hire a baby-sitter and explain the situation to her kids, and then she'd go with him to some cheap Italian restaurant and they'd pretend to love the linguine with clam sauce and talk about their upbringings and what they majored in in college. They'd talk about their failed marriages and their kids, and maybe they'd take a walk down the street and have ice cream, and they'd pretend to feel all young and carefree because they were eating mint chocolate chip, which they claimed never to indulge in, and they'd talk about how much better music was in their day and maybe, later, at her front door, they would kiss. Oh, God, what would it feel like to kiss? She hadn't kissed a man in years. She and Cliff did not kiss anymore. Occasionally, their lips would collide, their faces sliding away from each other as they struggled to make love. And they did struggle toward the end, pursuing it like some tiresome but necessary exercise. It was like the Lifecycle at the gym. You dreaded it, then liked it a little, then finally it was over. And when it was over, she appreciated the sweat and the effort and she felt noble, as if she had gone to church, done a good deed.

Finally settling on a bar, she ordered a hurricane, the city's must-have drink, and sipped it, standing on the street, watching people go past. The atmosphere reminded her of college, or Easters in particular. Sometimes when she thought of the Charlottesville of her college days, it seemed like a completely different place than where she lived now. She felt disconnected from the UVA students now. They all seemed so young and serious. Was she like that? Did she ever take college seriously? She did her work, she made her plans, she was responsible. But serious? She was serious about everything now, it seemed. Particularly her children. She didn't miss them, she realized, as she stood there watching the revelers. She needed a break from them, needed to escape the feeling that they were her sole purpose in life. There was a whole entire phase of her life when children didn't enter her consciousness, didn't influence her at all. She had had one abortion in college (not thanks to Cliff, nor anyone in particular, just some guy), and she never thought about that child, never mourned its loss, didn't even think of it as a child, in fact. Thought of it as a bad weekend.

Was she evil? Was she bad not to think of her dead child?

The drink went right to her head, and she decided to walk back to her hotel. She wanted to get in the bathtub and feel sorry for herself. She walked until she reached St. Ann, and she turned down it and started toward her hotel on Chartres. There was one stretch of street, beyond the hotels, that was quiet and empty. And just as she approached it, she saw two men walking in her direction. Her heart sped up and she thought she might die. She thought about crossing the street but it was too late. They were upon her.

"Excuse me," one said, "do you know what time it is?"

She looked around and could see no one near her. *How stupid is this,* she thought, *turning a corner and walking into this kind of danger. I have children at home.*

The men looked harmless, barely twenty, black, clean-cut, and she thought, *All criminals probably look harmless.* She recalled a self-defense class she had taken that had instructed her never to respond to a stranger's question, particularly if it was about the time. That was an old trap. She crossed the street, but they crossed it with her.

"Did you hear me?" one of the men said. "We wanted to know if you had the time?"

"No," Nora said.

"No? That looks like a watch right there on your arm."

"Well, actually, yes, but it's on Virginia time, which is an hour later, so it wouldn't be correct."

They stared at her as if she might be too stupid to rob.

Suddenly a sound came through, the blaring of a car horn. They all looked up. A car swerved in their direction, pulling up almost on the sidewalk. It was a cab, and the driver jumped out and said, "You need a ride?"

"Yes," Nora said.

He opened the back door for her and she got in.

"Jesus, lady," he said. "You were about to be mugged. Don't you know that?"

Nora didn't know what to say. She thought perhaps she could have talked them out of it, and she was strangely disappointed that she didn't get the opportunity.

The cab driver looked like Orson Welles in *Citizen Kane*. He had a wide forehead and black hair (retreating), and that wide, round baby face with intense dark eyes. Handsome in a babyish kind of way, and on the verge of becoming too heavy.

Could she date this man? Could she kiss him? she wondered irrationally.

"I'm only going two blocks," she told him.

"That's okay," he said. He put the car in gear and pulled away. "Did someone tell you it was safe to walk in the Quarter at this hour?"

"I . . . I don't know," Nora said. She had neglected to ask anyone.

"Well, it's not safe. Jesus, you tourists. This town is a nightmare. It's a Balkan state, for God's sake."

She didn't say anything. She was impressed by his knowledge of politics. As that thought was settling in her mind, she noticed a book on the front seat: *The Collected Works of Jung*.

"Are you a student?" she asked.

"No. I'm a teacher."

"You're a teacher and a cab driver?"

"I'm a public school teacher. Now do you understand?"

"You're pretty cranky, aren't you?"

"I told you, I'm a public school teacher. In New Orleans. Moonlighting as a hack. Would you be cranky?"

"Why don't you move if you hate it here?"

"Kid," he said, lighting a cigarette.

"Boy?"

"Girl. Six. Lives with her mother. Mother wouldn't leave here if there was a goddamned tsunami coming."

"Well, that's admirable," she said. "I mean, that you won't move away from your child. I have a six-year-old daughter, too."

"Why the hell does your husband let you walk around New Orleans alone?"

"Because he's fucking a waitress in Miami."

That shut him up.

He dropped her off in front of the Collier House and gave her his card. LEO GIRARDI, it said.

"Thanks, Leo."

"You ought to care enough about yourself to be careful," he said.

She smiled. "I'll think about that. It's deep, but I've got a lot of time on my hands."

# 3

The courtyard of the Collier House was beautiful, with the trickling slate fountain, the wrought-iron tables and chairs, flames flickering inside tiny votives, and wild, seemingly primitive greens growing up the sienna stone walls. Maybe it was her recent brush with violence, but the atmosphere had a deathlike quality to it. Not death the ugly way, though. Not death at the hands of pubescent muggers on a sidestreet. Death the way it was in literature, according to Thomas Mann or Faulkner or Byron. The place had the feeling of romantic decay, of poetic stagnation and virtuous descent. She found it exciting and invigorating. She thought that if she sat out here long enough, and perhaps smoked a cigarette, or a joint, she could write a poem. She had not done that in years.

Strangely, she was not particularly upset by her mishap on the street. She did not believe it, for one thing. Despite Leo Girardi's harsh warnings, she simply couldn't believe those men had been about to rob her. It was the small-town Virginian in her, but she still thought of muggers as being a lot more menacing than these boys. They didn't have a weapon. One of the kids had on a Chicago Bulls sweatshirt, like the one her son had. Even if they had asked for her belongings, she had the sense that they would have done it as politely as possible. It was stupid to think that, of course, and she knew perfectly well that people who had never experienced violence had a hard time picturing it happening to them. A nimbus of disbelief surrounded her, and she was certain that that made her the perfect victim. She would have to try harder to feel afraid.

She did not want to go to her room yet. It was pleasant out in the courtyard, and the honor bar looked inviting, all those different-colored bottles glistening under a pale yellow light. She contemplated the selection and finally poured herself a gin and tonic, which seemed fitting. She dropped a slice of lemon in it and licked her fingers, and stared up at the stars, which were out in force, sharp pinpoints of light across a violet-black sky. She felt young, suddenly, and it occurred to her that something good could happen to her.

She walked to the back of the courtyard to be nearer to the fountain, and as she turned a corner she noticed someone sitting at one of the tables. It was a woman, hunched over a book, reading in the dim light and sipping a glass of wine. A calico cat rubbed against the woman's leg, and every now and then she reached down to pet it, never taking her eyes from the book.

Her hair was dark, turned under, kept away from her face by a hair band. She wore a dark suit with a short skirt, and her legs were crossed, one of them swinging back and forth to an inaudible rhythm. She was slight yet imposing, and Nora knew right away that no one else could project that image. No one else could dominate a space that way, with so little effort, with so little stature.

"Poppy?" she said in a near-whisper.

The woman looked up, but slowly, as if she fully expected to hear her name spoken. For a long time she stared at Nora, without a sense of recognition.

"Oh, God," she said. "Poppy, it's me, Nora Braxton. Nora McCabe, I mean. From UVA?"

Poppy's face came to life now, and she stood and said, "Nora? Why are you here? And why are you blond?"

Nora laughed, and they hugged, and swayed back and forth, patting each other between the shoulder blades. Poppy was still so slight, it was like hugging a child. Her perfume was instantly familiar. Her laugh sounded like the trickling water.

"I can't believe it," Poppy said, over and over.

"Me either," Nora said. "Are you here because of Simone?"

"Sort of," she said. "That's why I'm at the hotel—because Simone asked me to come. She's picking up the tab. It's a ridiculous luxury because I live here now."

"You *live* here?"

"I live in Metairie, just outside of town."

"Since when?"

"Six months ago."

"I thought you said you'd never come back here."

"I said a lot of things," Poppy admitted. "I was in college, Nora. You said you'd never dye your hair or have plastic surgery."

"I didn't have plastic surgery."

"It looks good, though," Poppy said, touching Nora's hair lightly with her fingertips, as if afraid the color might come off on her hands. "How does Cliff like it?"

"Cliff and I are getting divorced."

"Oh, God. I'm sorry."

"Hence the hair," she admitted. "I'm having a break-down."

"Well, if that's the worst you do . . ."

"It's the worst I've done yet. I make no promises."

"Sit down," Poppy said, gesturing, putting her book away.

They sat and stared at each other across the table, the candlelight making them both look younger than they were. And healthier, probably, Nora thought. She was certain she had dark circles under her eyes and broken blood vessels in her face, but she was hoping that she looked just as unblemished as Poppy did in this light. Poppy was still pretty in a way that scared her, for reasons she couldn't name. Simone wasn't like that. Simone was wispy and flighty and model-pretty, not a threat to anyone, just a pleasure to be around. But there was weight to Poppy, a significance to her that was subcutaneous and hard to define. Whereas Simone always made Nora feel free and adventurous, Poppy kept her anchored, reminded her of the importance of serving, eventually, a purpose of her own definition.

Had she done that yet? Other than procreating, had she put forth any theory in her life and set out to prove it? She doubted it, and for this reason it was a little bit difficult to meet Poppy's clear, knowing gaze.

"Tell me everything," Poppy said. "What the hell got into Cliff?"

"I don't know. He made a lot of money? Started feeling old? Never should have married me in the first place? Take your pick. Is it ever really that fascinating why men leave their wives?"

"Young meat is involved?"

"Twenty-eight, I think."

"The bastard."

"What are you gonna do?"

Nora shrugged, feigning a stoicism that was far from convincing.

"How long ago did this happen?"

"A few months. It still feels new. It isn't the affair that I mind so much. It's that he had to run away in shame, like a criminal. He left town owing money to the state of Virginia. Sixty thousand plus in back taxes. If he steps over the state line again, he'll be arrested and do time."

"You should turn him in."

"I can't afford to have my children humiliated that way."

"But Nora, he betrayed the state of Virginia. What would Mr. Jefferson say about that?"

"Jefferson was a slave owner."

"Don't start with that."

They laughed, and Nora was amazed to find she had a sense of humor about this living somewhere inside her, like a crack of light under the door.

"Do you hate him?" Poppy asked.

"Yes, I hate him," Nora said. "Not just him, either. The gender at large. I even hate gay men. I hate women who *look* like men. I hate the Pope."

"The Pope's too easy."

"Anyway, I'm trying not to stay there. It's not a good place to be, hating men, because, of course, they are attached to penises. And I have always been a fan of those."

"It's the best place to go for a penis," Poppy agreed.

"What about you?" Nora asked.

"I'm married," Poppy said quickly, as if to get it over with. Nora tried not to look surprised, because she knew Poppy wanted her to take it in stride. But it was hard to do. Among other things Nora remembered from their days in college, Poppy had vowed never to get married.

"Really?" Nora said evenly. "Tell me about him."

"He's in New York," Poppy answered. "We're separated."

"I'm sorry. How long . . ."

"Five years," she said. "That we've been married. Only six months apart. I'm not sure we'll get divorced, but probably. He doesn't want to, but . . ."

Her voice trailed off and she sipped her wine, staring into it, then dipping her tongue into it like a child. Nora watched and waited. She didn't know what to ask, or where to look.

"No children," Poppy said. That was obviously the next thing to ask. "You and Cliff had some, didn't you?"

"I have a girl, six, and a boy, thirteen."

"That's good."

Nora shrugged. "Well, I'm not a great mother. But they're pretty good kids, so . . . I guess I'm not the worst, either."

"You always downplay your abilities, Nora. Why did you do that? You know how capable you are. Everyone knows it."

Nora looked at her, a little stung by what sounded like a criticism. It was odd, the way it came out, flat and undeniable, as if it were something they had often discussed, though she couldn't remember ever doing so. In fact, she did not think of herself as someone who downplayed her abilities. She thought of herself as someone who had no particular abilities to play down. And even as she had that thought, she realized they were the same affliction.

"I don't know," Nora said. "Do you think that's my tragic flaw?"

Poppy smiled. "I'm not sure. Let me think about it."

She looked away and drummed her fingers on the table. The fountain trickled, keeping time like a clock ticking. When Poppy looked back at Nora, she was not smiling. She said, "I think your tragic flaw is your sense of equation."

"My what?" Nora said, stifling a laugh, uncertain if she was supposed to find this funny.

"Things need to equate in your world. You've always been that way. That's what you've always pursued. And you're not going to find it because it's not there. The world is in a state of imbalance."

"I don't understand what you mean. I need things to be fair, I guess. Everyone wants that."

"But not everyone expects it."

"You're the one who turned someone in for violating the honor code."

"That was a matter of *honor,*" Poppy said. "That's different from fairness."

"How?"

"Oh, I can't explain it right now. Maybe ever. It's something I understand because of having grown up here."

"New Orleans? The most corrupt place on the planet?"

"Honor and corruption are vital to each other."

Nora downed the last of her gin and tonic and began chewing the ice. It was a nervous habit. Poppy was making her nervous, but in a good way, causing her to feel agitated and alive and ready to debate.

But now that she was engaged, ready to pursue these issues, these criticisms, Poppy yawned and stretched.

"I have to go to bed now," she said. "I need my energy for facing Simone tomorrow. We both do. You know she'll have us on plantation tours or at the Rock 'n' Bowl or hang gliding or something. There's no escaping that girl's energy."

"I'm really glad to see you, Poppy. Simone didn't tell me you were coming."

"She likes surprises, doesn't she?"

They hugged and kissed, and walked in opposite directions across the courtyard to their rooms, agreeing to meet for breakfast at the same place in the morning.

When Nora walked into her room it was freezing cold, the air conditioner blasting. She turned it off and put on a sweater and sat on the edge of her four-poster bed, wondering why she felt uneasy. It was something Poppy had said. Not about her tragic flaw. She didn't really care if wanting things to be just and equitable was her tragic flaw. She'd cop to that any day. She saw the same instinct in her own daughter and felt glad that she might have passed that on to her. The only thing she was really afraid of was being devoid of virtue.

But maybe that was it. Poppy had informed her that honor was different from fairness, in a way that made it clear that honor held dominion over the other. In that context, the need for fairness sounded like a superficial concern, a childish pursuit. Someone playing in the sandbox of virtue, while the true defenders were elsewhere, defending the beachhead, surrounded and undaunted by the struggle.

She picked up the phone and dialed her mother's number. Boo sounded frightened when she answered.

"Hello, Mother? It's me. What's wrong?"

"What's wrong?" came Boo's gravelly voice, already angry and accusatory. "It's way past eleven. Have you lost your mind?"

Nora glanced at her watch, surprised that it was so late, albeit an hour earlier than back in Virginia. Where had the evening gone?

"I'm sorry, Mom. I just went walking around, and then I ran into my old friend Poppy Marchand . . ."

"Walking around? In New Orleans? What kind of fool did I raise?"

"I'm in the Quarter, Mother. It's safe here." Shame flooded her as she thought about her encounter with the two men on the street, hating the notion that her mother could be right about something.

"All right, sister. You just keep waltzing around, acting like the world owes you a favor, and see what happens."

"How are the kids?"

"Well, I don't know. They're asleep. They waited all night for you to call, and eventually I just had to say you probably got busy and you'd call in the morning. Annette was pouting when I put her to bed. And Michael? That boy is out of control, Nora Kay. He might need professional help."

Nora felt nauseous and dizzy, thinking of her children sitting by the phone waiting to hear from her. How could she have neglected them? Further evidence, she thought, that she was starting to lose control of herself. There was a time when she could not even bear to be away from them. Years when she and Cliff would go out to dinner or a party, and she'd run to the nearest phone to check on them. It irritated Cliff; he thought she was overly connected to them.

"Do you really think they can't cope without you?" he would ask. "My God, Nora, how will they ever evolve into fully-functioning adults? You act like they're disabled in your absence. That's a form of ego, you know. Megalomania."

This topic had come up in couples counseling many times. Nora was too connected to the kids, he claimed, and she countered that he was too disconnected. The therapist said both of them were right, to a degree. Nora used to sit there thinking, *If we are this much at odds and both right, then we shouldn't be together.* She wished she had said that, at least once, so that Cliff's departure wouldn't hang in the air like the last word.

"What's wrong with Michael?"

"He's rude, that's what. He told me to shut up tonight."

Nora smiled. Of course he told her to shut up. No one on earth talked more than her mother, and got less said in the process.

"And what did you say to him?" Nora asked.

"I told him I'd shut up when I felt like shutting up."

"Mother," Nora sighed, "you can't engage him at his level. He's a child. He needs guidance. You need to explain to him . . ."

"You've done too much explaining, that's your problem. The boy should have been spanked when it would have done some good. But now he's too big and he's ruling the roost. He knows it, too, sister. Don't think he doesn't know who runs your household."

Nora knew there was no hope of winning this argument. She decided to move on.

"But they're okay, right? Basically, they're fine?"

"They're as fine as two children can be who've been taken out of school and dumped on their grandmother without a good explanation."

"It won't kill them to miss one week of school. And you're always saying you want to spend more time with them."

"I'd like to visit them, Nora Kay, not raise them. I'm through with raising children."

"You only raised one, Mother, and I wasn't terribly difficult."

"Excuse me, are you forgetting your brother? Maybe you have put him out of your mind, but I haven't."

Nora felt her throat closing, as if she were having an allergic reaction. She knew it was the rage again, tightening in her chest and around her neck. Of course she had not forgotten Pete, her little brother who had died when he was only two.

She was six at the time. The boy had tried to crawl out of his crib in the middle of the night and had fallen on his head. A fluke thing, the doctor later said. One in a million probability. He had fallen hard and cracked his skull, and no one had heard him. He lay there on the floor all night, his brain swelling, the life leaking out of him. He existed in a coma for a while and finally slipped away. Her family had never fully recovered, and even now Nora had nightmares about it, blaming herself for not coming to his rescue. It seemed to her back then, and now, that she had heard the sound of him hitting the floor. Her bedroom was next door and she had heard the commotion, the distant thud. But it had barely registered in her consciousness and she had gone back to sleep. That was something she had never told anyone. She knew that if she told her mother, she would be opening herself up to the blame she already carried squarely on her own shoulders.

"I'm sorry, I didn't mean that," Nora said.

"No, I should hope not. The things that I have lived through. You think your divorce is so tragic. Well, I tried to warn you. And losing a husband is nothing compared to losing a child. You just think about that."

"I do think about it, Mother. But are my children all right?"

"They are alive, Nora Kay. They aren't sick. They miss you and they don't listen to a thing I tell them to do. Your son acts like his father is the second coming. Won't hear a word against him. What's this about him going to live with Cliff? He can't live with that man. That man is a criminal."

"He's not going to live with him, Mother. It's just a fantasy he has. He's thirteen, and he imagines anybody would be better than me. He imagines his father would understand him. And while we're at it, you shouldn't be saying anything bad about Cliff. It's not fair to them."

"I will speak my mind," Boo announced. "I will say whatever I feel like saying. You can't tell me to shut up and neither can your son."

*This is lunacy,* Nora thought. *Leaving my children with this woman. She is so clearly insane.* When her father was alive, he used to tell her this. When they fought he would put Nora in the car and drive her around and say, "Doctors have told me your mother should be committed, but I can't do that to her. And I don't want to raise you alone. A nervous mother is better than none, don't you think?"

Once she had asked her father why he married her. He said, without missing a beat, "Because I thought she was the most beautiful woman I had ever seen. And I still think so." Remembering that, she still felt the pain she had felt then. Even as a child, she knew that wasn't a substantial reason to marry someone.

Suddenly her mother said, "Poppy Marchand?"

"What?"

"You said something about Poppy Marchand?"

"Yes, I ran into her . . ."

"I thought you were going to visit Simone."

"I am, but Simone got delayed, and then I found Poppy here, staying at my hotel."

"Well, thank the Lord for small favors. I always liked that girl, Poppy. She's from good breeding. Simone was crazy. She wore all that makeup. Too much mascara, made her eyelashes look like tarantulas. But Poppy, now, that girl was grounded. I feel better knowing she's there."

Her mother had met Poppy only a couple of times and exchanged no more than a dozen sentences with her, but she had picked up right away that Poppy was from old money. Maybe it was the pearls Poppy used to wear in those days, real ones, swinging carelessly around her neck like costume jewelry. The fact that Poppy's father was a judge impressed Boo, even though Poppy's father was fairly famous for being a corrupt judge, one who took kickbacks and manipulated his courtroom accordingly. Her mother didn't know that about him, but she probably wouldn't have cared. A judge was a judge.

"Now, that Simone," her mother went on, "she's just trouble. She's never going to amount to anything."

"She's a model, Mother. And now she's a big restaurant critic, too. She does a spot on TV. She's very successful."

"Money can't give you class, sister. And that Simone is from trash as far as I can tell."

Nora bristled and tried not to enter into this debate. Her therapist was always telling her not to take her mother's bait, but her therapist didn't know how inviting that bait was. She tugged and Nora jumped, even after all these years. Her therapist called it the marionette syndrome. Nora didn't like to think of herself in those terms, but where Boo was concerned, it was fairly undeniable.

Simone, of course, was not from trash. Her father was some high-level executive at a movie studio, and she had been raised among actors and politicians and royalty. She had gone to school in Europe. She spoke French. Quite a contrast from Nora's own upbringing, the daughter of a traveling salesman in southern Virginia, a place so small it rarely showed up on a map of the state. Lewiston was a one-horse town, and the horse was not particularly healthy. She thought of her children staying there, sleeping in Boo's one small guest room, in a tiny postwar house near the highway. It was all her mother could afford after her father's death. For all his concern about family, her father had not provided for them. He died without life insurance, and with no savings and a lifetime of debt. No one felt up to blaming him, though. His death had been so prolonged and painful and humiliating. Prostate cancer. The slow withering away, being attacked by the cells in his penis, a kind of ironic demise, Nora thought, given how much Boo claimed to detest "the act." Both of her parents were devout Christians, Baptists, no less, which led them to all manner of nutty ideas about sex. Her mother thought of it as a necessary evil, and her father was somewhat obsessed with it—while denying its importance, of course. This made for a closet well stocked with pornography and a threat on her life if she ever slept with a man out of wedlock.

"You tell Poppy I said hello," Boo said. "And you stay close to her and keep your distance from that Simone."

"Tell the kids I'll call them tomorrow."

"Well, I don't want to get their hopes up."

"I will call them, Mother."

"Annette chews things. Did you know that?"

"Yes. It's age-appropriate."

"Well, it's not appropriate in my book. She chewed up the edges of my *TV Guide*."

"Give them a kiss from me. Remember, Michael doesn't eat breakfast."

"Everyone eats breakfast in my house, sister."

"Good night, Mother."

She hung up the phone and sat on her bed, her thoughts scrambled, floating about, trying to reassemble themselves. She knew, of course, that one day she would end up in another therapist's office, with Michael and Annette pointing fingers at her for leaving them with their insane grandmother.

"It all started when my mother went to New Orleans," she could imagine Annette saying. And it would just get worse from there.

# 4

Nora and Poppy met for breakfast in the courtyard.

It was a little after nine, and they were sipping their chicory coffee and orange juice, nibbling on homemade biscuits and jam. The air was already close and hot. The smells of the city crept over the walls. It made Nora think of Venice, a place she had visited once with Cliff, on a business trip. He had gone there to study Italian cooking, thinking he might try to open an Italian restaurant with authentic Venetian cuisine. Venice had been beautiful and romantic, but an odd, oppressive stench seemed to take hold of the place. Nora felt that her face was constantly contorted, warding off a bad smell that loomed but never quite materialized.

Poppy buttered her biscuit and said, "Louisiana should secede, probably. It's not like any other state. We should stop pretending to play by the rules."

"But why are you back here?" Nora asked. "I mean, if you hate it so much?"

"I don't hate it. I used to. Now I accept it. I was raised here and I guess I'm kind of infected by its influence. But I can't claim that it has anything to contribute to the rest of the country."

"What do you do here?"

Poppy stared at her biscuit, driving the butter into its flesh. She said, "I teach school. I teach art at a middle school in Metairie. My father died two years ago and left me his estate. I don't ever have to work again, really, but I want to stay busy."

"I met a teacher last night. My cab driver. Leo Girardi."

Poppy immediately stopped buttering and looked at her. "Leo?"

"Yes. You know him?"

She nodded. "He's an old friend. But I don't talk to him much anymore."

"Why not?"

Poppy didn't answer. She concentrated on her biscuit, and finally, when she spoke again, said, "I don't paint anymore, either."

"Why not?"

"I can't," she said. "It's like . . . I don't remember how. I can't explain it."

"When did this happen?"

"Around the time I left Adam. I'm sure it's just temporary."

"Was he an artist, too? Maybe you were competitive."

"He's a plastic surgeon. He spends his time making women's breasts bigger and sucking fat out of their thighs. It's not an honorable profession."

"What about burn victims and that kind of thing?"

"Oh, yes, burn victims. That is what he always used when

he felt he had to justify his calling. To be fair, he did special-
ize in putting scarred people back together. But that's just an
excuse. I happen to think we should just live with what God
gives us, even if, for some reason, He decides to give us scars.
Our scars are our medals, in a way. How noble is that, trying
to wipe away the business of living?"

"God?" Nora questioned, certain she had not heard right.
It was not a name she associated with Poppy.

"Well, whatever higher power you believe in. For me, it's
God."

"Since when?"

Poppy licked some jam off her fingers and said, "My life is
different now."

"Different how?"

Poppy shrugged and looked into her coffee cup.

"You know where chicory comes from, don't you? They
used to add it to coffee back during the war, when the crop
was bad and it tasted like shit. Chicory was supposed to make
it taste less like shit. Most of New Orleans cuisine is based on
poverty, the desire to keep from starving. They ate anything
that crawled past their house. Crawfish? That's swamp trash.
Catfish live in the mud. So do lobsters. Alligator meat, turtle
meat, nutria, for God's sake? That's a rat. Smart people do
not eat these things. They eat steak."

"Well, Simone will probably have something to say about
that. Now that she's this big food critic."

"That's so ironic," Poppy said. "Simone was the person
who would eat the dining-hall crap, no matter how vile it
was. She was born with an impaired palette. And now she's
writing about food, and considered the expert on cuisine.
How did that happen?"

"I don't know, Poppy. How did I end up divorced? How
did we both end up alone?"

"That is not the point," Poppy said.

"So why are you and your husband separated?" Nora asked.

"We can't overcome our differences."

"What are your differences?"

"Religion," Poppy said.

"But you're not religious."

Poppy reached inside her blouse and pulled out a silver cross. She thrust it at Nora, as if to ward off a vampire, and after a second she tucked it back in.

"Poppy," Nora said. "You have got to be kidding."

"I'm not."

"How the hell did it happen? Who got to you?"

"Nobody got to me," she said. "Except Jesus."

Nora felt like throwing up. Her throat burned as the chicory coffee came back up. This could not be happening. The memory of all those ranting, angry people in her church. Her parents' ridiculous screaming matches, always playing out in that strange religious vernacular. Those horrible, frightening pictures of Jesus all over the house. The Bibles. The lectures, the accusations, the eyes of God, always looking down on her in judgment. Poppy could not believe those things.

"Are you in AA or something?" Nora asked. She recalled that Poppy had been a big drinker.

"No. I am one of those lapsed Catholics, and I just got unlapsed. Don't worry, I am not going to start proselytizing. It's my own private concern. But in answer to your question about Adam, that's it. He's Jewish."

"So was Jesus," Nora said.

"Oh, really?" Poppy said sarcastically. "News to me."

"But why would his being Jewish be a problem? I mean, you knew he was Jewish when you married him, didn't you?"

"I wasn't a Christian then. And I actually don't consider myself to be married because we didn't take the sacrament . . ."

"Oh, for God's sake, Poppy. Stop! This is utter nonsense."

"Not to me."

They stopped talking abruptly, like quarreling lovers. Nora looked away, and was surprised to find that tears were welling in her eyes, and her throat felt tight with grief. She did not understand how this could be happening, or why it upset her so much. They sipped their coffee and accepted a refill from the porter, and still they did not talk. They listened to the sounds of the city coming to life, a steamboat whistle in the distance, trucks rumbling through the Quarter, the ground shaking as if it were liquid at the center. Which, in New Orleans, of course, it was.

Finally Nora said, "Poppy, I'm sorry. I have issues with religion. And I'm feeling very strange right now, anyway. My life is . . ."

She couldn't finish the sentence. She wanted to say "out of control," but that wasn't really it. Her life just didn't feel like it was hers. She felt like she was living someone else's existence, in some circumstances set up by someone who hadn't the slightest idea of what she, Nora, wanted or cared about. Who came up with calligraphy, for example? Who wanted to marry a guy with an MBA? Who had given birth to two children and let one of them turn into a teenager? It was a mystery how any of this had happened, and how it had taken her this long to feel the impact.

"Don't worry about it," Poppy said. "I know it's a shock. I can't explain it. Well, I can, but it would take too long."

"You don't need to explain."

And it was true. Nora felt, despite her protestations, that she understood perfectly well. She could still remember the days when she was little, saying her prayers at night, praying to the God her parents assured her was in control of every tiny detail, and she felt relieved that it was all up to Him, and not her.

Anyone would want to believe that.

After breakfast, they parted. It was understood, at that point, that they needed a break from each other. Nora claimed she wanted to do some work (she had brought some invitations with her), and Poppy was going to visit some old friends in town. And, in fact, Nora went back to her room fully intending to get at least half of the one-hundred-fifty-invitation order finished. But she made it through only two when she felt overcome with the desire to call her children. She rang her mother's number again, but the answering machine picked up. Boo's voice reverberated in her ear, like the voice of a schizophrenic God, the God of the Old Testament:

"If you want to leave a message, do it after the beep. You have to talk loud and clear and leave your number. If I don't understand what you're saying, I can't call you back. Thank you."

Nora smiled. It was her mother's perpetual state of admonishment. She was already angry at the caller, before he or she had a chance to speak.

Nora said, "Hi, Mom. Just me again, hoping to talk to Annette and Michael."

She paused, wondering what else to say.

"Hi, kids," she said. "It's Mom. Having a great time in New Orleans. It's very hot. Hope you're doing okay and listening to Grandma Boo. I'll be home soon. I'm at the Collier House, and Grandma has the number . . ."

There was a loud beeping sound, and the machine cut her off.

She hung up the phone and stared at the walls. They were the color of ripe bananas. The molding and the ceiling were white, like meringue balanced over a cream pie. The painting on the wall was a modern, psychedelic depiction of zoo animals. It was pleasantly anachronistic in the antique setting. *What the hell am I doing here?* she thought.

She got out a book of Faulkner's short stories and started to read. She was embarrassed by her desire to read Faulkner in New Orleans. (She had brought Tennessee Williams, too, and John Kennedy Toole.) Her eyes skimmed over the words, and she tried to remember how she had once felt about literature. In college, she had actually found it exciting. It had made her feel hopeful and alive. Even the authors she hated (Thomas Wolfe, Bernard Malamud, George Eliot) made her feel challenged and envious. She wanted to write. She wanted to create stories and have her thoughts communicated in English classes. When she read people she did like, her heart would speed up and she felt light-headed. Faulkner, in those days, seemed like a personal friend. Someone she should have married. She would have put up with the rage and the alcohol. Flannery O'Connor, Chekhov, Tolstoy, Nabokov, Jane Austen, Ralph Ellison . . . these people made her dizzy with the desire to talk back, to speak her own truth. She had written some short stories in college and even had some published. But once she started dating Cliff, her desire to do anything important dwindled. From the time she met him, she understood that it was he who was going to be important, and she was simply going to feed off his success. For a while she had pretended she was going to keep writing. She even jotted down some thoughts in a journal. But chasing after Cliff's affection had become a full-time job. She married him right out of college, and then she had embarked on the fifteen-year marathon of making him happy. Obviously she had not succeeded.

She wondered if it counted that she had satisfied him for a while. In the early days—and especially right after Michael was born—she seemed to be enough for him. He was gentle with her, considerate, even worried. He encouraged her to go to work. She shouldn't be sitting around, cooped up in the house with a kid, he said, not with her drive and intelligence. But she felt that his encouragement was just a test, that the right response was to say, "No, I want to raise my children. I don't want to hand them off. This is enough for me. Really."

Though it wasn't, of course, and she now knew it wasn't enough for him, either. Now she realized he had been begging her to have another life, something to talk about at the dinner table other than diaper rash and Mommy and Me. She refused to go to the place of blaming herself for the demise of her marriage. But she knew that she had, in fact, cheated herself by trying to be too good. If Cliff had wanted an obedient soul, after all, he would not have married her. She was feisty enough when they first met. It was the children that had smoothed out her rough edges, made her dull. She didn't blame them, and she didn't blame herself. That left only Cliff. She blamed him for everything because he had behaved badly. Yet her staunch devotion had not paid off, and it did not make her feel good about herself. When the dust settled, there she was—a martyr, and there was nothing worse to live with than that.

The thing was, she didn't want Cliff back. The truth was, he had bored her. His restaurants were silly. Oh, yes, they made a lot of money, but the food was simplistic and dull. He always gave a theme to his places, the first one being modern Southern cuisine, the second one Cuban, the third upscale Mexican, the fourth Italian. They all did well because he explored only the surfaces of those cultures, giving people food they could recognize, setting it in a context that made them feel well traveled. She could see him manipulating people. The restaurants weren't a bad thing, as business schemes went, but Cliff didn't really care about the food, and that gave her an insight; she was on to him. It was as if he were tricking people. Making fun of them. And if he was making fun of them, then, what about her?

Perhaps she had actually married Cliff because he was so boring and predictable. Her parents' volatile marriage had made her yearn for something more peaceful. She wanted no surprises. She and Cliff never fought, at least until the end, and even then the fights were polite and articulate. Once when she was needling him about something, he wheeled on her and said, "I won't have that charge leveled at me."

Stunned by his polite reaction, she had simply screamed, "Fuck you, you asshole."

And he had turned and walked out, into the rain. He disappeared until three in the morning, and when he returned she attacked him with affection, and they made love on the floor of the bedroom. She was sorry, he was sorry, they wouldn't do this again. They stayed in love for days after that. But Cliff's unpredictable nature went on a long vacation after that, and did not resurface until he stopped paying taxes and met the waitress.

Nora could not concentrate on Faulkner now. She did not care about literature, and she missed that passion. She was not passionate about anything anymore. Passion seemed dangerous to her, yet she missed it. She examined the prose and tried to feel a stirring in her heart, but instead of taking flight, the words landed like lead, dull thuds with no echo. If she could not get excited about literature anymore, then what was left?

The phone rang. She picked it up quickly, on the first ring, even though in Cliff's absence she had trained herself to wait until the second or third. She had done this in the early days after his departure, always thinking it would be him and not wanting to seem too eager. It was never him, of course. And it wasn't him this time, either. It was Simone.

"Nora Kay? Is that you? I'm here, at last."

"Simone? Where have you been?"

"I had a last-minute assignment in L.A., and I couldn't get away. I'm so sorry, honey."

"I ran into Poppy Marchand."

"I meant to tell you she was coming."

"Did you know that she's completely crazy?"

"Oh, yeah, the religion thing."

"You knew about that?"

"Yes. I'll explain later. Can I come over?"

"Sure, of course."

Nora went to the bathroom and put on makeup, as carefully as if she were about to go on a date. It was a well-known fact that women always dressed and primped for other women, not men. Men had no taste. Men wouldn't know a Jill Sander suit or Stephan Kelian shoes from Gap wear. They certainly couldn't appreciate the natural makeup approach. (They actually believed women weren't wearing makeup, and as a result believed that they preferred "natural beauty"—as if there were such a thing.) Simone was particularly difficult to dress for. She was the arbiter of taste, one of those people who could look good in anything. She didn't wear style; she gave style to what she wore. She had been a model ever since she was sixteen, but had never actually become a "super model." That was a leap she couldn't quite make because, as she often complained, she wasn't willing to "take that many drugs and sleep with other women." She let her modeling career fizzle out, and somehow replaced it with a calling in the haute cuisine industry. It had all started when she wrote a whimsical piece in the *Los Angeles Times* called "What Models Really Eat." The piece was well received, and no one was more surprised than Simone to discover that she could actually write. No one except Nora, who tried very hard not to let any bitterness fester. *She* had been the writer in college. Well, she hadn't actually done much writing, but she intended to, and she appreciated and chased after fine prose. Simone hadn't cared at all about that kind of thing.

Still, Nora told herself, she would never have wanted to be a food critic. It seemed a fatuous occupation, a genuinely silly use of language. And though Simone was often witty and insightful, the fact was, she was just talking about food. How much could be said on that subject?

There was a knock on the door and Nora opened it, prepared to have her own appearance judged, but instead she was taken aback by Simone's. She was so thin that it actually made Nora's heart skip a beat, in a kind of empathetic arrhythmia. Her hair, which had once been long and black, was now short, curly and red. Her face was still strikingly beautiful, her eyes a pale gray, deep-set and kind. Her lips were full of collagen, but they wouldn't have looked so bad if her cheeks weren't so sunken in. As it was, she almost looked freakish. Nora stood there with her mouth open, not knowing what to say.

Simone said it for her.

"I know, I look like something from *Star Trek*."

"What happened?" Nora asked as Simone breezed past her into the room.

"It's a long story."

Simone pulled off the red hair, which mercifully turned out to be a wig. Her own shiny black hair tumbled down to her shoulders, giving color and definition to her otherwise hollow countenance. Nora felt she could breathe a little easier, but she was still worried.

"I am a bona fide mess, Nora Kay," Simone declared. She sat on the bed and fished in her purse for a cigarette. Nora didn't bother to object. She thought Simone should ingest something, anything, even tobacco.

"Are you sick?" Nora asked.

"No, not the way you're talking. I have been . . . not well. I'm in the throes of a trauma or two."

"Why are you in disguise?"

"Because of the job," she said, twirling the wig around on her index finger like a Frisbee. "I'm not supposed to go anywhere looking like myself. If I get recognized, then my food-reviewing days are over. For obvious reasons, if they see you coming, they treat you different."

"Oh, right."

"It used to be just restaurants where I couldn't look like myself. Now I'm getting so well known, I can't look like myself anywhere. It's out of control, Nora. How did I end up in this profession? I don't even care about food."

"Obviously," Nora said, gesturing toward her thin frame.

"Please. I am trying to gain weight."

"Are you anorexic?"

Simone took a drag of her cigarette and said, "I am someone who can't eat. If that's the term you want to give it, okay. I mean, I want to eat. I think about eating. Hell, I eat for a living. But something just happens, and I can't do it."

"Are you in counseling?"

"No, Nora, I figured I'd just pray a lot. Of course I'm in fucking counseling. But it's so complicated. You, on the other hand, look fantastic. Divorce suits you."

"I am also having a breakdown. Although not as bad as yours, I think."

"And Poppy's a goddamn Catholic now. Can you believe it?"

Nora sat by Simone on the bed, waving the smoke away.

"What are we all doing here?" Nora asked. "Are we here because of your condition?" A short wave of her hand indicated Simone's thinness.

Simone chewed on a fingernail and took a long time answering. Finally she said, "In a way, yes, but not the way you're thinking. I'll explain it all at dinner tonight. This is the weirdest time of my life, and as I don't have a husband or anything, I figured I should just get my oldest friends together. You know, to help me out, moral support, that kind of thing."

"Absolutely. You should have called sooner."

"It's all very recent."

"How did you find Poppy?" Nora asked.

"I've been talking to her and emailing her for a couple of years."

"You *have?*"

Simone nodded. "She married a great guy. Adam. He's worked on a lot of girls I know. Pretty famous plastic surgeon."

"She's leaving him."

"Yeah. She's crazy now. I watched it happen, her whole demise."

"Why was she talking to you, not me?"

Simone ground out her cigarette and said, "She's afraid of you, Nora."

"That's ridiculous."

"You're an intimidating person."

"*I* am?"

"You always seemed to have your shit together. You knew what you wanted and you went and got it. That's intimidating."

"It was an illusion."

"Well, now we know."

They sat in silence for a moment, and Nora felt suddenly disoriented and uncomfortable. It actually hurt her feelings that people thought that she was solid and together, that she knew what she wanted. She was fairly impressed that she had hidden her weaknesses all this time, but it actually made a knot grow in her stomach when she thought of how much her friends had missed the point of her, how badly they had understood her. All this time, all this bonding, and they weren't even connected to the person she really was. They had no idea.

She was also feeling selfishly threatened, jealous that Simone's breakdown was now going to take precedence over hers. She had wanted to indulge in a weekend of analyzing her own plight, and here sat Simone with a greater and more urgent set of afflictions. It didn't seem fair; on the other hand, Nora thought, it might do her good to think about someone else's problems.

"We should do some sightseeing," Simone said. "Let's go get Poppy and get on one of those horse-and-buggies."

"Oh, really. Do we have to?"

"Yes, we have to. We have to do whatever I want this week. It'll be fun. It'll be familiar, me getting my way."

"Yes," Nora said and smiled. "It will."

And as she followed her friend out the door, she felt that familiar sense of childhood comfort, the freedom of not being in charge.

# 5

The buggy ride was exactly what it was supposed to be—
tacky, touristy, benignly annoying. Nora found herself enjoy-
ing it. It reminded her of childhood vacations, the only times
her parents were ever remotely content, when they had gone
to Williamsburg and Jamestown and Monticello and Appo-
mattox, and in later years to Myrtle Beach and Nags Head
and sometimes Carrowinds, a big amusement park in North
Carolina. Her parents always took the cheapest, easiest route
to anything. They stood in line for hours for free tours, and
they saved coupons, and they went to dinner at five o'clock at
steak-and-seafood chains to take advantage of the early-bird
discount. They stayed at a Days Inn or a Motel Six, and Nora
grew so accustomed to them that she felt certain the sealed
toilets, paper-covered glasses and small soaps were signs of

sophistication. In a very real way, growing up with her parents was like being taken on the buggy ride of life. So this morning's trip felt familiar and soothing, sweating in the humid air, feeling the sun pressing down on her face, sipping a beer and being rocked from side to side. Even the faint smell of manure comforted her.

The driver drew their attention to this and that historic site, and Simone, who had taken this ride before, filled in the blanks.

"This here," said the driver, "is the haunted house. Now, N'awlins has plenty of haunted houses, but this is the most famous one."

Simone said, "The infamous Madame Delphine Lalaurie. She tortured her slaves, beat them, chained them in the attic. You're supposed to be able to hear them screaming at night."

"Now, the house was destroyed by a fire in 1834, and that's when Madame's ugly secret was discovered."

Simone said, "She barely escaped with her life. The neighbors tried to kill her on the spot."

The driver said, "Who's givin' this tour, babe?"

"You are, handsome. Go ahead."

Poppy, who had been staring resolutely at her lap the whole time, finally looked up as if she had been awakened from a trance. "Why don't you take us past the projects?" she said. "Why not clop on over to the cemetery, where about fifty tourists a year are robbed and murdered? And maybe, while you're at it, take us past the criminal courts building, where all the judges are taking kickbacks, and then the gambling casinos, which are bankrupting the city, and then the KKK headquarters . . ."

The driver said, "Lady, this is my tour, my bu'iness. You want the bad-news tour, go take it yourself."

"It's dishonest," Poppy said, "the way they peddle this city."

Simone lit a cigarette and said, "Poppy, when did you grow these opinions?"

"She's always had opinions," Nora piped up, a little too eagerly, always ready to take on the role of peacemaker. "Remember in college? She was a communist."

Poppy laughed. "It was the eighties. Anyone left of Franco was considered a communist."

"Still, you were always protesting, and writing op-ed pieces in the school paper. I forget. What was your big complaint?"

"South Africa," Poppy said. "Enslavement has always bugged me."

"They're better now, aren't they?" Simone asked.

"Oh, yes. Black people get to ride the bus out of the ghetto."

"You know me, Poppy. I've just never been political."

"What does that mean?" Poppy demanded. "That's like saying you're not an organism. Everything is political, and if you choose to isolate yourself from the issues of your time, you are, in effect, being political. That is a political stance. A stance of apathy. It adds to the problem, and that is your contribution."

Simone thought about this for a moment, blowing tobacco smoke into the air. "I see your point. But I happen to think I've made more of a contribution than that."

"Like what? Writing about food? Modeling? Making people feel bad about the way they look?"

"First of all, food is important. Good food is more important. It's an art."

"Please."

"It is important to eat well, Poppy. Why deny yourself plea-sure? Is that a healthy way to live? Is that self-love?"

Poppy ignored this question and asked instead, "What about modeling?"

"Beauty," Simone replied. "Also important."

"Whose standard of beauty, though? Starving women? That's beautiful?"

"The public responds," she said.

"They are bombarded. They are told what to think."

"Oh, mercy. So the masses can't think for themselves? Lis-ten to yourself. And besides, people do understand the differ-ence between looking and being. They can look at a fine painting without wanting to go home and make one. You can look at a model and admire her without wanting to be her."

"That's ridiculous."

"Look, remember when Princess Diana died?"

The driver said, "If y'all are interested, that's the Old Ur-suline Convent, oldest building in the Mississippi Valley."

"Of course I remember when she died," Poppy said.

"And Mother Teresa died the same week? And who got the most press?"

"Diana, which is thoroughly disgusting."

"No, it's not. People loved her because she was beautiful. People want and need and crave beauty. All those dresses were a service to the world. Mother Teresa in that potato sack—she didn't value beauty. And the people know that is wrong. That is not self-love, to walk around in a sheet with your face all shriveled."

"She healed people! She fed them when they were starv-ing!"

"So did Diana! And she did it in a Chanel suit! Are you telling me Mother T's got a higher spot in heaven because her face looked like a baseball mitt?"

Nora listened and squirmed, trying to think of something neutral to say, when Poppy began to laugh. She snorted into her fist and then got the giggles, and Simone followed suit, her loud laugh echoing off the walls of the buildings and down the street. It scared the horse and he jerked forward.

"Y'all calm down now," said the driver.

Nora smiled, suddenly remembering that Simone and Poppy had always gone at each other this way. For hours it seemed, back in that house on Vinegar Hill, sitting at the kitchen table, dunking bags of tea into hot water, or sometimes sipping scotch. Their voices would resonate, waking up the floaters or the people next door, who yelled for silence. But they wouldn't stop, and Nora would sit watching them as if it were a spectator sport, wishing she had enough nerve or opinions to join in.

Why had she forgotten those evenings? Over the years she had smoothed out the edges, and in her memory everyone had been made polite, reserved, respectful. But they had been boisterous in college; of course they had. Maybe she had, too. Maybe she had taken away her own edge in reconstructing the past.

When Poppy finally had stopped laughing, she said, "Simone, what is all this self-love business?"

"I'm in therapy," Simone said.

"Ah. Well, it seems to me that this country is a little too afflicted with self-love."

"You're wrong. You're talking about narcissism. That is a totally different thing. Narcissism is rooted in self-loathing."

"I don't believe that. I think that people are inherently flawed, and we should acknowledge that and stop all this self-aggrandizing."

"Holy moly! Inherently flawed? That's the best part, Poppy. That's where the challenge is. You're an artist, think about it. Is a perfect painting beautiful? Is it even possible? And when people try to re-create human beings in art, they know it is important to capture that imperfection."

Poppy said, "Have you ever seen Michelangelo's David?"

"Yes, I have, and the man is standing like a faggot. With that slingshot over his shoulder? Right. He's going to kill a giant? He's a fucking hairdresser. He's going to mousse Goliath to death."

"He is a bit precious," Poppy conceded.

"What about Degas?" Nora said suddenly. She wanted to be in this debate.

They looked at her, waiting.

"Those ballerinas are kind of perfect," she said.

"Pedophile," Poppy said.

"Cross-dresser," Simone suggested.

"Clearly the man is obsessed with prepubescent girls."

"I think he was traumatized by a tutu as a child."

"The Napoleon House," the driver said. "They have real good muffulettas. Y'all hungry?"

"I think he wants us to get out," Nora said.

"That's fine. I'm hungry."

They got out at the corner of Chartres and St. Louis, at what appeared to be a dilapidated bar. Nora had not yet adjusted to the old charm of the city. Everything seemed dirty to her, and dangerous. In Charlottesville, you knew what a restaurant was before you went in. Mostly big chains or family-run diners. She would never go into a place like this in Virginia. It just wouldn't make sense. Once inside, she saw the plaster was crumbling off the walls, revealing aged brick underneath. The floor was concrete, and the air was blue with smoke. There were tables pushed right against each other, and there was a long bar, full of drinkers even though it was barely noon. These were not beer drinkers either. Martinis, scotch, margaritas. A ceiling fan stirred the smoke around and made a shadow like a starfish on the floor.

They sat away from the bar, trying to escape the pollution and the boisterous chat of the locals.

Simone explained the Napoleon House to Nora.

"The mayor and Jean Lafitte the pirate and a whole bunch of other people built it for Napoleon after he was exiled to Elba."

"St. Helena, actually," Poppy said.

"He had a bunch of supporters here, and they wanted to bring him over and give him a nice place to live. It was originally the mayor's own house. He was going to give it up! That's how much they loved the little guy. But Napoleon died in 1821, without ever setting foot inside."

A waiter in a white shirt and black bow tie approached them with menus, but Simone waved them away. "Three muffulettas and three Pimms."

Nora said, "I don't recognize any of that."

"You'll like it," Simone assured her.

"It's pleasant," Poppy said, "to eat greasy meat and drink potent liquor in the home of a despot."

"You said it," Simone said.

"Who was Jean Lafitte?" Nora asked.

"A pirate," Poppy said, "who is given credit for doing almost anything of merit or notoriety in this city. It's mostly apocryphal. He was a pirate, for God's sake. He didn't hang around the city. He hid in the swamp like a good outlaw."

"There are plenty of outlaws in this city who don't hide out," Simone said.

"That's true," Poppy admitted. "My father was one."

They looked at her. Nora felt a little breathless, as if she were about to hear something sacred. Poppy never talked about her father, except to say that he was a bad man, and that she had nothing but unpleasant memories of her up-bringing. She was raised by him and a black maid named Es-ther. Her mother had died under mysterious circumstances when she was a child. An unexplained fall down the stairs. Drunk, perhaps, or maybe a "My Last Duchess" scenario, she thought, remembering the Browning poem. Or was the duchess strangled? She used to know that poem by heart. Now she knew nothing substantial.

"Did you ever make peace with him?" Simone asked.

Poppy stared at her. "In my way."

They didn't talk for a while. The Pimms came, a sweet golden liquid with cucumbers floating in it. Then the muf-fulettas arrived and Nora ate hers quickly, ravenously. She thought she had never tasted anything so good. It made her forget about the restaurant's crumbling walls and the smoke and the water bugs scuttling across the concrete.

When they had finished eating, Simone lit a cigarette and said, "Now. We have to talk."

"What about?" Poppy asked. She had eaten only half of her sandwich and had made no mess at all. Nora felt like a slob, olive confetti splattered around her plate. She put her napkin over it.

"About why we're here," Simone said.

"In New Orleans," Poppy asked, "or on the planet?"

"Can I go to the bathroom first?" Nora asked, standing.

"No, Nora Kay. Stay put."

She sat back down. Simone's expression was gravely seri-ous. Nora wasn't sure she'd ever seen her look this way. She glanced at Poppy, who was starting to recognize the same thing.

"It was nearly a year ago," Simone said, as if she were about to tell a fable. "I was in New Orleans on assignment.

Seduction in the South, or some damn thing, was my topic. I was supposed to write about a romantic evening in New Orleans. Restaurant, hotel, dance spot, buggy ride, so on. It was my last night here, and I went to this place on Bourbon Street, a dance club called Oz. It's a gay bar, but a lot of straight couples go there. I thought it might be interesting to include the place in my article. Anyway, I danced a little, had a beer, and started walking home. It was around eleven o'-clock. The streets were pretty crowded still. I decided to walk down Pirates Alley, over by St. Louis Cathedral. It's listed as the most romantic walk in the city."

She paused here to take a drag from her cigarette. Nora could see that Simone's hand was shaking.

"So I was walking along there, and I realized that someone was walking behind me. I didn't pay much attention at first. Then the next thing I knew, he had his hand around my throat and I was up against the wall."

Nora sat paralyzed. She did not want to hear the rest. She did not want to know that this thing had happened, this terrible big thing. It was starting to happen now, that her life was collecting tragedies like bugs in a net. But maybe it wouldn't end badly; maybe there was a way out of this tale. She waited and hoped.

Simone said, "I couldn't breathe, so I couldn't scream. He explained what he wanted me to do, and I did it. I was afraid I was going to die."

"He raped you," Poppy said.

Simone nodded. "In a number of ways. It was horrific. I won't go into the details, but that wasn't even the worst part. And thinking I might die right there and be a body in the alley, next to the homeless guy—who did not one thing to help me, by the way—that was not the worst part either. When it was over, he gave me a lecture. He told me I shouldn't be walking around New Orleans by myself. It was a dangerous city. He told me not to be stupid. I stood there nodding, agreeing with him, saying I was stupid. I just kept yessing him like crazy, hoping he would let me live. And finally he walked away. Just walked. He felt no urgency."

She paused to take a sip of Pimms, but her momentum was going now, and she did not back off her story.

"I walked to the hotel, to the Collier House, in fact. And I told the clerk what had happened, and he called the police, and so on and so forth. Just like a bad TV movie. All the uncomfortable questions and the humiliating exam at the hospital. I had to take the AIDS cocktail as a prophylactic measure. That's part of the treatment for rape these days."

"Oh, God," Nora said suddenly. It was all too much to hear.

"I'm okay," Simone said. "I've been tested, and so has he. But that's another story. You'll hear it all at the trial."

"Trial? They caught him?" Poppy asked.

"Yes. And the trial is Wednesday." Simone paused. "And that's why you're here." She exhaled a long breath and smiled. "There. That wasn't so bad."

Nora shook her head. Her eyes were clouded with tears and she was finding it hard to breathe. "I can't believe it," she said.

"Neither could I," Simone said. "Even when I tell it, it sounds like something that happened to another person."

"Why didn't you tell us?" Poppy asked, and there was a degree of indignation in her voice.

"I couldn't. I don't know. I was ashamed."

"You did nothing wrong! *He* should be ashamed."

"Yes, but the human psyche's a weird little number, isn't it?"

Poppy stood and put her arms around her friend. Simone started to cry in earnest then, and Nora cried, too, watching them. She cried for her friend's pain and anguish, and she cried for her own helplessness, the fact that she could not even make a move toward reassurance. She had nothing at all to say.

# 6

In the afternoon, the heat became unbearable. Blistering. There was nothing to do but lie down in the cool hotel room and wait for it to pass. Nora tried to hypnotize herself by staring at the ceiling fan slicing through the air. She did not want to feel anything. She held off her emotions like two hands trying to hold off a hurricane. They were coming, but she would make them wait. She learned this trick when Cliff left her. Everything was battering at her, but she became skilled at emptying herself of all emotion, creating a void inside. She would retreat there; for hours at a time she could lie there and think of nothing at all, feel nothing. It was a useful skill, and she didn't even know how she did it. If she could explain it, she could make a million.

She exhausted herself into a fitful sleep, dreamed stupid

dreams filled with talking animals and people from her childhood; when she woke up, she was crying. How could any of this be? How could she, who had stepped so carefully around life, be smack-dab in the middle of it? How could so much pain have tracked her down? She realized this was not her own pain, but there was such a slight difference. She realized, too, that she had arrived at a point in life when things happened from which she would never recover. There would be more things like this. Cancer, soon, as they all entered their forties. More divorces. Troubled children. Unfaithful men. Menopause. Dead parents. Epiphanies.

She wanted none of it, yet she did not want to be dead. She felt stranded and alone, here in the middle of her life. She did not know what to do.

She was ashamed to admit that she did not want to go to the trial. Her selfish thought was, *I have had enough*. My own pain is still too fresh. I can't bear it. But she knew that this was such a bad thought, if she gave any weight to it her soul would be irreparably damaged.

Boo would say, "I told you she was trash."

"She was raped, Mother," she would spit back.

"Some people go looking for trouble."

She shut down the conversation. There were enough troubling discussions with Boo that were real. She didn't need to start making them up. But she couldn't really help it. Sometimes she felt she carried her mother's personality inside her—the ugly reprimands, the skeptical eye, the constant criticism.

What Nora could not believe was that this happened to Simone of all people, who had never put a foot wrong, had never had anything bad happen to her, could negotiate her way out of the tightest spot. Being raped was more like something that would happen to her, Nora. She wasn't sure why she felt that way. Perhaps because she was nearly raped once, in college. She had been so grateful to be in the company of a football player, she actually believed he wanted to leave the party so he could see her apartment. (He said he was looking for a place in that complex.) So she took him there, and the next thing she knew, her hands were being held down, and she was on the bed, and he was on top of her and shushing her. She could not move at all. He could have killed her if he had wanted to, snapped her neck at will. Somehow she thought to bite him, on the cheek. He screamed and jumped up, concerned, no doubt, about his perfect countenance. She ran out and he left. That was all. She never told anyone. Why would she? It had been humiliating, and it had been mostly her fault.

A distant sense of anger stirred in her, and for the first time she realized that, no, of course it had not been her fault. She took a man to her room, that was all. The rest of it was his crime. And certainly Simone was not to blame for what happened to her. It was horrible, that was all.

With a jolt, she thought about her encounter with the two men the night before. What if they weren't going to mug her at all? What if they had had something else in mind? Now she was scared, and she pictured Leo Girardi's round, reassuring face, and she felt immensely grateful and affectionate toward him. She wanted to track him down and give him a bigger tip.

A knock on the door made her sit up, her heart hammering. But it was only Poppy, of course, coming to see how she was doing.

"I'm all right. It's Simone we should be worried about," Nora said.

"She's taking a nap, but I couldn't sleep."

"Me either."

Poppy moved into the room and began pacing. Her usually neat hair was disheveled and it swung around her face, obscuring her expression. She fingered her silver cross and stared at the carpet as she walked.

"What are we going to do?" she asked.

"What do you mean?"

"We have to do something about this," Poppy said.

"Well, we're going to the trial, I guess."

"Yes, but we have to take care of her. We have to make sure she's okay."

"I don't know how to do that."

"Me either," Poppy said. "I've been praying for her, ever since we got back from lunch. But that is so . . . nothing. Prayer is not really a useful exercise. God is going to do what He wants, and all we can do is ask for the strength and wisdom to understand it."

Nora said, "I don't really believe in God."

"I know, but that doesn't matter to Him."

"It doesn't?"

Poppy shook her head. "His grace is there, whether we believe in it or not."

"I think Simone will be okay," Nora said, eager to get off this subject. "She seems pretty together. She's had some counseling."

"You don't understand, Nora. You really don't. When something like this happens, it gets inside you and it festers. You start to nurture it, the bad feeling, because you're so afraid if you let it go, it will come back and kill you."

"How do you know? Has anything like this ever happened to you?"

Poppy stopped pacing and looked at her with an expression of mild surprise. Nora rummaged through her brain, trying to recall some dark part of her history Poppy might have once shared in college. Some awful fact revealed over too many beers at a party or in a bar. God knows what Poppy had once told her that she had forgotten, or had never absorbed in the first place. Nora had been so preoccupied in college, so intent on getting good grades and graduating and marrying Cliff. It was completely possible that all manner of important information about her friends had skimmed the surface of her mind and gotten lost in her own commotion.

"Bad things have happened to me," Poppy said. "Not exactly like that. But I know what she's going through."

"Oh," Nora said, and she wanted to hear more but felt it was inappropriate to ask.

"What I really want to do is give her the Bible. I want her to be open to God's help. I want her to turn to Him. It's her only hope."

"Well, that's not necessarily true. There's therapy and support groups, and drugs, too. Antidepressants . . ."

"I called my husband," Poppy suddenly announced.

"You did?"

She nodded. "I was so upset, I didn't know what else to do. Adam has worked a lot with battered women. He used to run this free clinic, where he did cosmetic surgery for women whose faces had been damaged by physical abuse."

"That's admirable," Nora said. She wondered why Poppy had characterized her husband as a superficial man, concerned only with enlarging women's breasts.

"So I asked him what to do, how to handle this. You know what he said? The only cure for this kind of pain is time. He said, 'Poppy, you have to let this run its course. Don't try to fix it. It's not fixable. There's no fast cure.'"

"That sounds reasonable."

"But it's just bullshit!" Poppy exclaimed, her voice breaking like a child's. "That's no consolation to Simone. God, I could just kill her. All this time we've talked on the phone and emailed each other. She let me go on and on about my marital problems, and all the time she was sitting on this terrible secret. I'm so ashamed of myself."

Poppy started to cry. Nora didn't know what to do. She felt cold and indifferent, even though she had shed her own tears only moments before. Now she felt her defenses returning, and she actually felt angry about Poppy's display of emotion. All this faith in God, and here she was, just as weak and clueless as anyone.

Something rumbled in the distance, like the footsteps of God, coming to punish her for her cynicism. But it was only thunder, of course, rolling at a low, ominous pace.

Poppy wiped her face with the back of her hand and said, "It's going to rain."

"Yes, I guess it is."

"Didn't she understand how dangerous this city is? Hasn't she seen the statistics? You don't go walking down Pirates Alley by yourself. I tried to tell you all about this city. I tried to explain that it's hell on earth. No one would listen."

Nora had nothing to say about that. She had committed her own indiscretions here. As if the thoughts were somehow connected she said, "Tell me again how you know Leo Girardi."

Poppy looked at her as if she had suddenly started speaking in tongues.

"Leo?"

"Yes, he gave me a cab ride the other night. Remember?"

Poppy nodded, as if she had some vague recollection of that.

"I'd like to find him again," Nora said, "to thank him."

"Thank him for giving you a cab ride?"

"Well, he sort of rescued me. It's a long story."

Poppy nodded and said, "Leo is good at rescuing people."
She sat down on the bed and crossed her legs, swinging her
foot back and forth in a sort of nervous gesture. She stared at
the wall for a moment before speaking.

"Leo was my first real boyfriend in high school. We were
very close. We thought we'd get married. Daddy didn't like
him, of course. He was poor. His father was a janitor, of all
things. His mother was a maid at a hotel in the Quarter. But
they were good, sturdy people. Daddy wanted none of that.
They weren't 'our kind' of people."

"Did he interfere?"

Poppy smirked and said, "Daddy always interferes."

Nora did not bother to remind her that her father was
dead.

Poppy said, "There was an incident, when we were seniors
in high school. We got very serious and we were going to
elope, but Daddy found out about it and put a stop to it. First
he offered Leo money to stay away from me. Leo took it. I
couldn't believe it. He said he was only going to use the
money to take me away and marry me. But . . . things conspired. It never happened. I don't know if he gave the money
back. I'd like to think he did."

"Wow," Nora said. "Imagine that."

"It's not so hard to imagine. Leo was dirt-poor, and Daddy
was a very powerful man."

"No, I mean the coincidence of me getting in his cab."

Poppy smiled. "It's not all that fortuitous. New Orleans is
a small town. That's what people forget. It feels like a big city,
but that's only because of the tourists. The people who actually live here, they barely make up a respectable population.
Everyone knows everyone else's business. It's odd, because
the city has all the detriments of a small town, and all the
detriments of a city. It's the worst of both worlds."

"It's funny, the way you talk about it. I'm surprised you ended up back here."

"You can't escape your history," Poppy said, as if that were an immutable truth.

"I think I escaped mine," Nora put forth, not at all convinced, but hoping it was true.

"Really? You still live in Virginia."

"But nowhere near my mother."

"Still, have you escaped her? Do you not feel your whole upbringing walking around with you? America is this strange, nomadic place, where we jump from city to city as if changing the landscape will somehow eradicate the past and improve our dispositions. In other cultures, you don't have that choice. Here we are afflicted by the possibility of distance. We think it's an answer, but it's really just a diversion."

Nora thought of Cliff, running away to Miami with June Ann, trying to start over with a new identity, trying to pretend that he didn't owe money to anyone, trying to forget he had children to take care of. When would it hit him? Did he wake up in the middle of the night in a cold sweat, regretting the fact that he had deserted his obligations? She hoped so, but she didn't feel she could count on it. She suspected that Cliff slept just fine, convinced he had gotten away, proud of himself for covering his tracks.

"But you don't know how to get in touch with Leo Girardi now?" Nora asked.

"I'm sure he's in the phone book. People don't try to hide in this city. There's no point."

Nora nodded, trying to appear detached. Poppy chewed on a fingernail, appearing to be deep in thought. Nora waited, though she wasn't sure what for. Eventually she realized she wanted Poppy to leave so that she could track down Leo. She had his business card, but for some reason felt strange calling him at the cab company. As if she didn't want his dispatcher to know.

"What else did your husband say?" Nora finally asked.

Poppy shrugged. "The usual stuff. He wants me to come home. He still loves me. He wants to come to New Orleans and talk things out."

"Is he coming?"

Poppy shook her head. "I forbade it."

"Does that really work? Forbidding men to do things?"

"We'll find out, I guess," Poppy said, and it was clear that she wanted her theory to be tested.

**Poppy finally left, and the thunderstorm arrived in full force.** Buckets of rain thundered down on the roof, on the slate patio, against the windows. For Nora, it was a soothing sound. She always enjoyed a storm because it limited her options. There was nothing to do when a thunderstorm was happening. No talking on the phone, no taking a bath, no going outside. She could only sit and listen, flinching at each flash of lightning, counting until she heard the thunder. Annette was deathly afraid of storms. Whenever one occurred at night, Nora always awoke to find her daughter creeping into her bed. Back when she was still married to Cliff, these visits made him cranky. He'd say, "Why the hell do we have a three-bedroom house if our children are going to sleep in our room?"

"It's only when it storms," Nora would say.

"It storms a lot in Virginia. Why don't we just move her in for the summer?"

Annette seemed to frustrate and confound Cliff. She had been a fix-it baby. Their marriage was already troubled when they decided they should either break up or have another child. Nora had read all the articles in *Parenting* and *Redbook,* and she knew it was wrong to have a child for this reason, but she wanted another one and decided to close her eyes to the onslaught. If Annette had been a boy, things might have been different. Throwing a baseball, coaching Little League, being a Boy Scout guide, might have gotten them through a few more years. But Annette had arrived, as feminine as any little girl could be, and she scared the daylights out of Cliff. From the moment she was born, she was aloof. She did not want to be held, did not want to be taught or guided. It was clear she intended to figure things out for herself. She taught herself how to sleep through the night at six weeks, how to walk at eleven months, how to read at age four. She never said so, but it was apparent that Annette thought her father and brother were inferior examples of humanity. So clumsy, so needy, so desperate for her attention. She ignored them to an almost pathological degree. She focused instead on her mother, as if she had an innate understanding of the female psyche, the woman's struggle. She felt a kinship with her mother. She called her mother to kill spiders or to help her reach something on a high shelf. She did not want to be dependent on men. She didn't trust them.

Was this something Nora had inadvertently communicated to her? Had she sent those signals to her at an early age, possibly even in the womb? She hoped not, and yet she was secretly proud of her daughter's stern defiance and independence. She never had to worry about Annette. She did worry about Michael, who rattled around in his existence like a loose marble. Life baffled him. He seemed to be held hostage by the mercurial nature of being alive. From an early age, Michael was hesitant to attempt anything, already anticipating his own failure. He seemed almost paralyzed. He tried out for sports teams and quit before the final cut. He studied just enough to get by. He noticed girls from afar. Lately he had started to show an interest in music, making a cautious attempt to play the guitar. But he hid these efforts behind his locked bedroom door. Whenever Nora asked how it was going, he denied knowing what she was referring to. Michael was allergic to risk, it seemed, and Nora simply did not know how to talk him out of it. She didn't know how, she realized, because she felt she shared that affliction. For some reason, Annette regarded her mother as a brave and adventurous person, but that was a mother she had created in her own mind.

"I like having a mother who works," Annette had announced when Nora started her calligraphy business. "You said you always wanted to write, and now you are!"

Nora had laughed, and it took her a moment to realize that Annette honestly did not understand the difference.

"Well, honey, that is not the kind of writing I meant," she admitted. She felt incapable of deceiving her daughter.

"What kind, then?"

"I wanted to make up stories. You know, write books."

"So, write books," Annette said, as if it were that simple. "You know how."

"No, I don't really."

"Well, I'll tell you. I read books all the time. You start with chapter one. You don't have to say 'Once upon a time.' You can just start writing about imaginary people, and you can make them do and say all kinds of things."

"It's not that easy, sweetheart."

"Yes, it is, Mom. I've read these books, and some of them aren't all that good. You just start giving people names and making them do things. Like something scary happens to them. Or something magic. And it all ends up okay. You should put a cat in there, too, or a dog. There's always a pet or something."

Nora had laughed, admiring her daughter's raw and, as usual, linear interpretation of literature. But was she so far off? Something happens. There's a pet. It all works out. This sort of wisdom was exactly what had frightened Cliff. Nora recalled, with a chill, how Annette had interrogated him one morning at the breakfast table not long before he ran away. Out of the blue she had said, "Daddy, would you leave Mommy if you thought you could get away with it?"

Nora had been packing the kids' lunches at the counter. Cliff was reading the paper and shoveling cereal into his mouth, disconnected from his environment. Michael was still loitering upstairs, getting dressed.

Cliff said, "Annette. What on earth would make you say that?"

"I dunno. But would you?"

Nora paused and waited for his answer. She wanted to know.

"You have an incredible imagination," Cliff had said.

"No, I don't," Annette said. She seemed to have that understanding of herself. She was too attuned to details, too busy analyzing reality and putting it all in a meaningful order. She could not give herself over to flights of fancy. And this was when Nora realized that all her nagging suspicions about Cliff and his waning interest in her were real.

Cliff had refused to answer the question, and had gotten up to go to work, leaving the house about twenty minutes earlier than he needed to. After he was gone, Nora sat down at the table across from her daughter and said, "Why did you ask that question?"

Annette shrugged, unwilling to answer. She picked the marshmallows out of her Lucky Charms, and Nora was glad her daughter had not answered. It was something Annette had overheard him saying on the phone, probably. The end of their marriage had come to stay; it hovered over them like a dark cloud. She could not hide from it anymore. Her daughter had already embraced the knowledge.

Annette had been conceived as an answer to their problems, and in the end, she had lived up to that promise. She had arrived as the truth teller. She had let them know, in no uncertain terms, that the game was up. The lie was exposed. The only thing left to do was to act.

That seemed so long ago, a memory shrouded in all the events that had followed it, a whole lifetime of things that had come after, but, in fact, nothing had come after. Months ago, that was all. Not even a full season.

The storm was going away, so Nora felt safe picking up the telephone. (Was there really any danger in being on the phone during a storm, she wondered, or was this some leftover superstition from her childhood?) She dialed 411 and asked for Leo Girardi, a residence in New Orleans. The operator couldn't find it. "Try Leonardo Girardi," Nora suggested.

"In Saint Bernard's Parish," the operator said. "Hold for the number."

It rang and rang. Finally, a small voice answered, a little girl, about Annette's age.

"Girardi residence," she said.

"Is your father there?"

"Yes," she said.

"Can I talk to him?"

"Who are you?"

"Just a friend."

"My father has lots of friends."

"I rode in his cab," Nora said, feeling a bit foolish that she needed to explain herself to a child. "What's your name?" she asked, hoping to gain equal footing.

"Nicole. They call me Nicky, but I hate it."

"Are you six?"

"Yes, of course. How old are you?"

"I'm thirty-seven," Nora said, surprised at how old that sounded. "My name is Nora."

"Well, I'll tell him, but he might not want to talk to you. He's not really a phone person."

"Give it a try, okay?"

The kid dropped the phone with a clank. Nora waited for a long time. She could hear the television blaring, and she thought about hanging up, but suddenly Leo's voice came on the line, dark and deep, severe and sure of itself, just as she remembered it.

"Yeah, this is Leo. Who's this?"

"Hi, this is Nora Braxton. You gave me a ride in your cab the other night."

He said, "I give a lot of people a ride in my cab."

"I was about to be mugged. You saved me."

There was a long silence and she thought once again about hanging up. Then he said, "Oh, yeah. How are you? Are you okay?"

"Yes, I'm fine. But I've been thinking about what happened, and I feel I didn't thank you adequately enough. That is, I didn't give you a big enough tip."

He laughed. "You don't have to tip me for saving your life."

"I'm friends with Poppy Marchand," she said.

There was a pause. She could hear him exhaling.

"How do you know Poppy?" he asked.

"We went to college together. We shared a house in Charlottesville, at UVA."

"I'll be damned," he said.

"She's here now. She's at the hotel where I'm staying, but she also lives here."

"Yeah, I heard she had come back. Her old man is dead, thank God. Judge Marchand. He was a piece of work. Did you know him?"

"I might have met him once. At a parents' weekend, or graduation."

She was lying. She had not, to her knowledge, ever clapped eyes on Judge Marchand.

"Well, tell her I said hi," he said, sounding as if he wanted to end the conversation.

"Okay, but I'd like to see you again."

"Why?" he questioned.

Nora cleared her throat. "Well, I think you kind of saved my life. At least, you saved me from something terrible, anyway, and I'd like to buy you a drink."

There was a pause. She could hear the TV still, and then the loud screeching of his daughter's voice, demanding his presence.

"I'm playing chess with my daughter right now."

"Oh," she said, thinking she had never played chess with her daughter.

"I'm taking her to her mother's around ten tonight. Her mother lives in the city, so I could meet you after that."

"Where?"

"Harry's Corner Bar," he said, "on Chartres, just past the convent."

"Oh, great. I'm at the Collier House. That's not far."

"So, I'll see you there," he said, not interested in her geography.

"Okay, but . . ."

He hung up. She sat holding the phone, wondering what

she had gotten herself into. She felt she wanted to tell someone about this idea, to get someone's permission. She called
Poppy's room, but got no answer. She called Simone's room,
and after several rings she picked it up, sounding sleepy.

"God, I'm sorry, did I wake you up?" Nora asked.

"No, not really. I'm just resting."

"Well, I was thinking of going out this evening, and I
wanted to make sure you would be okay."

"I'm fine. I'm going to stay in. I thought we could do
something, but now that I'm in my room, I feel like staying
here."

"You don't sound so good."

There was a long pause and finally Simone said, "I have a
big day tomorrow, Nora. I have to meet with the district attorney and be prepped for the trial. So, you could say I'm not
doing so good."

"Oh. Right," Nora said, wanting to kick herself. In fact,
she did slap herself on the forehead in a gesture of admonishment.

"But after that, I'll probably want to go out and do some
drinking. So we can celebrate tomorrow."

"Celebrate?"

"Us being here. Me being alive. That kind of thing."

"Yes, right."

Another long pause ensued, and Nora realized she just
didn't know how to talk to her friend anymore. Was this normal? Was she being a coward?

Simone anticipated her thoughts and said, "Nora, nobody
knows how to talk to a rape survivor. I'm used to that. So
don't worry about it."

"It's not that, really . . ."

"Yes, it is. It's like having cancer or something. I don't expect you to understand. I'm glad you can't understand, and I hope you never have to."

"I just want . . . I want to be a good friend."

"You are a good friend," Simone said. "You're here."

Simone hung up then, and Nora felt grateful to be released. But she didn't feel so much better about herself. She had come here thinking they were going to have a nice vacation. If she had known the purpose of the visit, would she have come so willingly? In her heart she suspected that she was a terrible coward, and that she would have been hesitant to be a part of this.

She had never liked to look at anything really ugly. Once Cliff was injured in a skiing accident. Skiing in rough terrain, he had hit a rock, broken his ski pole and driven it several inches into his leg. The doctor had put a tube into the wound to help it drain, and Nora was supposed to clean the area around the tube every night until it was removed. But she couldn't. She had stood there, paralyzed, with cotton and alcohol in her hand, as Cliff urged her on. "It's not on you, Nora. I'm the one who has to feel the pain." But that was the point. It was other people's pain she couldn't endure. Her own didn't frighten her. She had chickened out, and he had grabbed the alcohol from her and cleaned his own wound while she waited outside the door, covering her ears so she wouldn't have to hear him yell. No wonder he lost faith in her. The waitress would probably clean his wounds. The waitress was made of stronger stuff.

It was the worst thing in the world, Nora thought, the worst thing you could possibly learn about yourself—that you have no courage. But maybe it was an acquired skill. Maybe courage could be learned.

◆ ◆ ◆

*She started to get ready at seven o'clock. She knew it would be* a lengthy process. She showered, changed clothes three times, dried her hair, put on makeup, took it off, put it on again. She finally approved of herself in a black sleeveless silk dress and clogs. She watched PBS until ten o'clock, then tied an apricot-colored cardigan around her neck and walked out into the night. The air was damp and forgiving, after the fierce thunderstorm. There would be about an hour of coolness, she realized, before the heat moved back in to stay. Cars sloshed through puddles as they drove past. Tourists had returned to the streets, traveling in packs, dressed in their shorts and oversized T-shirts and baseball caps. Looking at them, Nora feared she was missing the point of life. But maybe they were just as doubtful, just as miserable after they got home.

It seemed like a long walk, only because she was thinking of Simone and her situation. She kept picturing the crime, Simone walking down a quiet street, then hearing footsteps, then feeling herself thrown against a wall, her whole life about to change. What did she think of in those moments? Did she try to fight back? Simone was tall and strong. Could she have kicked the guy, scratched him, bitten him the way Nora had bitten the football player? Did anything like that occur to her, or did she just freeze and submit? It was hard to imagine not having the impulse to fight back. It was not a question Nora had thought to ask, but it had been simmering in her mind. The guy didn't have a gun or a knife, after all. Couldn't she have taken him? Maybe he was big. Maybe it all happened so fast. She didn't really want to know the answers to these questions, and she was ashamed of herself for thinking them. She was ashamed that somewhere in her brain a question had lodged itself like a piece of shrapnel—couldn't Simone have prevented it?

She finally arrived at Harry's Corner Bar. Walking in, she could see that the evening was not going to evolve as she had planned. She thought the clubs would be crowded and lively, but this one was mainly empty, except for a few stalwarts at the bar, and some locals playing pool at the other end of the room. She felt conspicuous here, like an alcoholic out on an evening prowl. The jukebox was playing loud, a CCR song, "Fortunate Son." She liked the song, and she felt vaguely cheered by it. It reminded her of college parties, those days when people crowded into the living room of their house, clutching plastic cups full of beer, talking all manner of non-sense, laughing, dancing, trying to get drunk. In college, the goal of the evening seemed always to be getting drunk enough to forget what you were doing, something to which she never subscribed. What the hell was the point of that? That was why in her fourth year she gave up drinking and got stoned instead. She found that she didn't forget so much when she was smoking pot. The drug seemed to slow things down, to intensify rather than obliterate. And there wasn't the hangover to deal with the next day. Just a dull aching in her lungs and a scratchy throat. When was the last time she had smoked a joint? A few years after Annette was born, she thought. Cliff had brought one home and they had smoked it and played Scrabble, and eventually collapsed in fits of giggles on the floor. The munchies had hit them and they had made banana bread, which was rubbery and awful, and they ate it right out of the pan, pulling it apart with their fingers. She smiled, remembering it, wondering if it hadn't been their last happy time together. Did Cliff still get stoned, but now with the waitress?

She sat at the bar, and the bartender swooped down on her immediately.

"What's your pleasure?" he asked.

She laughed. "Do bartenders really say that?"

"It's late and I'm bored," he admitted.

"I thought this city was always at work," Nora said.

"It's boring around here," the bartender said. His hair hung down past his shoulders, and there was a paltry goatee fomenting around his mouth. "Jazz Fest was last week. That was wild. Now everyone is tired."

"I'll have a Bloody Mary."

"No, you won't. We make 'em from scratch here and I'm too lazy to do it."

"Oh. Well, how about a martini?"

"Done," he said.

He started mixing, pouring liquids into a silver shaker, and a man with a leathery face approached her and said, "You having a good time here, little lady?"

"I don't know. It's too early to tell."

"You an East Coast girl? You look like a New Yorker."

"No, I'm a Southerner."

"God bless you. Give this woman a drink on me," he instructed the bartender.

"She hasn't had her first one yet," the bartender said.

"No matter. She needs another."

The bartender put two martinis in front of her and stood there, as if he wanted to watch her drink. She sipped the first one. It was ice-cold and delicious. She ought to drink more, she decided, feeling the gin turn from cold to hot as it slid down her throat.

"Gonna be hot tomorrow," the bartender said.

"You should be used to that."

"You here on vacation?"

"Not really. Although sort of, I guess."

"What do you think of our city?"

"I almost got mugged yesterday," she said, biting into an olive.

"No shit. In the Quarter?"

"Yes, over on St. Ann's, I think."

"Yeah, you gotta be careful. Pretty girl like yourself, walking around alone."

She blushed. It had been ages since anyone referred to her as a girl, let alone pretty. She felt embarrassed by how much she needed to hear it. Two more sips of the martini and she felt like she wanted to ask for details. *What's pretty about me? The blond hair? My eyes? They were blue until I was six, then they turned this strange blue-green color. But they are okay, aren't they? Am I fat? Would you leave me for a waitress?*

Fortunately, she didn't say any of this.

Instead she said, "My friend got raped."

The bartender seemed surprised to hear it. A look of concern spread across his face.

"In New Orleans?"

"Yes, a year ago. They caught the guy. The trial is on Wednesday."

"Goddammit," he said. "This place is going to hell in a handbasket. Well, I hope they fry the bastard."

"They don't have the death penalty for rapists, do they?"

"They oughta," he said, taking a swig from a bottle of water. "Women get the short end of the stick, don't they? I mean, guys can't really get raped. I guess they could, but most of the guys I know wouldn't mind. Sorry if that sounds tasteless."

"I've heard worse."

"But damn, to force a woman to have sex? That's just wrong."

Nora stared at him. How old was he? Barely twenty-one, she had to think, given how much trouble he was having sustaining facial hair. Was this how the younger generation saw things? Force a woman to have sex, pay with your life. Did she ever think in such absolutes? Even now, she wasn't sure what she wanted to see happen to Simone's rapist. Jail, certainly, for a long time. But death? She did not feel that kind of rage yet. Maybe she would when she laid eyes on him.

"Is she doing okay, your friend?"

"Oh, yeah, she's fine," Nora said, and then she was a little disturbed at how cavalier that sounded. But Simone *was* fine. Until she told them about the rape, Nora would never have guessed anything had happened to her. Except that she was painfully thin. And on the phone, she had sounded drugged. But so what if she was? It was okay to take painkillers when you had your wisdom teeth out. Wouldn't it be okay to take a sedative to recover from being raped?

Suddenly the bartender looked up as the door opened and said, "Leo, my man! How's tricks?"

Leo Girardi headed toward the bar in a lumbering gait. He was a little heavier set than Nora remembered, and not quite as handsome. She had fantasized him into some kind of Harrison Ford–esque hero, and now the reality of him was coldly disappointing. She felt a sudden urge to leave.

He sat beside her without looking at her and spoke instead to the bartender. "Hey, Jess, slow night?"

"Pretty damn slow. Leo, this here is my friend, the martini drinker. I don't know her name."

"Nora," she said to Leo, and he finally looked at her and smiled.

"I know Nora."

"Damn, it's a small town. What's your poison?"

"One of those," Leo said, nodding at her martini.

She slid the extra one to him. "I can't finish the one I have."

He sipped it and studied her as he drank. She did the same. His face looked a little more attractive now, not quite so doughy, and his dark eyes were very pretty—feminine, almost—deep-set with long eyelashes. She tried to picture him in high school, when Poppy knew him. Nora could imagine him about twenty pounds lighter, with more hair, long the way boys wore it then, swept over one eye, wearing a tie-dyed T-shirt and ripped Levi's. She liked the image.

"How's it going?" he asked.

"Oh, fine, I guess."

"You didn't bring Poppy with you."

Nora felt uncomfortable, wondering if he had only come here with the hope of being reunited with Poppy.

"No, I didn't. She wasn't at the hotel when I left. We had kind of a stressful day. She's married now, you know."

He nodded. "I heard she left her husband."

"Oh, well, I'm sure they're trying to work things out."

"Like you and your husband?"

"No, we're not trying at all. He's in love with someone else."

"Amazing," he said, looking at her.

"Why?"

"Well, you seem like perfectly fine wife material to me."

"You don't know me."

"No, and you don't know me." He took large sips of his drink and wiped his lips with his sleeve. "What did you call me for?"

"I told you, I wanted to thank you."

"Yeah, but that seems kind of strange to me."

"Well." She didn't know what else to say. She tucked a

strand of hair behind her ear, the way she used to in high school when she had long hair. Now it seemed foolish, as she had almost nothing to tuck. "What do you teach?"

"Excuse me?"

"In school. What do you teach?"

"Ethics," he said.

She nodded, but thought he was probably kidding. She had never had an ethics class. She didn't realize there was such a thing.

"What kind of ethics?" she asked.

"Kind? There's no kind of ethics. You can't place a value judgment on ethics, odd as that might sound. I present moral dilemmas and ask my students to construct a response. That's all. Your ethics are what they are. That's what they learn. Even the absence of virtue is a form of ethics. If you reject altruism, if you reject belief, that is an ethical position. Your ethics in that case are called nihilism. A rejection of all accepted norms and principles is a code of ethics. If that weren't the case, then philosophy wouldn't exist. Descartes, for example, decided it was necessary to doubt everything in order to formulate a single belief. Martin Luther, Meister Eckhart, Socrates, Hegel, Kierkegaard, they all thought it was their duty to deconstruct existing beliefs. So people of their time thought of them as unethical."

Leo took a sip of his drink and continued talking. "But people like the Buddha and Kierkegaard would say that the only unethical stance is the absence of a stance. That is, the lack of consciousness. Kierkegaard called such people aesthetes, a word he borrowed from the Greeks. Meaning, people who only seek pleasure and who reject consciousness. He thought such people were not actually alive."

"Aesthetes," Nora said. "You mean, like, artists?"

"A common misconception," Leo said, though he didn't clarify.

"So you're telling me that murderers are ethical," Nora said. "Murderers and rapists."

"Depends on your murderer," Leo said. "In a sense, most murderers are ethical in that most murders are crimes of passion, not a way of life. But let's take your average serial killer. He certainly is ethical. The same guy who would kill a dozen prostitutes wouldn't think of killing a guy in a bar fight or running down a cop. He has his own code of ethics. Which is not to say that such a person is moral."

"Well, what makes a person moral?"

"Morality is usually linked with spirituality. Unlike ethics, which are merely linked to a code of principles, often but not always aligned with a social contract."

"What about evil?" Nora asked, feeling the drink traveling through her from her head to her fingertips. "What about that?"

"Oh, well, that's complicated."

"Tell me."

"Everyone has a different definition. I call it the active denial of self. And the active denial of self results in the active destruction of anyone else's sense of self. Hence, Hitler. Hence, Stalin. Of course, Kierkegaard thought of the active denial of self as despair. But I think despair and evil are inevitably linked. Bertrand Russell thought that evil was a byproduct of boredom and that both these things were cousins of fatigue. Imagine that. Fatigue!"

"So maybe Hitler only needed a good night's sleep?"

"Exactly," Leo said, grinning.

"Where does God figure into all of this?"

Leo rubbed a thumb across his bottom lip and stared

at the bar, at the circles of condensation left behind by his glass.

"Here's what I think about God," he said. "It just doesn't matter. It doesn't matter if anyone believes. Of course He exists, if in no other form than in what Jung describes as the collective unconscious. You know, the common human experience. Those symbols we all recognize. Those experiences we all understand. So maybe that's God. But it's like believing in gravity. Whether or not you believe in it, it's there."

"So you believe God is there."

"I never think about it. I know I don't have to. I know He doesn't require it. The Buddha said it is pointless to contemplate unanswerable questions."

"But aren't most ethical questions unanswerable?"

"No. Only the question of God."

"Then I guess what I'm wondering is, what makes people behave well? I mean, what stops them from doing bad things?"

Leo laughed. "Obviously, nothing. People do bad things all the time."

"But horrible things. Unthinkable things."

"Well, there's no such thing as an unthinkable thing. But that takes us back to ethics. Most people behave because they are ethical—that is, they enter into a social contract. I won't kill you if you won't kill me. If someone deviates from the ethical or social contract, that person is punished."

"Not always."

"There are loopholes," he said. "Things aren't black and white."

"No, but . . ."

"And speaking of that, why do we associate black with evil? Black is the presence of all colors. While white, the color of purity, is the absence of color. Why, then, do we value absence over presence? I'll tell you why. Because presence is too frightening. Which is why we drink."

Nora wanted another sip of her drink, but his comment forced her to abstain. She sat still, crossing her hands in her lap. She was aware of being dressed in black. What did that mean, ethically or morally speaking, she wondered.

"Okay," she said, "here's a question. What would make a man leave his wife of many years for a barely legal waitress?"

Leo smiled and said, "I'm sure you're just making up an example. But, not knowing the details, I'd have to say boredom, which brings us back to Kierkegaard. Or maybe he'd say lack of consciousness."

Nora felt brave enough to sip her drink, then said, "Was this Kierkegaard married?"

Leo shook his head. "He broke off his engagement, which was a seminal moment for him. He felt that he sacrificed his love for the sake of purity, much as Abraham attempted to sacrifice his son for the sake of God."

"God spared Isaac."

"Yes, but Abraham was prepared to kill him. Think of it. Do you mind if I smoke?"

Nora shrugged, though she did mind, and the fact of Leo's smoking lowered him in her estimation somehow.

He noticed her expression and smiled.

"You're thinking, what's an ethical guy like me doing smoking a cigarette."

"They're your lungs," she said.

"Yes, they are my lungs. And my ethics are my own. I'm on the same page with Jung, who believed that the attempt to keep the shadow side at bay would ultimately be the destruction of us all. He believed that the dark and the light had to coexist, and that any attempt to deny the darkness was futile and ultimately fatal. At the very least, it resulted in shallow and unrealized individuals."

Jess put full martinis down in front of both of them and winked at Nora, for some reason she could not fathom. Her own martini was still half-full, but she was happy for the second one. It meant the night would last longer.

Nora said, "Do you have any ideas that are your own? I mean, everything I'm hearing comes from some text book, some genius with a foreign name."

Leo laughed casually, unconcerned, though Nora had meant to put him on the defensive.

"Well, as the man in Ecclesiastes said, there's nothing new under the sun. Actually, that's a saying he stole from the Egyptians. The sun sets and the sun also rises. Even Mr. Hemingway borrowed from his predecessors."

Nora yawned, trying to sort out her thoughts. She was considering the countenance of Kierkegaard, whose thin face and disheveled hair she thought she remembered from college textbooks. He looked not unlike Elvis in a cravat, as she recalled.

"Do you think people are better off believing in God?" she asked. "I mean, are they happier?"

Leo stared into the ember of his cigarette and said, "I don't think people are happy, or that they're meant to be. And I think that's just fine. I think 'happy' is a concept invented by advertisers. It's a recent phenomenon, the pursuit of happiness. Even when Thomas Jefferson was peddling it, he was really talking about something else. The absence of dread."

"What constitutes the absence of dread?" Nora asked.

"Well, Kierkegaard thought . . ."

"Fuck Kierkegaard," Nora said suddenly. "What do *you* think?"

"I think, as he did, that dread comes from the horrible

specter of freedom. It's no coincidence that the freest country in the world is the most violent. And that's really what I think."

"Are you free?" she asked.

"Yes," he said, "I am. And that's why I drink so much."

Nora noticed that the room was swirling around her. And she knew she was in a foreign city with a virtual stranger, knew perfectly well that she wouldn't see him again, so she felt at liberty to ask an inappropriate question.

"Is that why you took the money? Because you were free?"

His eyes narrowed as he looked at her. "What money?"

"From Poppy's father."

His face grew still, and he stared once again at the burning tip of his cigarette.

"I didn't take any money," he said.

"Poppy says you did."

"Is that what she thinks?"

"I don't know. It's what she told me."

A thought germinated in Nora's brain. Maybe this had all been a matter of miscommunication. Leo had not taken any money. They had parted for all the wrong reasons. And in her inebriated state, she thought herself to be powerful enough to bring them back together. She would do that, and this act would make up for all the selfish acts she had committed in the last few days and months, maybe in her life. She had originally sought out Leo with the notion of a careless affair. But now she was confronted with the possibility of doing a remarkably good deed. Which meant that she must be ethical. Underneath it all, she had good intentions. Like the heroine of a Jane Austen novel.

"I can't believe Poppy told you about that," he said, his face turning solemn.

"She didn't tell me any details. Just that her father gave you money to leave her alone. She'd had some drinks when she told me."

"He offered," Leo said. "I didn't take it. She knows I didn't take it. I told her about that. I told her her father was a bastard. I begged her to go away with me, but her connection to him was too strong. And I know why, too. Goddamn her. Now she's found Jesus and she's defending her father? That's enough to make you stop believing in God or ethics or anything. We were both screwed up at the time. But I came out of it and she didn't. Goddamn her."

"How were you screwed up?"

"It's a long story," he said. "But she didn't tell you about the baby?"

Nora looked at him, at a loss for words. Finally, she shook her head.

Leo shook his head and sipped his drink again. His cigarette had burned down to the filter.

"There was a baby?" Nora asked.

"No, no baby. That's part of her fantasy."

Nora squirmed in her seat, moving the slightest distance away from him. He was bent over toward his drink, and now the fluorescent lights behind the bar settled on his face, making him look surreal.

"Did you love her?" Nora asked.

He turned his face toward her. It was bathed in bright pinks and greens. His eyes were stern and solid, and only the muscles around his mouth moved.

He said, "Of course I loved her. What else could explain it? You asked if I believed in evil. Indeed, I do. I think love is evil. This kind of love, between a man and a woman, devoid of spirituality, anchored in nothing but a kind of recognition of ourselves in another person. It makes you a stranger to yourself. It makes you lie and cheat and steal, and keeps you awake thinking of more ways to lie and cheat and steal. It makes you examine the limits of your behavior, and if you are far gone enough, then you act on them. God, why did you get me started on this?"

He drained half of his new martini and lit another cigarette. Nora felt frightened. She wanted to go home.

She cleared her throat and said, "So murder is ethical but love isn't? That's what you believe?"

He turned his face away from her and said, "I've told you. I don't believe."

Leo didn't talk for a long time, and Nora respected his silence. She sipped her martini and listened to the music on the jukebox—Smokey Robinson singing "You Really Got a Hold on Me"—and when Jess came around with the check, she picked it up. By the time she had finished paying, Leo was willing to look at her again.

"I'm sorry," he said. "I'm in a bad mood."

"Well, okay," she said with false cheer. "Moods are allowed."

"I'm drunk," he said.

"So am I. I'll go home now."

"I'm going to walk you."

"No, I'm fine."

He shook his head. "It's dangerous here. I'm going with you."

As Nora headed out of the bar with him, she wondered where the danger was—with or without her companion.

The streets were empty, the tourists finally having retreated. Leo walked her the four blocks to her hotel. She thought of his defense of serial killers and wondered if he had ever considered such a calling for himself. That was probably ridiculous, she decided, as she moved through the soft, damp night, the song of the crickets guiding her home. As she approached the wrought-iron gate of her hotel, Leo stopped, keeping a respectable distance. He hadn't said a word during the journey.

She couldn't help thinking about Simone, being thrust against a wall by her rapist, her airway cut off by a single, strong hand, and all the moments of her life leaking away from her, heading toward some kind of cosmic drain, where all life choices go to swirl around and die, none of it amounting to much in that moment between knowing and not knowing, between the stirrup and the ground.

"Well, it was nice talking to you," Leo said, swaying on his feet.

"You're not going to drive home, are you?"

He shook his head. "I've got a friend a few blocks from here."

"What about your daughter?"

"She's taken care of."

Suddenly he smiled, and his face changed entirely.

"I feel good," he said. "It's been ages since I had a talk like that. I used to talk that way with Poppy."

"Well, I guess those days are over."

"I guess so," he said.

"I mean, she's found Jesus now."

Leo smiled. "She used to think of me that way."

"Like Jesus?"

"Yeah."

She waited for him to elaborate, but he didn't.

"Well, that's something," Nora said. She wanted to sleep.

Leo moved toward her and said, "How long since you've been kissed?"

"Not that long," she lied.

"I'd like to kiss you anyway."

"Why?"

"Because you listened to me talk about Kierkegaard. Not a lot of people will do that."

"Well, I didn't enjoy it all that much."

He leaned forward and kissed her, calmly and politely, on the lips. Something in her stirred. She felt suddenly desperate. She felt afraid of how much it made her feel, how all these sparks attacked her, these repressed memories of being alive in her body, doing what the body wanted to do. She had been ignoring it for a long time.

"Yeah," he said, when it was over. "That is what I miss."

"Good night, Leo."

She took out her key. He said, "Strange, isn't it? You live all this time. You have sex and you have babies and you get old. And what you miss is the simple stuff. When I was a teenager, kissing was just a pain in the ass, the thing you had to do to get a woman to sleep with you. But now, it's a mysterious thing."

"I guess so," she said.

"Sleep well," he instructed her, and he squeezed her arm and walked away.

She went into her cool hotel room, and she felt pleasantly drunk and ready to talk. She called her mother's number. Boo answered in a gravelly voice.

"Mom? It's me. I know it's late. How are the kids?"

"Insufferable," Boo said. "I don't know what you think you're doing with them, but Annette has a smart answer for everything, and Michael won't even leave the house."

"Why do you want him to leave the house?"

"I asked him to mow the lawn. Know what he said to me? He doesn't know how. The boy is thirteen years old and he's never mowed a lawn? I had to go out and do it myself. Honestly, Nora, what kind of children are you raising?"

Nora was contemplating an answer when there was an obvious scuffle on the other end. She heard her mother negotiating with someone else. A high-pitched voice broke through, and then Annette was on the line.

"Mommy," she said. "Mommy, is that you?"

"Yes, honey. It's me. How are you?"

"Terrible," Annette said. "She hit me."

Nora's blood ran cold. She remembered being hit by her mother. Hit on the legs with the fly swatter, hit on the butt with a spoon, hit in the face with her mother's bare hand. Her own children had never been hit by an adult. Only by their peers, in nursery school.

"What do you mean, honey?" Nora asked, her hands starting to tremble.

"I didn't want to go to bed after *Rugrats,* and she said I had to, and when I asked her why, she hit me in the face. Mommy, she hit me!"

"Let me talk to your grandmother."

"Violence is wrong," Annette reminded her.

"Yes, it is. Let me talk to your grandmother."

Annette said, "But also, we saw some fireflies. It was cool. When are you coming home?"

"Soon, honey. Let me talk to your grandmother."

"Love you to pieces, Little Meeses," Annette said. It was part of a rhyme she and Nora said every night.

"Love you back, Cracker Jack."

"Love you more, Corner Store."

"Let me talk to your grandmother."

Annette went away and then Boo came back on.

"Mother," Nora said, "did you hit my daughter?"

"I swatted at her. They are too spoiled, Nora."

"You do not hit my children."

"I tapped her."

"You don't tap my children. My children are not tapped."

"Then, why don't you come home and raise them your-self?"

"I'm needed here," Nora said authoritatively, because she was still a little drunk and her real purpose for being there was secreted away, safe to her.

"Well, you do what you have to do, and I'll do what I have to do," Boo said.

"Don't hit my children. That's not okay."

"Fine, whatever you say."

At this point Boo turned the phone over, and to Nora's surprise it was Michael's voice that came on.

"Mommy," he said, "I tried calling Daddy, but he doesn't want me. He says it will be too complicated to have me. What's going on?"

"I'm coming home soon," Nora said, "and I will take you and your sister to play miniature golf."

"Daddy says things are just too complicated."

"And maybe they are," Nora said. "Michael, you and I did not leave on good terms. But I want you to stay with me. I love you, sweetheart."

"Mom," Michael said, "let's try to get this worked out 'cause I want to be with Dad this summer."

"You're not going to be with your father. He can't support you. I don't know if he even has a job down there."

"He does, too! He's managing three restaurants."

"That's what he says," Nora said, wondering if there was any truth to it. Knowing Cliff, there probably was.

"What, you think he's lying? You never had any faith in him."

"Watch your mouth," Nora cautioned. "You don't know any-thing about your father and me. I mean, our lives together."

"Oh, no. I only lived with you my whole life."

"Then, tell me why he left."

"Because he loved June Ann more than you."

Nora felt like being sick. Of course he knew that. Either Cliff had told him or he'd figured it out. Maybe she had even blurted out that fact in his presence. She couldn't stand it that her son had so much information. She thought she had sheltered him. *But how dim you are, Nora,* she said to herself. *You have sheltered them from nothing.*

"Listen, Michael. When I get home, we're going to have a long talk."

"Great. I'll put it on my calendar."

"You want to have your Sony PlayStation taken away?"

"I don't give a shit about that," he said.

"Michael Braxton . . ."

"Mom, Grandma Boo is crazy. You were raised by her? I can't believe you can chew your food and drive and vote and stuff. She's a lunatic."

"We will talk about this later. Don't let her hit your sister."

"I really want to live with Dad, but he doesn't want me."

"So why do you want to live with him, Michael? I want you. Live with me."

"You're not a guy."

"I'll try harder, okay?"

"You're such a goof," Michael said, and she actually heard a laugh.

Then there was a dial tone, and Nora sat on her bed for a long time, listening to it, wondering where the hell her life was going. Was she out of control, or was she finally figuring out how to live?

She drew a bath and crawled into bed and slept very well. Nothing disturbed her until it was morning and she could hear people talking out in the courtyard, discussing the heat, which had predictably returned.

# 7

Margaret Marquez-Pratt was the assistant district attorney in charge of Simone's case. She was their age, but seemed younger. She walked with that plodding, athletic gait of someone on the intramural field hockey team. Nora could imagine her playing quarters at a college bar. Her suit made her look like someone who was pretending to be a grown-up. Black, with a leopard-skin print blouse, thick stockings, black pumps, no jewelry, no makeup.

She scared them. Nora, Simone and Poppy followed her back to her office without speaking. Even Simone, who never met anyone she couldn't charm, made no attempt to chat with her.

The office was bare and depressing. It had a metal desk, a bulletin board, no photos, nothing decorative. On Mar-

garet's desk sat an old push-button–style phone, which she
immediately disconnected and said, "It's the only way to do
business, to cut off the line. Have a seat. Y'all want water or
anything?"

"No, thanks," Simone said.

Simone sat in a stiff-backed metal chair. There were no
chairs for Nora and Poppy, and Margaret made no attempt to
find any for them. She sat behind her desk in a black leather
swivel chair, her arms crossed, a curious smile focused on
them.

"Usually I do the interview in private," she said.

"I want my friends here," Simone said.

Margaret raised her hands in a gesture of surrender.
"Whatever."

Margaret took out a pack of cigarettes and said, "Now, I'm
going to smoke. Is that okay with everybody?"

"Fine," they all said in unison.

Margaret took a moment to flip through the file.

"The *People* versus *Quentin Johnson*. Forcible rape. You understand the charge, or do you want me to read it to you?"

"I think I get it," Simone said.

"It means he forced you, even though he didn't have a
weapon."

"His hands around my throat were pretty impressive," Simone said.

"I understand, but what we're talking about is a gun, knife,
lead pipe. That would be aggravated rape. Now, this charge
carries a responsive verdict, which means the jury can find
him guilty as charged, guilty of attempted forcible, guilty of
simple, or guilty of attempted simple rape. Or not guilty."

No one said anything to this. Suddenly Nora found herself
speaking.

"What the hell is a simple rape?" she demanded.

Margaret looked at her, her smile still in place.

"Where the victim was drugged. I don't think Simone was drugged. Were you?"

"No, I don't think so."

"But what does simple rape mean?" Nora continued, surprised at the amount of anger she felt, and at her willingness to express it. "It was easy to accomplish? It was less complicated than all that pesky life-threatening stuff?"

Margaret finally lost her smile and said, "It's just terminology."

"It's lousy terminology."

Simone reached back for Nora's hand and said, "It's okay, sweetie."

"No, it isn't."

"Let's not rediscover America here, all right? I just want to get this over with," Simone said.

Nora felt embarrassed, having been admonished by her friend when she really meant to help. She avoided looking at Margaret, and looked at Poppy instead, certain that she would understand her anger. But Poppy was staring out the window, as if she had not heard any of this.

Margaret looked back at the files, then up at Simone. "You had a lot to drink that night."

Nora bristled but kept her mouth shut.

Simone said, "No, I didn't. Not before the rape. I drank a lot after it."

"The doctor said he smelled alcohol on your breath."

"Yes, I drank after I got back to the hotel. I was a wreck. The hotel clerk kept giving me wine. It took the cops at least an hour to arrive."

"Two hours," Margaret said.

"Whatever," Simone said.

"And the cops took you back to the crime scene and you couldn't identify it."

"I was drunk," Simone said. "And upset."

"Okay."

Nora glanced at Poppy again, with no success, and then a sudden, disturbing thought swept over her and she wondered if Poppy knew about her and Leo. Had she seen them in front of the hotel? There wasn't much to see. It was just a kiss. But was the whole thing a bad idea? Was it somehow hostile to seek out the company of Poppy's high-school boyfriend? Nora felt she had no moral barometer anymore.

Margaret said, "So you talked to this guy in the club?"

Nora was surprised to hear Simone say, "Yes, we spoke briefly."

"So you knew the guy?" Margaret asked.

"No. We exchanged small talk."

Simone shifted nervously in her seat. Poppy tore her eyes away from the window and looked at her friend, as if this detail had finally caught her attention.

Nora didn't know what to think. She had assumed the man had been a total stranger, someone who had sneaked up behind her in the alley. She was sure it didn't matter. It was just different, that was all.

Margaret stared at the file in front of her for a long time, then said, "I want to do this without your friends. If that's okay."

"It's not," Simone said. "I need them here."

Margaret leaned over her desk and said, "I know you need moral support. But here's the thing. Whether you mean to or not, you alter your story according to who's listening. You leave out a fact here, a detail there, because you're afraid of being embarrassed. You might not even feel yourself doing it, but it happens. Okay? The goal is to get this guy put away. That's what I'm here to help you do. And it would all go much faster if you'd just take my advice."

Simone gave a slight nod, and Nora felt angry all over again.

She said, "Look, it's Simone's case, and she should handle it however she wants to."

"No," Margaret was quick to say, "it's the people's case. We chose it. We are prosecuting, not Simone. She's a witness. She's the victim. It's our job to get the conviction, and that's what I'm trying to do."

"But still . . ."

Simone said, "I am not a victim. Don't refer to me that way."

Margaret took a deep breath and said, "Look, Ms. Gray. I am a feminist from way back. I have been in my share of marches. I am not deluded about the way the system works, about the way women are mistreated or misrepresented. I did not write these rape laws, and I do not like them. I don't approve of how the jury system works either, but it's what we have. Now, you might not want to be a victim. You might want to be a survivor, and that's admirable. But that's not what the jury's going to want to see. They don't want to see you dry-eyed, composed, a year's worth of counseling and you're back together. They want you crying, trembling, passing out from grief and shame. That's what they're going to understand. I'm not saying you have to do that. I'm just saying that for the next few days, you are a victim and you need to start thinking of yourself that way and give your best performance. Then, when we get this guy convicted, you can go home and be a survivor and a feminist. You can be a goddamned honorary man, if you want, but not now. Not here."

Nora felt her throat constrict, so much anger was flooding her at once, and she thought of her husband and his waitress, and how she had probably been thinking of herself as a victim all this time, and that she had been figuratively raped (maybe, sort of), and that she wanted to be a survivor, too. It was a different way to go, and it infuriated her that Margaret was taking away her friend's dignity. As if it were an easy thing to replace.

She waited for Simone to argue, but she didn't. Instead she gave a slow nod and said, "You're right. You're right."

Margaret looked at Nora and Poppy. It took them a second to realize they had been dismissed.

"There's a café right next door," Margaret said.

They didn't speak as they walked down the steps of the court building and onto the sidewalk, turning in the direction of the café. They had nothing to say, and the din of the traffic and some distant construction would have drowned out their voices anyway. This was the real thing, where people tried to live real lives. This was not the tourist version; here there were bail-bondsmen offices across the street, and the police station around the corner, and boarded-up restaurants, and gas stations that looked ready to be robbed. Nora felt afraid, even in daylight. She was happy when they finally arrived at the Justice Café.

"They must be kidding," Poppy said after reading the sign.

"I guess they have a sense of humor about the criminal justice system."

"I guess you'd have to," Poppy agreed, "to survive."

They went into the café, which was empty except for a painfully thin man wearing a flannel shirt (despite the heat) and a Saints baseball cap. He seemed overjoyed to see them.

"What can I get you ladies?" he asked.

"Just coffee," Poppy answered for both of them, eliminating the possibility of eating anything in there.

The tables were wobbly and had red-and-white-checked vinyl tablecloths with a history of food stains and cigarette burns on them. There was golf on the TV, and after serving them, the thin man went back to watching it. Nora wondered if he had had a recent illness or was in the throes of one. Perhaps he was dying, and this was how he intended to spend his final days, sitting in a café and imagining himself teeing off with Tiger and the other guys. It was too sad to consider.

Poppy said, "Simone is not telling us the whole story."

Nora looked at her. This was what had been on Poppy's mind as she stared out the window.

"What do you mean?" Nora asked.

"You heard. She was drinking. She knew the guy."

"She just spoke to him."

"She never told us that."

"Does it make any difference? She was still raped. She could have been on a date with him. It wouldn't matter."

Poppy said, "I agree, but the point is, she's lying."

"Maybe she was embarrassed."

"You don't understand, Nora. You always had your head up your ass about people."

Nora flinched, as if she had been struck. She was too surprised by Poppy's words to respond.

Poppy said, "In college it made me insane, your naïveté. It's how you ended up married to Clifford Braxton, the biggest liar on the planet. You couldn't catch him at it, so you didn't suspect him. You think he wasn't sleeping around on you all through school? Everybody knew it."

Nora felt her neck muscles tighten. She wanted to scream, the way she did in a nightmare, where her mouth opened and no sound came out and her chest ached.

"You were that way with Simone, too. Simone always lied to you. She made fun of you, the way you trailed around after her, like a lap dog. You were so obviously ashamed of your background, and you were so eager to escape it, even though you denied it. You studied hard and you dated the handsome guy and you focused on how your life would look after college. Not on what you wanted. Not on what you believed or who you were. That's how you ended up here, stranded, looking for an identity. You don't know who the hell you are without Simone or Cliff or someone to emulate. I hate having to tell you this, Nora, but I can't stand to see you getting sucked in again."

Nora sat still for a long time, her head thick with shock and sorrow, as if someone had just told her her entire life had never happened. That she had dreamed it. Like she had really been in a coma all this time, a vegetable on a respirator. She had contributed nothing. She had done nothing except breathe and ingest.

Nora said, "Why don't you just snap my spinal cord while you're at it?"

Poppy actually laughed. "Okay, I'll give you that. You were funny sometimes."

"Thank God I was something."

"I get frustrated with you because you won't see things. I want you to be a whole person."

Nora said, "Look at you, Poppy. Are you a whole person? All this God and Jesus crap. That's your identity? At least I don't run and hide behind mysticism and dogma."

"It's the opposite of that. I have come out of hiding. I used to hide behind sin."

"Please."

"You don't understand where I've been, Nora. You don't know what I have to apologize for."

"You stood for something once. You hated your father, you hated New Orleans, you were going to be an artist, you were

going to reinvent yourself. And what did you do? You can
back here and started over from scratch. You don't even
paint."

"Painting is an act of vanity."

"That's crazy."

"I have committed a mortal sin!" Poppy said, loud enough
to make the man look away from the golf game. "And I have
to atone for it. That is what I am doing. It's a lifelong
process."

"What sin, Poppy?"

Poppy's face had turned red now, and a strand of hair had
fallen away from its perfect configuration, and that single
dark strand drifting over one eye made her look suddenly
loose and crazy. She said, "My father . . . my father . . ." And
then she said, "Leo . . ."

Nora looked up at her, afraid that her face had suddenly
flushed, too, and that her guilt was surrounding her like an
aura.

*You did nothing,* she reminded herself. *You kissed a man,
that's all.*

"What sin?" Nora asked again.

"My father's dead," she said, "and Leo has made his peace,
but I am the only one left. I have to finish the job."

"What job?"

Poppy began to cry. She grabbed some napkins and held
them against her eyes for a long time, and when she took
them away, there were mascara stains under her eyes. Nora
leaned across the table and wiped them away.

"I'm sorry," Poppy said. "I didn't mean to attack you. It's
all so much to bear."

"We'll get through it," Nora said, with no evidence at all to
support her belief, except that she had gotten through everything else in her life, and she did not feel diminished.

◆ ◆ ◆

*When they got back to the criminal courts building, Simone*
was standing in the lobby with Margaret. They were chatting
as if they were old friends, holding Styrofoam cups of coffee
and laughing. The lobby was full of heavyset black women
and police officers and white girls who looked young enough
to still be in school. Nora and Poppy caught a few stares as
they walked through. Nora wasn't sure what it was about
them that made them stand out. Maybe it was how uncomfortable they looked, how obvious it was that they did not belong here.

"Oh, here are the girls," Simone said cheerfully.

"Thanks for your cooperation," Margaret said, offering her
hand. They shook it, feeling awkward but not knowing what
else to do. Nora had the sense that Margaret knew a lot more
about the world than she did, and that inside she was scoffing
at her, and at Poppy and Simone. She imagined Margaret going home to her roommate or lover or spouse, kicking off her
shoes and saying, "What a bunch of idiots I had to deal with
today. These UVA girls. What a waste of an education."

Or maybe Margaret was alone. Maybe her work was her
life. Did she wrestle with all the same dilemmas—have I sacrificed my personal life in exchange for my career? Should I
have a baby? Should I write a book? Suddenly Nora thought
of those invitations she was supposed to finish, and it alarmed
her how quickly and easily she had abandoned her work.

It was starting to get dark as the three women walked outside, but only because another storm cloud had moved in.
Nora glanced at her watch and saw that it was approaching
four o'clock.

"I feel like shopping," Simone said. "How about you?"

"Why not," Poppy agreed.

They caught a cab and went back to the French Quarter.

For a long time they wandered in and out of clothes shops and antique shops, picking over the curious offerings, laughing and joking about what they could and couldn't live without. It felt like college, and it was easy to forget what they were all here for. Simone was clearly not interested in talking about what had transpired in that off-limits office. And Nora and Poppy were too afraid to ask. Simone was cheerful, and they did not feel willing to interfere with that.

The rain had come and gone by the time they made their way back out onto Jackson Square. The street musicians were coming out again, and a few fortune-tellers were setting up shop.

Simone said, "Oh, we have to have our tarot cards done."

Poppy shook her head and said, "I don't believe in that."

"Neither do I," said Simone, "but it's a hoot. We have to do it while we're in New Orleans. Come on, it'll be fun."

Simone chose a woman with Coke-bottle glasses and a small dog situated on her lap. They sat in lawn chairs next to her, and the woman said, "The heat's back."

"Excuse me?" Simone said.

"The heat. It's back."

"Oh, yes," Simone agreed. "Does that mean anything?"

"It means summer's coming."

She started shuffling cards with tanned, pudgy hands, their backs riddled with age spots. The dog remained so still in her lap, Nora thought he might be dead.

"It's ten dollars to have your palms read, fifteen for the tarot, and we'll take it from there if you want more. Who wants to go first?"

"I do," Simone said.

As the woman dealt out the beautiful, mysterious cards, she said, "It's important to remember that these cards do not predict the future. They simply present you with possibilities

which you may embrace or reject. Tarot teaches us how to
deal with various opportunities. It is not what's going to happen. It's what may happen. Understand?"

"Yes," said Simone.

"Because you are in control of your life. Don't ever forget
that. You are what you are because of the conscious and sub-
conscious choices you have made."

Simone stifled a yawn, then said, "No offense, it's been a
long day."

The cards looked crazy and frightening. Nora was certain
that nothing good could come of this conglomeration, but as
she laid them out one at a time, the card reader looked un-
alarmed. She stared at them for a long time, lighting a cigarette and blowing her smoke straight up into the air, toward
the clouds. She said, "Well, you have a lot of opportunities
coming your way."

"Who doesn't?" Simone said.

"A lot of people don't. Sometimes the cards are consistent
and unvaried. They suggest a smooth course. But you? You're
in for some ups and downs. Just remember, there are no
tragedies in life, only opportunities."

"Okay," Simone submitted. "Let's hear about them."

The card reader pointed and said, "These are all cards of
the minor arcana. You already have money, you have luck,
you have pain, and you have peaceful resolution. But here is a
card I want to focus on. The Hermit."

"That's not me," Simone said. "I am so not the Hermit."

"Girl, do you have a hearing problem? These cards aren't
literal. The Hermit is the wise spirit within us. Everybody has
that. Some folks don't listen to it."

She drummed her finger on the picture of a man, head
bent, staff in hand, holding out a lantern.

"He stands at the precipice but he does not step over it.

The Hermit is the ancient spirit who lives in us through the collective unconscious. The universal mind that guides us through the darkness with clear light. It is the deepest part of ourselves, the part that knows what to do in times of decision. When we encounter the Hermit, we should take it as an indication that the answers we seek can be found within our own hearts."

Poppy looked up and said, "That is true of any encounter."

"Yes, but the tarot tries to alert us to a situation in which we will have to use those forces."

"Go ahead," Simone said.

The reader pointed to another card and said, "This is the Wheel of Fortune. It's rare that you get these two cards together, as they are both part of the major arcana. This card represents the circular nature of time. What goes around comes around. The sphinx at the top represents success and good fortune. The devil at the bottom is there to keep us alert, to help make us aware that all things are subject to change."

"Oh, this is nonsense," Poppy said. "And it's pagan. The tarot cards are based on ancient pagan rituals and beliefs. It's blasphemous."

The card reader suddenly looked in her direction and said, "You have your own penance to pay. Try not to interfere."

Poppy just stared at her. Nora looked back and forth between them, wondering what to do.

The next card the reader pointed to looked pretty dire. It showed a man facedown with several swords in his back. It was called the Ten of Swords.

"This doesn't look good," Nora heard herself whisper.

"Every card is good," the reader said, "if you choose to see it that way. The Ten of Swords represents a potentially difficult situation. A card predicting loss and release. A new awareness that the difficulty is finally past. It seems negative, but it is a card of hope and an indication that troubles will not be permanent."

"No troubles are permanent," Poppy said.

"Tell me more," Simone insisted.

"This is the card of judgment," the reader said. "It says that a judgment will be found in your favor. Judgment speaks of a time of reckoning, a time of bringing to light those things which were hidden. What is your judgment of yourself and your own self-appraisal?"

"I don't know," Simone admitted.

"Whatever is up in the air, it will come down on your side. But it will mean nothing until you judge yourself, until you absolve yourself of what you know you have done. Justice does not come from the outside. It comes from inner peace. You cannot find the answer you are looking for on the outside."

"Why not?" Simone asked.

"I told you, all scores are settled within one's soul, within the psyche. You may have justice on the outside, but it is in here," the reader said, stabbing her own chest with her index finger. "This is where we find peace."

Her little dog barked and Simone said, "Is that all?"

"I worry about you," said the reader. Her eyes seemed abnormally large behind the glasses. They seemed capable of seeing something on another plane, in a parallel universe. Now that the dog was awake, his eyes seemed to bear the same trait. Nora shivered and pulled her sweater around her shoulders. It was hot, but a chill had settled inside her and she couldn't stop shaking. "I worry," the reader continued, "because you are not open. At this moment, you are closed to possibility. And anyone who is about to face this many challenges needs to be open. Otherwise, it will turn to pain."

"I've had pain," Simone told her. "The thing about it is, it doesn't kill you. It just hurts. These days, if something doesn't kill you, it doesn't impress me."

"Well, all right." The reader sat back and sighed. "That'll be fifteen dollars."

Simone gave her twenty and told her to keep the change. They walked back across Jackson Square, silently contemplating what had just happened, wondering how to respond. Nora thought she should laugh, but no one else seemed to favor that idea. Finally Simone said, "What an obnoxious old hag."

Poppy said, "What did you expect, Simone? It's voodoo nonsense. That's her way of feeling powerful. Pretending she has answers she doesn't. Ascribing some sort of mystical authority to a bunch of playing cards. It's completely amoral."

"You mean immoral," Nora corrected her. "There's no such thing as an amoral world."

Poppy stopped walking and looked at her. "Where did you hear that?"

Nora felt momentarily confused, and then she realized she was quoting Leo Girardi. Her attempt to steal his philosophy had given her away.

"I don't know . . . it's just something I heard once."

Poppy stared at her long and hard. Her eyes were dark and piercing, and any notion Nora had that Poppy wouldn't mind her connection with Leo went up in smoke. She felt frightened and desperate to hide her actions.

"Let's stop talking about it," Simone suggested. "I'm hungry. Let's go to Nola. It shouldn't be crowded. It's still early by New Orleans standards."

The restaurant Nola was right up the street in the Quarter. It was, in fact, already crowded, a large group of people hanging around the bar, waiting for tables. But Simone spoke briefly to the maître d', and suddenly a man in a suit came out, and then the sous-chef himself, and they were being led like royalty to the finest table in the house.

"Emeril's a friend," she told them as they sat down.

"Who?" Nora asked.

"Emeril Lagasse. He owns this place, as well as several other places in town. Possibly the best chef in the country. I'd judge him that way, anyhow. I have said so in articles. That's why I get treated so well."

"I thought food critics weren't supposed to identify themselves," Poppy said, as if the special treatment unsettled her some.

"True," Simone said, "but it's too late in this restaurant. They already know me."

The waiter brought over complementary champagne and appetizers, a delicious crab concoction that Nora ate so quickly she was startled to find it gone. She had never tasted anything like it. It was so good it brought tears to her eyes. Looking over, she saw that Simone had barely touched hers.

"Did you like it?" Nora asked.

"Of course. It's fabulous. But I have this eating problem."

"Don't you eat anything?"

"Enough to stay alive, I think."

"Did this happen after the rape?" Poppy asked.

"No," Simone said. "It had started before then. It's just gotten worse. I think because it is my work, and because I feel like such a fraud, making my living the way I do. Even when I was modeling, I could eat. But being a restaurant critic has kind of done me in. It's hard to explain."

Simone eagerly sipped at her champagne and lit a cigarette. She glanced nervously around, as if expecting to see someone she knew. Suddenly she said, "Oh, dear God, girls. How did we end up like this?"

Nora and Poppy looked at her, knowing what she meant but not wanting to acknowledge it, and certainly not wanting to talk about it.

Poppy said, "Things aren't so bad. I am not unhappy."

"But it is not how we envisioned ourselves. Remember in school, when we felt like great things were in store for us? I guess UVA made us feel like that. Everyone there acted as if they were so anointed, so privileged. I guess we were. I guess I felt those expectations hovering over me."

"But you were born privileged," Nora said, hoping that didn't sound too insulting.

"I was born to money," Simone objected. "We never had any kind of pedigree. My father just went to some half-ass college in Arizona. He always longed to be taken seriously as an intellectual, someone with taste and dignity. The movie industry lets you pretend you have that. But he knew he was on the outside looking in. Lately, he's been replaced by young Harvard MBAs. His job has dwindled down to nothing. He knew his lack of education would catch up to him eventually. He's still rich, but he's not part of the elite. He's not in the club."

"Well, the club sucks," Poppy said. "My father was always in it, and I can tell you the kind of thing that goes on there. Not good. You should consider yourself lucky."

"Oh, I do," Simone said. "And there's nothing like almost dying to make you feel like the luckiest person on earth. I know I have learned lessons, but I don't see why I had to nearly die to be taught. Wasn't there an easier path?"

Poppy said, "God has a divine purpose for our lives, and it is best not to question it. You just have to have faith."

"Oh, Poppy, you know I love you. But this religious horseshit is starting to annoy me. Since when did you believe in this crap? Why give up your power like that? Why hand it over to some bearded guru in the sky, who fucked things up in the first place? Tell me, what is the divine purpose for Quentin Johnson? What does that wise one have in store for him?"

Poppy gave no answer to that. Nora sensed that she certainly had one but had lost her desire to share it with the nonbelievers. A waiter took their order and they sat in silence for a while, listening to the lively chatter in the restaurant.

"Boy, that Margaret Marquez-Pratt is a piece of work, isn't she?" Simone eventually said.

"She's tough," Nora agreed.

"You ought to sick her on Clifford Braxton," Simone said. "He'd come back to town and pay his taxes and a few other people's to boot. And he'd leave that waitress slut in a by God New York minute."

"I'd just as soon hire a hit man," Nora said.

"No, you wouldn't," Poppy interjected. "You don't really hate Cliff. You say you do, but you don't. You want him to come back. You'd take him back tomorrow."

"Poppy, how can you say that? It's completely untrue."

"Then, why do you still wear your wedding ring?"

Nora blushed and looked down at the wide gold band on her hand. It was a hard question to answer. In a way, she felt she had no legal right to take it off until they were really divorced. But she recovered from her embarrassment long enough to say, "Why do you still wear yours?"

"Because I still have hope," Poppy answered.

"You think Adam is coming back to you?"

"I left him," she said simply. "And I may go back. It doesn't look good, but it could happen. I pray for it."

"What do you pray for?" Simone asked. "That he'll find Jesus?"

"No. That Jesus will find him."

"Wait, Jesus doesn't lose people, does He?"

"I don't want to have this discussion. You're just being glib."

"I'm always glib. You know that."

Their food came, and it was so unbearably delicious that they couldn't talk while they ate. Nora feasted on some tender duck that fell away from the bone and a soothing pile of creamy polenta mixed with a tangy collection of greens. Poppy devoured her catfish, and even Simone made some progress with her lamb.

"Oh, this is delightful," Simone said. "The lamb is tender and petulant, while the mashed potatoes are sensually flavored with garlic and rosemary. They are nicely complemented by a mango relish, giving an ethnic quality to an otherwise thoroughly American meal."

Nora giggled. "Are you serious?"

"It's how I'm supposed to talk about food. I told you my job was ridiculous."

"But how can lamb be petulant?"

"It can't, of course. I'm just expected to find creative adjectives. You have no idea what it's like to do this day after day. I feel like such a liar. I want to say, it's food, it's dead meat, it's mushed-up vegetables, it turns to shit in a matter of hours."

This got a laugh out of Poppy, and she pushed her plate away.

"That article would get some attention," she said.

"Believe me, one day I'm going to have a breakdown and write it."

"Well, my food was great. I never get to eat like this," Nora said. The champagne had gone to her head and she felt happy, despite the previous tensions she had sensed circling them like a flock of buzzards.

Poppy and Simone giggled some more, drinking their champagne. They were finally starting to relax. Nora was starting to feel better about being here, about her decision to come to New Orleans. She was suddenly visited by the memory of Leo's kiss, and she could do nothing to stop her face from flushing.

"But seriously, here's a question," Poppy said. "Did you know the guy or not?"

Simone's smile faded and she said, "Quentin Johnson?"

Poppy nodded.

"I didn't know him. I told you, I talked to him briefly at the club."

"Actually, you didn't tell us that. You told Margaret."

"Well, I figured you'd hear it at the trial."

"So, you weren't with him or anything."

"No, Poppy. For God's sake, he asked me for the time and he offered to buy me a drink, which I declined. That's it. Does that mean I deserve to be raped?"

"No one's saying that," Nora volunteered quickly.

"I think Poppy might be saying it."

"No, no. Of course she isn't. Look, Simone, even if you were dating him, even if you went back to his apartment, whatever, you still had the right to say no to him. It doesn't matter at all if you knew him or not. Rape is rape."

"Yes," Poppy said. "Of course, that's true. I was just wondering."

"Well, try to stop wondering," Nora said. She felt herself shaking with anger. She had never spoken to Poppy that way. For some reason, she had always been afraid to.

"All right, forget I said anything."

Another pall fell over the evening. They skipped dessert. Simone tried to pay the check, but she was told the meal was on the house. Finally they left, after touring the restaurant to thank everyone involved.

They walked back to the hotel in silence. Nora tried to think of other things, but there was no comfortable place to let her mind rest. The thought of her children staying with her mother made her nervous. Any thought of Cliff was out of the question. Thinking of her meal just made her remember the awkwardness, and the way Simone had barely touched her food. The only thing that cheered her slightly was thinking of the days on Vinegar Hill, when they were all careless and confident of their connection to each other. The days when they didn't question that connection. The days when friendship was enough. Now there seemed to be standards and restrictions. She felt she had to earn her right to be among them, and she wasn't sure how she was doing.

They parted inside the courtyard, each claiming to be terribly sleepy. Simone said, "Well, the trial is at nine A.M. tomorrow. We can have a quick breakfast and take a cab together."

"Do we get to be in the courtroom?" Poppy asked.

"Yes, but I don't. As a witness, I can only be there for voir dire, the jury selection and closing arguments. And, of course, my testimony. I'm relying on you guys to take notes and tell me what happened."

"We can do that," Nora said. Her calligraphy business had taught her how to write quickly and clearly. She could keep a neat and beautiful account of the whole thing, like a monk inscribing a Scripture.

"Okay, so good night."

Poppy and Nora both hugged Simone. Then they went to their cold, air-conditioned rooms. The light on Nora's phone was flashing. She called her message center and had two messages. One was from Boo, her raspy voice intruding on the evening like a jackhammer outside the window:

"Your children are fine, and I have decided not to bother teaching them any discipline. That's your job. Michael has settled down some, and Annette still has a very smart mouth, but that's for you to deal with, not me. I assume you're still coming back on Friday, like you said. Okay, well, tell Poppy I said hi."

Nora smirked, registering the omission of Simone.

Then there was a male voice talking, and her heart jumped around inside her chest. It sounded like Cliff, the same brusque, confident tone, the tone that suggested she had disappointed him without meaning to. It took her a second to realize that she was imagining this, and that the voice sounded nothing like Cliff's. In fact, it was softer and more solicitous, almost shy:

"I just wanted to call and say I was thinking of you. I was hoping you'd be in and maybe we could get together because I really liked seeing you last night. If you have any free time tomorrow, get in touch with me. I'd like to see you again. Well, I guess that's it. I hope I'll talk to you soon. And don't go walking around by yourself, okay? I might not be there to save you."

He never identified himself, but she knew it was Leo. She played the message back several times, and she lay on the bed listening to it, as if it were some pleasant dream she had the ability to revisit, over and over, until it became real.

## 8

"All rise for the Honorable Louis LaSalle."

Nora jumped to her feet and realized that everyone around her was a little slower to rise. She had the feeling she might be arrested if she did not behave herself in the courtroom, but the people around her, including Poppy and Simone, seemed to feel no such trepidation. They seemed skeptical, even grudging in their attempt to show respect.

The courtroom was nicer than Nora had expected it to be, even though the decor obviously dated back to the fifties. The walls were paneled, the gallery seating was done in a dark-red vinyl and the chandelier that hung down from the ceiling was a minimalist globe. There was a portrait on the wall of some grizzled judge, with a look of avuncular concern. There were two attorney's tables, just like on TV. At one sat Margaret Marquez-Pratt, looking very professional in a gray suit with a cream-colored blouse. Her hair looked more styled today and she was wearing lipstick. Beside her was a young man, another attorney, wide-eyed and fresh-faced, as if he had just walked out of law school. His hair was prematurely gray and blown dry. His face was very round, made to look more so by the large round glasses he wore. Nora certainly would not want her fate to rest in his hands, though Margaret seemed perfectly capable of getting her job done.

At the other table was the defense attorney. He was older but had one of those youthful Southern faces, full of guileless curiosity and well-meaning determination. He wore a seer-sucker suit, and his mousy brown hair defied his obvious efforts to comb it down. Then, next to him, was Quentin Johnson. Nora tried not to stare at him, but she couldn't help it. He was nothing like the monster she imagined. He was not a large man, probably no more than five feet seven or eight, no more than a hundred fifty pounds. He wore a starched white shirt and tie and black dress pants. He was handsome, with coffee-colored skin and sleepy eyes and a straight posture. Right away Nora knew this trial was going to be problematic. She was Simone's best friend, yet, looking at the defendant, she had trouble believing this man had committed any terrible deed. The troubling questions resurfaced in Nora's mind about whether Simone could have fought him off. For one thing, Simone was taller than he was, and arguably stronger. No doubt she was smarter. Couldn't she have reasoned her way out of the situation?

*Don't think like that,* she reminded herself. After all, no one had heard the facts yet, and she couldn't pretend to know what it felt like to be surprised by violence on a dark street.

The men who had nearly mugged her had appeared equally harmless.

She glanced at Simone, who kept her gaze fixed straight ahead. She was wearing a loose-fitting floral dress, with her black hair caught up neatly at the back of her head. No jewelry, no makeup except for a pale-colored lipstick. She had never seen Simone dressed this way, and it disturbed her. She had obviously been coached by her attorney. But what was so wrong with that? The object was to get this man convicted. And if Simone needed to change her image to realize that goal, then that was fair enough. No doubt Quentin Johnson had done the same thing. Surely he didn't walk around in the world wearing a shirt and tie.

The judge, the Honorable Louis LaSalle, was a short, heavyset man with a mean, jowly face. He wore black-rimmed glasses pushed up on his forehead, a shirt and tie under the ubiquitous black robe. He reminded Nora of a preacher, and she fully expected him to give a benediction or ask them to open their hymnals to a certain page. Instead he gave a dismissive wave, and everyone sat down again.

"Okay," Louis LaSalle said with a heavy sigh. "Let's get through the docket as fast as we can. We have a jury trial today. Where is Marcus Solomon?"

"Your Honor, if I might make an argument in favor of rearranging the docket," Margaret said, standing. "The victim in the case of the *People* versus *Quentin Johnson* is from out of town, and we need to get to her case so she can return to work. She cites financial hardship . . ."

"We all have financial hardship, Ms. Marquez-Pratt. I'm sure Marcus Solomon is not being paid for his time spent in court."

"But Your Honor, if you would consider . . ."

"Ms. Marquez-Pratt, we are not going to spend my time with you telling me how to organize the courtroom. Now, where is Marcus Solomon?"

A heavyset black woman, badly dressed and harried almost to the point of tears, rushed forth.

"Your Honor, Mr. Solomon assured me he would be here on time. As of this moment, I cannot account for his whereabouts. However . . ."

"He is up on armed robbery, is he not?"

"Yes, sir, though the people have offered a plea of carrying a concealed weapon, which we are prepared to accept. Or we were prepared to accept . . ."

"So his lack of appearance indicates a violation of bail . . ."

"Yes, sir, but he lives in Saint Bernard's Parish, so maybe he hit traffic."

"I live in the Parish, Ms. Forster. The people should at this time consider withdrawing the plea."

Suddenly there was a scuffle at the back of the courtroom, and a young man rushed to the front. He was breathing heavily, wiping sweat from his brow. He couldn't have been more than eighteen, a tall black man wearing jeans and a Chicago Bulls T-shirt.

"Here I am, Your Honor."

"Good of you to make it, Mr. Solomon."

Nora caught her breath. She recognized him right away. It had been dark, yet she knew that face. He was one of the men, one of the three who had asked her for the time on St. Ann Street the night she met Leo Girardi.

Marcus Solomon and his attorney whispered for a few moments, and then they stepped forward together.

"At this time, Your Honor," said the attorney, "we are prepared to accept the plea. We request probation of no less than twelve months."

"Mr. Solomon, you are aware that you are pleading guilty to a charge of carrying a concealed weapon."

"Yes, suh," Marcus said, in a tone that sounded purposely submissive, almost slavelike, Nora thought.

"No one has coerced you in any way to accept this plea?"

"No, suh."

"You understand that I could sentence you to as much as one year in county jail."

At this Marcus looked surprised and leaned over to consult with his lawyer. Then he nodded and said, "Yes, suh."

"Given that this is your first offense, I sentence you to one year of probation. During which time you are to report to your parole officer on a twice-weekly basis, and you are to abide by all restrictions placed on you by the court. Understood?"

"Yes, suh."

It occurred to Nora that this man was about to walk out of court, having brandished a gun somewhere, having nearly robbed her or done something far worse. And the judge was about to put him back out there, to do further harm. It wasn't fair. It was scary, in fact. She looked at her friends, but they were staring straight ahead, not really listening.

Nora stood, before she realized what she was doing.

"Your Honor," she said.

She could feel everyone in the courtroom turning to look at her.

"May I approach the bench?"

Louis LaSalle looked at her. "Who are you?"

"I'm . . . I'm no one, really, but I'd like to approach the bench."

More out of surprise than anything else, the judge waved her forward. She felt her heart hammering as she walked through the swinging doors, past the lawyers, up to the judge's bench.

"Your Honor," she said. "I'm a visitor from out of town, and the other night, I was walking down St. Ann Street, in the Quarter . . ."

"Wait a minute. Who the hell are you?"

"I am Nora Braxton. I'm just a tourist. But this man, this Marcus Solomon, he tried to rob me."

The judge stared at her. "Did you report this to the police?"

"Well, no, but that's only because I was saved by a cab driver. I was a little bit in shock. But the thing is, you can't put him back out there. He's dangerous."

The large black woman was standing beside her now, breathing hard. "Your Honor, I object to this disruption," the lawyer said.

"I don't understand. Are you some kind of witness for the state?"

"No, I'm here on another case altogether."

"Your Honor, this is outrageous."

"I just can't stand by and watch him get released," Nora said. "I didn't realize he was trying to rob me at the time, but now I know . . ."

"Ms. Braxton, is it?"

"Yes, sir."

"Please go back to your seat before I have you evicted."

"But Your Honor . . ."

"Are you hard-of-hearing? Shall I have the bailiff detain you? Go away, now."

Nora went away. When she turned back, she saw her friends staring at her, both of them wearing a look of surprise and dread.

Nora kept on walking, past them, out of the courtroom, into the cavernous hallway. The criminal courts building was beautiful and stately, vast in its emptiness, in its lack of warmth. It reminded her of all those presidential homes and capitol buildings she had visited on field trips in Virginia. She knew she was in the presence of the law, and she knew it should scare her. It had, when she had first entered it that morning. But now that she had seen Marcus Solomon, she realized her connection to the legal system. Before, she had felt completely alienated. She had never been in a courtroom, had always gotten out of jury duty, had never even had a traffic ticket. Now here she was, tied into the legal system in a state as strange as Louisiana. Her breath was coming hard and fast. She walked straight to one of the large windows and looked out. The hallway was populated by lawyers and their clients, criminals and families of criminals, and, at the far end, a group of students on a field trip, she had to assume. She was not at all sure how she had gotten here or what she was doing.

The day felt all wrong anyway, and she had been embarrassed half the morning because she was not thinking of Simone at all, not thinking of her case, not worrying about the outcome. She was thinking instead of Leo. She had called him right before breakfast. He had answered in a brusque, harried tone.

"Yeah, hello?"

"Leo, is that you?"

"Yeah, it's me."

"Hi, it's Nora."

There had been a long pause, and finally he had said, "Oh, yeah, hi."

"I'm sorry I didn't call you back last night. I got in too late."

"That's okay."

He waited. She waited. She thought he might have something to say to her, but he didn't volunteer it. Maybe she had dreamed it, that sweet, solicitous quality she had heard in his message. What was going on?

"Well, you said you wanted to see me again, and I wondered if you were still interested in that."

Leo cleared his throat. She could hear his child calling for him, over the din of a television set.

"Yeah, look, I was kind of drunk last night. I mean, can we talk later?"

"Oh. Okay." There was another pause, and out of desperation she had said, "Yes, we had a few drinks last night, too."

"You and Poppy?"

"Me and Poppy and Simone."

"Who's Simone?"

"That's our other friend. We came to help her out. It's a long story."

"I'd like to hear it, but I have to take my kid to school."

"Okay, whatever."

"I'll call you later. Is that okay?"

"Yes, I'll be here . . ."

"So, good-bye."

And he had hung up, just like that. Everything that happened after that had seemed like a dream. She had had breakfast in the courtyard with Simone and Poppy. They had discussed the weather, how they had slept, how the trial might go, what they would do in the evening when it was over. She had heard it all but not been a part of it. She had stored it away. Her mind was stuck in that place, where Leo had quickly gotten rid of her.

Why had she put her faith in him? Had the whole episode with Cliff taught her nothing? Men were not to be trusted. They were always looking for a way out. They said things, and they made promises, and then they felt shamed by their confession, their willingness to be vulnerable, and they took it back. She hated him. She hated Cliff. She had promised herself never to trust another man. Even her own son was untrustworthy. He had turned on her. Why wouldn't he? It was what men did. She considered, briefly, the possibility of becoming a lesbian. But she didn't like women much better, and anyway, she did like having sex with men. Liked it better than being angry with them. She had thought of sleeping with Leo since she had met him. She wanted to see that happen. She was determined, despite his efforts to humiliate her.

Cliff had always said she was afraid of sex. She didn't think so. She was afraid with him, maybe, because he was so rule-oriented, so rigid in how he went about it. She had to do everything perfectly. There was no room for play. If she moved in the wrong direction, pushed when she should have pulled, sucked when she should have breathed, laughed when she should have kept quiet, he would tell her about it, in no uncertain terms. He would shut her up, angrily, and sometimes he would say, "Don't you know what you're doing? Are you new at this? For God's sake, pay attention."

Cliff had trouble coming. They both pretended it wasn't a problem. They pretended it was stress, it was fatigue, it was his blood-pressure medication, it was her own fault, her own unimaginative approach to sex. But it wasn't any of those things. The problem was that Cliff had trouble coming, and nothing she could do would have ever solved that. She didn't really care; she would have been patient. But he was so ashamed of it, he never gave her the chance to fix it.

Once they had tried to address the problem by buying sex toys. But it had all been so awkward and cumbersome and hilarious. Trying to get the vibrator to work, trying to figure out the butt plug, trying to slide on the edible panties, trying to get the penis ring on his cock, attempting to put a cough drop in her vagina . . . They had spent an entire week doing this, and it always made Nora want to laugh, and she felt that if they could only laugh about it, everything would be fine. But each failed effort made Cliff more angry and more embarrassed, and though she tried to reassure him, nothing ever worked. She tried to believe it wasn't her. All the magazines said it wasn't her. Therapists said it wasn't her. Everyone said it was some other deep-rooted problem, something connected to Cliff's childhood, or his work problems, or their unrealistic expectations. Nora didn't think she had unrealistic expectations. She thought that if he came in some form or another, once a week, she could be happy. Once a month, she considered, toward the end of it. She asked him, over and over, if he was really gay. She would have been glad if that were the answer. She could have released him, could have let him go without blaming herself. But of course he wasn't gay. He was able to fuck the waitress, and other women, too, she suspected, and some prostitutes, she ultimately discovered, finding his credit-card statement. (Hookers took credit cards? Yes, of course they did. They'd go out of business otherwise.) It was hard for her not to acknowledge that it was indeed her. Once, toward the end, she had asked him what was going on, if they could ever expect to have a decent sex life again, and he had said, "Look, Nora, I wish I were attracted to you, but I'm not. I still want to stay married, though. I love you. Lots of people have sexless marriages."

Nora had indulged this proposal at the time, for her children's sake, and also because she was too embarrassed to admit she didn't think she could do without sex. Wasn't it selfish to leave a man for that reason? Wasn't marriage supposed to be more than that? Her parents had hated each other, after all. She was certain they had stopped having sex long before she was conscious of what it all meant. They weren't happy but they stayed together. Her generation was supposed to be different, though. She was not all that experienced when she had first slept with Cliff. She had remained a virgin in high school, had slept with her first date in college, a soccer player named Frank, who was nervous and skinny with a penis so thin, she now realized, it hardly made an impression on her. Four others had followed, only one of which was a one-night stand, and then there was Cliff, who had functioned quite properly in college, sexually speaking. It was only later that he seemed to lose interest.

After the phone call Leo had left for her, she had had high hopes for sleeping with him. It seemed logical. It seemed like the right time. And it was a big deal to her, the first man she slept with after her marriage broke up. In the days when it was dissolving, she had imagined another scenario, finding some polite, soft-spoken man who was grateful to have her. Someone who would say, "My God, you have been so neglected. Let me show you what it is like to be appreciated."

Clearly, Leo was not going to be that man.

She continued to stare out the window, and suddenly she felt a touch on her shoulder. She turned and saw Simone standing there.

Her face looked beautiful, devoid of makeup, pale white and splotchy, daring and sophisticated. Her painted lips stood out, like a splash of color in the cold room with white walls.

"Are you okay?" she asked.

"Yes, of course I am," Nora said.

"What was that in there?"

"What was it? It was the truth. That man, Marcus Solomon. He tried to rob me."

"When?"

"The first night I got here."

"Well, Nora, you can't just announce that in court. You're supposed to go to the police."

"They're going to just let him go!"

"That's how it works. They might let Quentin Johnson go, too."

"I couldn't stand it."

"Neither could I, but we have to prepare ourselves. Look, I need you to keep it together. I need you to be in there for me."

Nora stared at her for a long moment. Then she said, "Poppy told me that you lied to me in college."

"Lied to you? About what?"

Nora shrugged. "You thought I was some hick, desperate to latch on to your identity. Is that true?"

"Of course not. Poppy is always trying to stir something up."

"Why did you invite her?"

"I don't know. We had been talking for a while, and I thought it would be nice for all of us to get together. I thought I would feel safer."

"Do you feel safer?"

Simone shrugged. "I'm sitting in there, just a few feet away from the man who raped me and tried to kill me. So, yeah, next to that, I feel safe."

"Simone, I'm so sorry. I do want to be a good friend."

"You keep saying that," Simone said. "So just go ahead and do it."

Nora looked at her, feeling young and vulnerable and stupid. As if Simone's innate sense of sophistication weren't enough, the fact that she had been raped, had come close to death, made her even more . . . what? Remote? Elusive? Interesting? Nora knew it was ridiculous to respect her friend for such a thing, much less to envy it. Yet next to Simone, Nora's problems seemed tawdry and trivial. Was there ever going to be a time when her own life would stack up next to her friends'? A crazy mother, a dead brother, a cheating husband—this was all soap-opera material. But when tragedy struck her friends, it was more the stuff of movies or novels.

"Tell me how I can be a good friend," Nora said, feeling disgusted with herself for admitting her inadequacy. Why should Simone lay down such rules? Why was she, Nora, always struggling to keep up?

Simone shrugged. "I don't know. Just be there. And don't ask so many fucking questions."

"What questions?"

"Why did I invite Poppy. What's going to happen at the trial. What was I doing wandering around alone in New Orleans."

"I never asked that last thing. It doesn't matter to me."

Simone ran her fingers along Nora's arm, as a lover might do. The hairs on the back of her neck rose. Human touch. It was a thing that she missed. Not that Cliff touched her anymore, toward the end. And not that her mother ever had. She honestly did not have a solid memory of her mother touching her with affection.

Despite Simone's admonishment, Nora wanted to know things. She wanted to know why Simone had never married, why she wasn't in love, if she planned to have children, if she liked her life, if she envied Nora's in any way. Not that there was much to envy, but she did have children, and she'd never been raped. Nora felt cold when she realized that this sentence might have hit the highlights of her life.

Out of a sense of panic, Nora found herself saying, "Were you scared? I mean, when he was doing it. Did you think you were going to die?"

"Of course," Simone said, and nothing more.

The jury selection was painful to sit through. Margaret Marquez-Pratt interrogated them on several issues. First she asked if they were familiar with the French Quarter. Then she asked if they would go there alone. Then she asked if they had ever known anyone who had been raped. Half the people in the jury box raised their hands. "Yes, my sister." "Yes, my mother." "Yes, my best friend, my cousin and my half-brother." Those people were immediately eliminated. Then Margaret asked how they expected a rape victim to perform on the stand. Everyone said they expected to see a rape victim cry.

"What if it's been a year since it happened? What if the victim has had counseling and she's better now?" Margaret asked.

"Even so," one guy said, "rape is such a terrible crime. How could she get over it? How could she talk about it without crying?"

Nora looked at Simone. Poppy had reached over and taken her hand. It was going to be a long day.

Then the lawyers asked the jurors about their children, their jobs, and the three friends sat there, watching one promising juror after another being released. It took most of the day, but finally a jury was chosen. They were four black men, three black women, two Hispanic women, one white woman and two white men.

"Go ahead and call your relatives," the judge said. "Tell them you're going to be on a jury tonight and maybe tomorrow. We'll break for an hour."

Simone stood and stretched. She said, "Let's go to the Justice Café for a sandwich."

They walked down to the café. The thin man seemed pleased to see them again, and he insisted on giving them grilled-cheese sandwiches on the house. Nora excused herself and went to the public phone. She called Leo and got an answering machine. Then she called her room and got a message. It was from Leo:

"Hi, Nora, Leo here. Sorry I was so dismissive earlier. But when my daughter's around it's hard to get my attention. You're a parent, you understand this. Anyway, you said you might be around tonight. My shift ends at eleven, and I'll try to call you. It would be nice to get together for another drink. So I'm going to try to call you later, but if I miss you, why don't you just try showing up at Harry's? After midnight, I guess. If you're not there, I'll understand. We'll talk later."

Nora felt relieved. She wasn't sure why she needed his attention. Maybe it was just an important distraction, something to keep the scarier thoughts at bay.

When she came back to the table, Poppy and Simone were staring at her, expecting something.

"How are your kids?" Poppy asked.

"Oh, they're fine," Nora said, feeling embarrassment that she had not thought to call them.

Nora sat down and said, "What was it like, seeing him again?"

Simone looked at her. "You mean Quentin?"

"Yes, that's what I mean."

Simone smiled faintly, as if she had just remembered a rude joke.

"He's smaller now," she said. "Partly because he seemed like such a monster in my mind. But I'm sure he's lost weight. I'm sure that was part of the plan. He starved himself in prison so that when he went to court he'd look too frail to hurt anyone."

"That's terrible," Nora said.

"Well, you can't blame him for fighting back."

"Does it scare you to look at him?" Poppy asked.

"Not now. Not really. What scares me," Simone said, twisting a strand of hair around her finger, "is how innocuous he seems. That maybe I was never in any real danger. I could have punched him in the eyes or in the throat. I could have screamed. I could have done a number of things. But I just froze, and I took my punishment as if I deserved it. As if it were a long time coming."

"Well," Nora said, shifting uncomfortably in her seat, "I'm sure that you didn't have your wits about you."

Simone stared straight at her and said, "I let it happen. You know why? Because I thought, well, it will be over soon, and I might live. Do you know how ashamed I feel, knowing that I didn't fight back at all? How willing I was to give up this part of myself in exchange for my life? And my life was never in danger. I just gave it up. I paid full price, even though I could have bargained. What the hell is that about?"

"You're not seeing things clearly," Nora offered, but Poppy said nothing. She kept her chin tucked, staring at her lap.

Simone said, "Men are willing to defend their honor. To the death. They put on uniforms and go off and fight and have their limbs blown off. For what? Some nationalistic ideal? But women, at the first sign of harm, are willing to surrender everything. And that is a terrible thing to know."

Poppy looked up defiantly. "Women are willing to die for some things."

"What? God?" Simone laughed.

"Their children," Nora said.

"But not themselves."

"We need to get back," Poppy said, standing.

"I wasn't willing to do any of it, girls," Simone continued. "I wouldn't fight *or* die. I just turned over the government secrets."

"Yes, let's go," Nora agreed, rising.

Simone was crying hard now, still rambling. "What do I see when I look at him? I see the devil, that's what. The devil is a small man in a white shirt. He's a punk. Did you realize that? And I made a deal with him."

"Stop talking!" Poppy shouted, her voice echoing off the walls. "You know nothing about the devil. Nothing."

The tone of her voice stopped Simone cold in her tracks. And for once in her life, she had no reply.

# 9

Nora and Poppy left Simone sitting in the hallway as court was called to session. Nora had volunteered to stay with her, but Simone had said no. She wanted both of them to be present for the whole trial so that they could tell her about it later.

"Besides, I'd rather just be alone until I'm called. I have to psych myself into crying," she had said.

Nora glanced over her shoulder as they walked away. Simone, normally imposing, looked so small and alone in the big hallway, smoking a cigarette, a book open on her lap. Poppy took Nora by the arm and said, "Don't worry about her. God is with her. She's all right."

"Oh, Poppy, how can you say that? Was God with her when she was raped? Couldn't He have helped her out then?"

"It doesn't work like that," Poppy said.

"I suppose it's all in His plan, is that right?"

"Yes," Poppy said, "in fact, it is."

"Well, I have to tell you, I could have come up with a better plan than that."

Poppy just laughed and said, "We'll have to agree to disagree on this."

They sat together in the first row of the gallery. Behind them was the defendant's family—his mother, another older woman and a young white girl who must have been his girlfriend. Nora could not escape the feeling that she was about to watch a sports event. Her heart hammered, and she was actually excited at the prospect of seeing it all unfold.

Margaret made her opening argument. It was similar to the process Nora had seen repeatedly on television. She paced in front of the jury box and gave a synopsis of Simone's story. A woman had come to New Orleans on business, had briefly talked to a local man in a club. They had shared a drink. They had danced together. Then Simone Gray had told the man she was going back to her hotel. He volunteered to walk with her, and Simone had accepted, knowing that the streets of New Orleans were not safe. But she trusted this man. He had disarmed her. He had given her no reason to be afraid.

Poppy leaned over to Nora and said, "Did you know that?"

"What?"

"They danced together and had a drink. And she let him walk her back? I never heard any of this."

Quentin's mother shushed them, as if they were at a movie. Nora was glad she was saved from responding. Of course she didn't know any of this. She knew what Simone had told her, and hers was a much different story. She wondered if Margaret had gotten confused. She decided not to judge, just to sit and listen.

"Then, when he got her on a secluded street, he attacked

her. The evidence will show that he choked her, threatened to kill her and violently raped her. You will hear from the night clerk at the hotel, who took her statement. You will hear his frantic call to the police. You will hear the detective testify to what he discovered when he reported to the call. You will hear the doctor's testimony. You will see photographs of Ms. Gray's bruised neck and arms. You will see the blood on her dress, from where she was violated. You will hear from the officer who made the arrest the next day, and you will hear from the DNA expert, who can positively identify that the semen samples found on Ms. Gray are consistent with the defendant's. What you will hear, ladies and gentlemen, is that this man is guilty. He earned Ms. Gray's trust, and then he betrayed her. On a dark, abandoned street, where he led her, he raped and nearly killed her. He offered to walk her home, to protect her from the criminals in the city. Little did she know that the defendant *was* the criminal. He was the person she needed to fear. But she didn't. And why? Because he charmed her. He deliberately made her trust him, so that he could violate that trust in the most heinous way. You will hear everything you need to hear to convince you that this man is a rapist, and he needs to pay the price for what he has done. I don't have to say more than this. Because the evidence speaks for itself. The defendant's actions speak volumes. And his actions need to be responded to. By you. It is up to you to make sure that a man like this is no longer free to walk the streets of this city, this place that you call home, that your children call home. Ladies and gentlemen, I trust that you will make the right decision. Thank you."

She sat down. The defense attorney sat still for a moment, letting a dramatic silence fall over the courtroom. He let the silence go on a little long, Nora thought. Finally the judge said, "Mr. Farrell?"

"Yes, Your Honor."

He stood and walked in a jaunty gait toward the jury box.

"Ladies and gentlemen, I am Bill Farrell, the attorney for Quentin Johnson. I appreciate that you are all taking valuable time out of your day to be here, so I will try to be brief. I am sure that you are aware that as the defense attorney, I don't have to make any argument. I don't have to say a thing. The burden is on the people to prove this case. Because my client is innocent. By law, he is innocent until the people prove otherwise. And they can't. Not one of their witnesses were there when the alleged attack occurred. All they know is what Ms. Gray told them. There is no positive proof in a case like this. There is only circumstantial evidence; her word against his. And you'll hear her story. It will be dramatic and upsetting. There might be tears. There might be rage. There might be some pretty convincing anguish going on. But what you won't hear from the people is the truth. Because only my client and the victim know what happened that night. Did Quentin Johnson talk to Ms. Gray that night? Yes, he did. Did he dance with her? Several times. Did he buy her a drink? Yes, quite a few, in fact. Did he have sex with her? Yes, he most certainly did. But it was not against her will. It was not forced on her. It was not a rape. Ms. Gray followed Quentin Johnson into the men's room. She locked the door behind her, and she seduced him. In the bathroom of this dance club, Quentin Johnson and Simone Gray had consensual sex. Maybe it got a little rough. Maybe she got scared later, felt guilty, felt ashamed and embarrassed about what she had done. And so she had to concoct this story of rape. But it wasn't rape. It was consensual sex, and that is legal in any state, between two adults. You will hear testimony that Ms. Gray was intoxicated that night. The doctor at the hospital smelled alcohol on her breath, at ten A.M. the next morning.

In her inebriated state, she made up a story, and she told it convincingly. She convinced the night clerk, she convinced the cops and she will try to convince you. But look at my client. Does this look like a violent man?"

"Objection," Margaret said casually.

"Sustained," the judge agreed.

"He is not a violent man," Mr. Farrell went on, without missing a beat. "He has no prior convictions. He had a good job in the Quarter. He has a family, a girlfriend, a child. He had no reason to put all of that at risk. Is he guilty of a minor indiscretion? Maybe. Perhaps. But he is not a rapist. He did not rape Simone Gray. And you must realize, when you listen to the evidence, that none of it proves anything. It's her word against his. And her story will not convince you beyond a reasonable doubt. Even if you think he probably did it, could have done it, you have to vote not guilty. Because they have to prove beyond a reasonable doubt that what the victim says is the absolute truth.

"Now, a lot of what you're going to hear will be confusing to you. They will give you a lot of medical jargon, a lot of legalese. Some of it even I won't understand. But it means nothing. No one saw anything. No one knows what happened, really. You cannot convict this man unless you are convinced that this story makes sense, that all the facts hang together. They don't. And you won't. Thank you."

"State can now call its first witness," the judge said.

"The people call Jeffrey Bloom, Your Honor," said the young man next to Margaret.

Jeffrey Bloom was a handsome blond man, clearly gay, dressed in a tweed jacket and bright blue tie. He looked nervous, and Nora wished for him to calm down. She found she was rooting for him, and was therefore hypercritical of his every move, even though she had no idea who he was.

"Mr. Bloom, will you tell the court where you were on the evening of May twenty-seventh, 1997."

"Yes, I was working at the Collier House. I am the night manager there."

"What time did you start work that night?"

"At ten o'clock."

"And you were still on duty at a little after midnight?"

"Yes."

"Did you see Simone Gray on the night of the twenty-seventh?"

"Yes, I did. She came into the office at around twelve-fifteen."

"Please describe her appearance at the time."

"She was wearing some kind of dress. Blue, I think, sleeveless. The first thing I noticed was that her face was all red, and streaked with makeup. She had obviously been crying."

"Did you notice anything else about her?"

"Yes. She was shaking. And she was having a hard time talking."

"Had you ever seen Simone Gray prior to this occasion?"

"A couple of times, I think. She stays at the hotel a lot."

"And she appeared markedly different than on previous occasions . . ."

"Objection. Leading the witness."

"Sustained."

"Will you please tell the court what Ms. Gray said to you when she walked in your office?"

"Yes. She said, 'Can you call the police? I've been attacked.'"

"Was she drunk?"

"No."

"Objection. He can't possibly have determined that."

"Sustained."

"I'll rephrase. Did she appear to be drunk?"

"No. She did not."

"And what do you base that judgment on?"

"She wasn't slurring her words or anything. She just seemed very upset. She was crying."

"Did you then call the police?"

"I did."

"At this time, Your Honor, I would like to play the nine-one-one call."

"Go ahead."

Margaret turned on a tape machine, and Nora felt her skin crawl as Jeffrey's frantic voice filled the room.

"This is Jeffrey Bloom at the Collier House. Could you send a policeman over here? One of our customers was attacked on the street."

"Is she there now?" a female operator said.

"Yes. She's very upset."

"Does she need an ambulance?"

"Do you need an ambulance? . . . No, she doesn't."

"Was she raped?"

"No, I don't think so." He paused and then said, "Yes, she says she was."

"Okay, we'll send someone right away."

The line went dead. Margaret switched off the machine.

"Can you tell us what happened next?"

"Well, she was really upset, so I asked if she wanted a drink or anything. She said she'd like some wine, so I gave her some."

"How much?"

"I don't know. Two or three glasses. It took the cops a while to come."

"Did you make another phone call?"

"Yes, about an hour later."

"Your Honor, may I play that tape?"

The judge nodded, and Margaret turned on the machine again. This time Simone's voice was audible in the background. The room filled with her racking sobs, and then Jeffrey's voice came back, even more frantic.

"Yes, I called earlier about a woman who was raped . . ."

"The police aren't there yet?"

"No, and could you ask them to hurry because she's completely hysterical and I don't know what to do."

"I'll call them again."

"Thank you."

Margaret let the room sit in silence for a beat after she turned off the machine.

"And what happened, Mr. Bloom, while you were waiting for the police?"

"I just kept giving her wine."

"How much did you give her, do you think?"

"She drank three quarters of a bottle, I believe."

Nora looked at the jury. A couple of them frowned at this and shifted in their seats. Poppy stared straight ahead, showing no emotion.

Jeffrey went on to say that the cops finally arrived, asked her a few questions and then took her away. He did not see Simone Gray again.

"Your witness," Margaret said.

Bill Farrell stood. "May I approach the witness, Your Honor?"

"Yes."

Bill glided across the room and came to a dramatic stop right in front of Jeffrey Bloom. He stared at him for a moment and said, "I really only have one question for you, Mr. Bloom. Were you present when this alleged rape occurred?"

Jeffrey looked at him. "No, I wasn't."

"So you didn't see this attack happen."

"No."

"You only know what Ms. Gray told you."

"Yes, but she was . . ."

"Thank you." He walked away, then turned. "Oh, one more thing. Have you ever been convicted of a felony?"

"Objection," said Margaret.

"Overruled," said the judge.

Jeffrey shifted in his seat and said, "Yes."

"And what was that conviction?"

"Robbery."

"I see. No more questions, Your Honor."

Margaret shot up. "Redirect, Your Honor."

"Go ahead."

"Would you please describe the circumstances of that arrest?"

"Yes. I was living with someone in San Francisco. When I moved, I took some stereo equipment which I thought belonged to me. We did not part on good terms, and so he called and reported those items stolen. I was arrested and convicted. It was all a misunderstanding. That is, on my part."

"Did you serve any time?"

"No, I got probation. But it was over ten years ago."

"And no convictions since then?"

"Not even a parking ticket."

"Thank you."

Quentin's mother said, "That man lying like a dog."

Nora shushed her.

# 10

Detective John Henley took the stand, wearing a leather jacket and a tie. He had a pocked face and heavy eyelids. Nora was confused for a moment, thinking that he must be part of the defense team, a friend of the rapist or some kind of snitch. But in a gravelly voice he identified himself as a police detective, the one on duty the night Simone's call came in. Nora could imagine Simone's discomfort, having to confess all to this man. His beady eyes—literally like dull black beads, or maybe coffee beans—had trouble landing on any location. He exuded hostility. In fact, given a choice, Nora felt she'd rather encounter the rapist in a dark alley.

The detective stated that Simone had been visibly upset, but also quite drunk. She had trouble speaking. She couldn't positively identify the scene of the crime. She kept wandering away and they had to chase her down and bring her back. But he also stated that clearly something terrible had happened to this woman. She was in an "exaggerated state of distress." It was consistent, he said, with the behavior of most rape victims.

When it was Bill Farrell's turn to talk, he strode up to the witness box in the same flamboyant manner and said, "Were you actually there when the alleged rape occurred?"

"No," said the detective. "I've never actually witnessed a rape of any kind. Otherwise, I'd be able to stop them."

The jury tittered. Nora couldn't help smiling.

"So all you really know is what Simone Gray told you."

"Yes," he said, "but I've been doing this for fifteen years, and I felt convinced that a rape had occurred."

"You said Ms. Gray was drinking. How did you determine this?"

"She told me," Detective Henley said.

"What?"

"She told me she had had a lot to drink, after the rape."

Bill seemed momentarily flustered. He said, "But she might have been drinking before."

"Objection . . . calls for speculation."

"Sustained."

Bill stood still for a moment, then shook his head and said, "No further questions."

Nora glanced at the jury again. They looked bored. Most of them were staring at the wall or their laps, as if they were planning a grocery list or events for the upcoming weekend. She wanted to shout at them to pay attention. She regretted all the times she had gotten out of jury duty.

While the DNA expert was on the stand, Nora allowed herself to daydream. The talk became very technical, and she couldn't follow it. She thought of Leo, wondering what he was doing, if he was thinking about her. Why had she fixated on him? She looked at Poppy and wondered if her connection to him was fueling her interest. If so, what was that about? Did she want to get back at Poppy in some way? That didn't seem logical. It wasn't like her, either. As far as she knew, she did not bear a grudge against Poppy. She wasn't pleased with the way her friend was behaving these days, with all that God talk, but that wasn't enough to make her spiteful. She had always loved Poppy. She had always suspected that Poppy could teach her how to live better, could make her more aware and in tune with her surroundings. She envied Poppy's intensity, her opinions, her passion about her surroundings and the human condition in general. Maybe she was attracted to Leo because Poppy's attachment to him years ago validated him in some way.

And it could be a savior complex. That's probably what her therapist would say. Leo was the first person in a long time who had come to her defense, who had protected her in a paternal way. And wasn't she allowed? Poppy had God, Simone had the entire New Orleans judicial system. Couldn't she have the benefit of a cab-driving ethics teacher for a while? She did not need to be saved forever. A single evening, in fact, would suffice.

She hated the silly, needy way it made her feel, wanting the attention of a man. She had started to doubt herself, to wonder if her clothes were too dowdy, if her blond hair looked silly and desperate, if she were clever enough to hold Leo's attention. He was smart, after all. She had been smart once, she thought, in college, when she spent a lot of time reading books. But lately she had let her intellect stagnate. Now she thought only about her children, tending to their various activities and play dates. They were turning her dull and it almost seemed intentional, as if they wanted her to be uninteresting, uninviting to outsiders. Were they plotting against her? Did they have her gradual demise in mind? Was it part of their long-term plan?

When Michael was a little boy, he used to say he wanted to marry her when he grew up. All little boys wanted that, she imagined, wanted to marry their mothers. But lately, she suspected that he wanted to marry someone completely unlike her. Now, she thought, he used her as a different kind of yardstick against which he would measure women. It wouldn't work, of course. He would try to defy her, but all men ended up marrying their mothers, one way or another.

Bill Farrell approached the DNA expert and said, "You weren't actually there when the rape occurred, were you?"

The woman looked at him and said, "I don't even live here. I live in Texas."

"So you didn't see anything happen?"

"Um, no, I didn't."

"No further questions, Your Honor."

Margaret hid a smile behind her fist.

The next witness was the doctor who was on call when Simone came into the ER. He looked very young. Everyone looked very young to Nora, and she wondered how the professional workforce had suddenly gotten younger than she was. For a long time she had existed in a world where congressmen and people in professional sports and even models and actors were all older than she was. Now they were a few years younger, and it made her feel crazy, as if the world were getting out of balance. But then again, she reasoned, this was probably how everyone felt, as time ticked away.

The doctor's name was Carl Zimmer. He looked very German, very Aryan, extremely bored and annoyed at having to be there. He looked like every fraternity brother she had ever known at UVA. She wondered, briefly, if he actually could have been one of them, some younger student she had ignored on campus. When he opened his mouth to speak, he had a distinct Southern accent, but not Virginian, or even Louisianan. It was more twangy, more like Texan.

Margaret asked him several technical questions, and he answered them in a dull, uninspired way. Yes, he said, he had examined Simone Gray the way he examined other rape victims. He had used the sexual-assault kit. He went by the book, by the numbers. He was required to do a pelvic, a Pap smear, take a swab for the semen sample, extract a pubic hair. Before any of this began, he had someone take a photograph of Simone's bruises. Yes, he said, there had been extensive bruising. Especially around the neck area, and on the upper arms. He had also done a rectal exam. He had done a swab, which had come back from the lab testing positive for blood. But there had been no apparent rectal tears. There were hemorrhoids, which he determined to be new, a result of a recent trauma.

"Objection," Bill Farrell said. "He can't be certain of that."

"Yes, I can," the doctor said.

"You need to be more specific," the judge advised.

The doctor said, "Old hemorrhoidal tissue has a different color and consistency. I could tell that this tissue damage was new to the patient."

"Thank you," said Margaret.

"Objection," Bill said. "He cannot state how new. Days, weeks, months?"

"Days, I'd say," the doctor answered.

"But he can't say how many days. Your Honor, I think we need to reexamine this line of questioning."

"You'll get your chance, Counselor. Sit down."

Bill Farrell sat down.

Margaret said, "Doctor, how many years have you been working in the ER?"

"Five," he answered. "If you don't count my internship. That makes it more like seven."

"So you have seen a few rape victims."

"A few, yes."

"And so, after your examination, could you make a decent judgment as to whether or not Ms. Gray had been raped?"

"Objection," Bill nearly screamed.

"I'll rephrase the question," Margaret volunteered. "What did the wounds on the patient suggest to you?"

"She had obviously suffered a kind of trauma. She was bruised, and bleeding, and she was hysterical."

"I have no further questions, Your Honor."

The doctor stood up, but Bill Farrell's approach made him sit down again.

Bill said, "Were you actually there during the rape?"

"Objection, Your Honor," Margaret said, standing. "I think we've established that law-enforcement and health-care officials were not present during the rape."

The judge nodded. "I think you've proved your point, Counselor. No one is claiming to have been present during the rape."

"I'd just like to establish, Your Honor, that all of this is secondhand information. A gynecological exam cannot determine whether a sex act was consensual or nonconsensual."

"Yes, we're all aware of that."

"So allow me to ask the question. Please."

The judge sighed and nodded. "I don't think I can stop you."

"You were not there during the alleged attack?" Bill insisted.

"No, of course not."

"Thank you. I have no further questions."

Bill went back to his seat. Margaret leaned over her notes, talked to the young man beside her, then said, "We'd like to call Officer Frank Porfillio at this time."

Frank Porfillio came forth. He was also young, tall and lanky, wearing a street cop's uniform. He had a goofy, Gomer Pyle face, and Nora worried that he would not be able to convince anyone of anything. She didn't even know why he was there, or what his testimony would be about.

She didn't have to wait long to learn, however. He was the policeman who had been patrolling Bourbon Street the next night, when Simone Gray approached him and said, "Can you help me? A man just went into that bar, and I think he attacked me last night."

Officer Porfillio said he agreed to detain the man and ask him a few questions. When he stopped Quentin Johnson, he immediately started to deny that he had done anything wrong, even though no one had accused him of anything. When he saw Simone Gray, according to the officer, he said, "I never saw that bitch before."

That was what he said, even though he now claimed they had had sex in the bathroom of the club, Oz. Nora smiled, thinking this was the turning point. They had him now. She reached over to touch Poppy's arm, but her eyes were glued to the back of the room, where a man in an expensive suit stood, looking eagerly from face to face. Finally his eyes landed on Poppy.

She whispered, "Oh, my God."

"Who is that?" Nora whispered.

Poppy simply shook her head and said, "I don't believe it."

She stood, and headed in his direction. Nora didn't know

what else to do, so she followed. Poppy took the man by the hand and led him out of the courtroom. Too dazed and confused to make a judgment, Nora followed.

Once they were out in the hallway, Poppy said, "What are you doing here?"

The man said, "It sounded like you were in trouble. I wanted to be here. I wanted to help out."

"How can you help out? This isn't about you."

The man looked at Nora and said, "Are you Simone?"

Before Nora could answer, Poppy said, "No, she's not Simone. You don't even know what's going on here. It was wrong of you to come."

"I'm Nora," Nora said quietly.

"I'm Adam," the man said, offering his hand. "Poppy's husband."

"You had no right to come here," Poppy said. "What the hell do you think you are doing?"

"Simone was out here a while ago," Nora said, thinking she could make peace. "She must have gone to the bathroom."

"Will you give us a moment?" Poppy requested.

"Oh. Well, sure."

She walked away, but she kept her eyes on Adam, the man Poppy had accused of betraying Christ. He didn't seem capable of betraying anyone. He was boyishly handsome with dark curly hair, not much gray, and round, prep-school glasses. He looked smart and sensitive, the kind of guy who was picked on in high school but triumphed in college. She thought it was considerate of him to come to New Orleans, looking for his wife. She couldn't imagine Cliff coming to find her anywhere.

Nora went into the bathroom but didn't find Simone. Instead, she combed her hair and put on lipstick. She wanted to give Poppy some time with her husband. She gave them plenty of time to walk away, to find a more neutral ground on which they could discuss their problems. But when she came back out, they were still standing there, just where she had left them.

She wandered up to them and said, "I guess we should go back in."

"I will," Poppy told her. "You can do what you want," she said to Adam.

Poppy turned away from them and went back into the courtroom.

Adam looked at Nora and said, "You're the one who lives in Charlottesville."

"Yes, I suppose that characterizes me."

"I'm so sorry about your friend," he said.

"Thank you."

"I work with battered women. I mean, I don't work with them. I put their faces back together. And I can tell you, there is nothing worse than having to deal with a woman who has been beaten, and who still believes she loves her husband. When people can't break away from abuse . . . well, that's a scary thing. Simone's case is altogether different. I want to help, but Poppy won't let me. She won't let me help her, either."

"I suppose that is who Poppy is. She doesn't want to be helped."

He smiled and said, "How well do you know Poppy?"

"We lived together in college. She was always smart. She had a lot of opinions."

"Opinions are one thing. Belief is another."

"She seems to have a lot of belief lately."

"Lately," he agreed.

"Why did you come here?" Nora asked.

He shrugged, loosening his tie. "I had some vacation time coming, and I didn't feel like being alone. Honestly, I haven't really known what to do with myself since Poppy left me. I've been putting off trying to have a confrontation with her. I guess this isn't the best opportunity, but this is what I needed to do."

"Has it been hard for you?" Nora asked.

He looked at her. He had warm, dark eyes, and he would have looked quite feminine if it weren't for his fierce, black eyebrows. He had perfect teeth and a square jaw, and from the way the lines formed around his eyes and his mouth, she could see he probably was someone who smiled a lot. He wasn't smiling now, though.

"It's been hell," he said.

"Yes, I'm recently separated myself."

"I'm just sort of confused. It wasn't as if we fought. We had a great marriage. Even after she found Jesus, I was willing to live with that. I'm Jewish, but I'm not religious. I don't want to convert or anything, but it's not as if I ever forced my religion on her. She objects to it in the abstract. It's like someone objecting to the place you were born, or your zodiac sign. I can't help it. I can't change it. I don't know what to do."

"Maybe it will wear off," Nora said, realizing immediately that the remark sounded a little simplistic.

He shrugged. "I don't know how you felt when you got separated, but everything is out of balance to me. I was meant to be married to her. I knew it the moment I met her. And these recent events make me feel like the earth has tilted on its axis or something. I don't want to be overly dramatic. But it's obvious we should be together."

The clack of heels coming down the hall made them turn. Simone was approaching them, moving fast and smiling, and

as if she had never expected to see a familiar face in these surroundings.

"Hey, Nora, how's it going?" she said, as if it had been ages
since they'd met.

"Oh, fine, I guess."

"Anything exciting in the testimony?"

"Not really." She noticed Simone looking at Adam and she
said, "This is Adam, Poppy's husband. This is Simone."

They shook hands. Simone stared at him, as if amazed by
his presence.

"Thank you so much for coming," she said, in her faux
Southern-hostess manner.

Nora resisted an urge to roll her eyes.

"Well, I didn't know what else to do. I am so sorry about
what happened to you."

"Thanks," Simone said, blushing a little. "The clerk just
told me that I'm up next. So why don't you come inside?
This is the main event."

"Are you okay?" Nora asked.

"I'm great. Let's go."

They all filed into the courtroom, as if they were about to
see a private screening of a rare film.

Nora and Adam sat in the front row, next to Poppy, and Simone took the stand. She waltzed up to the witness box,
looking confident, sophisticated, wearing a slight smile. Nora
thought she should look a little more miserable. Glancing at
the jury, she could see they thought so, too.

She stated her name for the record. Margaret asked permission to approach the witness.

"Ms. Gray, can you tell the court what you do for a living?"

Simone said, "I am a journalist. Mainly I write food and
travel pieces."

"And where do you live?"

"In Los Angeles."

"Are you from there originally?"

"Yes, I am, though I spent four years at college in Charlottesville, Virginia, at the University of Virginia."

"Have you been to New Orleans on more than one occasion?"

"Several times, yes," Simone said, tucking a strand of hair behind her ear. "I have come here to do some travel pieces."

"And where do you stay when you come here?"

"Always at the Collier House."

"When was the last time you were here?"

"Last May," she said. "It was May twenty-seventh."

"And what was the purpose of your visit?"

"I was asked to write a piece for a national magazine. The assignment was 'The Most Romantic Spots in New Orleans.'"

"Were you by yourself at the time?"

"Yes. I am always by myself on assignment."

"Did the magazine you were writing for tell you where to go, what restaurants to review?"

"Yes, they gave me a list. I came up with some other spots on my own."

"Do you recall where you had dinner on the night of the twenty-seventh?"

"Yes, I ate at Emeril's. In the warehouse district."

"Did you go home after dinner?"

"No. I decided to investigate some clubs on Bourbon Street."

"Why did you decide to do that?"

"I was trying to construct a romantic evening. I thought that a couple might want to go dancing after dinner, and I knew there were dance clubs in the Quarter."

"Did you go to a dance club after dinner?"

"Yes. I took a cab to Bourbon Street, and I wandered along there for a while. I decided to go into a dance club called Oz."

"Can you tell us where that is located?"

"On Bourbon and St. Ann."

Margaret produced a map, and Simone marked the spot with a pen.

"What made you choose that club?" Margaret asked.

"It was loud and crowded. I heard dance music coming from inside it. It seemed like a popular place."

"Did you notice anything unusual about it?"

"I don't know if it was unusual, but I could tell it was a gay club."

"How could you tell?"

"There was a sign on the door. It said, THIS IS A GAY CLUB. BE NICE OR LEAVE."

"And you still thought this was a good club to investigate?"

"Well, I talked briefly to the bouncer. He said that it was technically a gay club, but a lot of straight couples and singles came there because it had good music."

"Did this concern you at all?"

"No. I'm from Los Angeles, where there is a large gay community. Also, straight single women tend to feel safe in predominately gay clubs. I thought it was a good place to go."

"What happened when you went inside?"

"It was noisy and crowded. I went to the bar and ordered a glass of white wine."

"Had you been drinking prior to that?"

"I had a glass of wine at dinner. I am usually required to sample the wine at the restaurants I review."

"Were you drunk?"

"Not at all."

"What happened after you got your glass of wine?"

"I watched people dancing. I thought about the article I was going to write. Then I was approached by a man."

"Describe this man, please."

"He was a black man, about five feet seven, handsome, well dressed. He was very polite to me. He asked if I wanted to dance. I told him I didn't at the moment. Then he asked if I were visiting from out of town. I said I was. We started talking a little."

"What did you talk about?"

"He said he was local, and I asked him about what it was like to grow up in New Orleans. He said it was good. He'd grown up in the Quarter, and he managed a restaurant on Chartres. I asked if the crime were difficult to deal with, but he said the crime was no worse than any other place. He asked where I was from and I told him. He said that Los Angeles had its share of crime, but I told him I had never been afraid there. I had never encountered any crime."

"Then what did he say?"

"He asked me again if I wanted to dance."

"What did you say?"

"I said no, I was there on assignment and I was happy just to observe. He asked me what assignment and I told him. He said it would be a better story if I actually participated. 'Just one dance,' he said. 'It'll be over before you know it.' I finally agreed."

"You danced with him."

"Yes."

"What kind of dance was it?"

"A fast dance."

"Did you touch at all?"

"No."

"How long did the dance last?"

"I don't know. Three minutes or so."

"Then what happened."

"I had to go to the bathroom. He told me he would show me where it was. He led me up the back stairs to a balcony up top. He showed me where the bathrooms were. The women's room was locked, but the men's room door was wide open. There was only a single stall in there, so he suggested I go in there, and he would watch the door."

"Did you?"

"Yes, I went into the men's room. I was alone in there. I used it quickly. When I came out, he was still there and he asked if I wanted another drink."

"Did you?"

"No, but I told him I would split one with him. He bought a beer and poured some in a glass for me. Then we went out onto an outside balcony that overlooked Bourbon Street. It was busy below, and we sat out there for a while and talked and watched people."

"Were there other people on the balcony?"

"Yes. Half a dozen or so."

"What did you talk about?"

"He told me about his life, his job at this restaurant, his child by a former girlfriend, his dreams of owning his own restaurant. I told him a little bit about my job as a journalist."

"Did you have any physical contact?"

"No, not at all."

"Then what happened?"

"I said I wanted to go home. I was tired, and I was going to get a cab to my hotel. He asked where I was staying and I said a hotel at Chartres and Ursulines. He told me I was only four blocks from my hotel. And I told him I was worried about crime. He said he was walking in that direction, as he wanted to check on his restaurant. So he volunteered to walk me there."

"What did you say?"

"I said no at first. Then he said it was silly for me to take a cab when he could walk me safely in that direction. I finally saw the logic of that. I had no reason not to trust him. He had been perfectly nice all night. Besides, he was local. He had told me his name and where he worked. I didn't think he'd risk any of that if he intended to do me harm."

"Then what happened?"

"We walked out onto Bourbon Street. It was late, around midnight, but it was still pretty crowded. We turned left and walked down St. Ann's."

Margaret produced the map again, and Simone charted out their path with a marker.

"When we got to Royal Street, he suggested we turn right instead of left. I knew this was the opposite direction of my hotel, but he told me it was a better street to walk on. Since he was local, I trusted him. Then he said to turn left. I didn't realize we were turning left on to Pirates Alley. I thought it was another commercial street, because it was well lit. So we were walking. I had my arms crossed and I was looking at my feet. He was talking to me, and walking a few feet away from me. All of a sudden, he grabbed me by the throat. I was completely taken by surprise. He told me he wanted me to take down my panties."

Simone stopped and took a breath. Nora looked at Poppy, who stared dead ahead. Between them, Adam was watching the event with rapt attention. Nora felt nervous, her palms sweating. She suddenly felt the need to stop this somehow, but there was nothing to do but listen.

"Did you scream?" Margaret asked.

"I couldn't scream, or even breathe. His hands were around my throat and he was choking me. I couldn't believe how strong he was. I looked to see if anyone was near. There was a homeless guy a few feet away, but he didn't move. Other than that, we were alone. There was no one around. At that point, I realized this wasn't a dream. It was happening. I was going to be raped, maybe killed. I thought of my family, how I would never see them again. I was just so horrified. I felt hopeless."

At this point Simone stopped talking. She pinched the bridge of her nose and sucked in some jagged breaths.

Margaret said, "Take your time."

She did. Nora looked at the jury. Some of them had started to pay attention. They were looking at Simone as if she were some strange creature in a zoo, who might suddenly pounce out of the witness box and attack them. They seemed nervous, aware, and Nora thought that was a good sign. Finally Simone took a deep breath, pushed back her hair and continued talking.

"When he took his hand away, I tried talking to him. I told him he didn't want to do this. I asked him not to. I had a family. He said he wouldn't hurt me if I did what he told me to do. I tried to offer him my money. He got mad and he threw my purse on the ground. He said he didn't need money, he had a job. What he wanted me to do was take my panties down. I said no. He choked me again. Then, with one hand around my neck, he took his other hand and started pulling up my dress and pulling down my panties. At that point, I helped him. I just wanted to stay alive."

"Then what happened?"

"He raped me," Simone said. "I don't remember much of it, but he raped me, and then he took his hand away from my throat and turned me around. He penetrated me anally, and that hurt so bad that I screamed. When I screamed he stopped. He turned me back around. He said, 'I ought to kill you.'

"I told him he shouldn't. I was just a tourist and I was leaving the next day, so I couldn't be a threat to him. All I wanted to do was get on a plane and forget about it. He said, 'I don't care if you call me a rapist. I don't care what you call me. Just get out of town. And remember that this is a dangerous place. You can't go around talking to strangers. Don't be stupid.' Then he told me how to get back to my hotel, and he told me again not to be stupid, and he walked away."

"What did you do?"

"I walked back to the hotel, which was only a few blocks away. I went into the office and told the night manager to call the police because I had been attacked."

The interrogation went on, Margaret asking question after question. They covered the two hours during which she waited for the cops and drank more and more wine. They talked about the policemen who had asked her to identify the crime scene, though she couldn't. She talked about the four hours she had spent in the waiting room at Charity Hospital, and then the cold, callous way they had treated her during the exam, including the culmination of it, where they kicked her out of the hospital and told her to look for a cab stand. And she told about going back to her hotel, crawling into bed and thinking about suicide. She told about the AIDS cocktail she was forced to take after that, and the next night, when she went back to Bourbon Street looking for the assailant. She found him, and he denied knowing her, but she identified him by name and they arrested him. Then she went back to Los Angeles, and had not returned until this moment.

Simone was crying by then, her shoulders shaking as she sobbed, and the jury was watching her as if they had finally gotten to the interesting part in the movie.

Margaret approached her with some photographs, after she had shown them to the defense attorney. She said, "Ms. Gray, do you recognize these photographs?"

Simone took them and stared at them for a long time. Even from this distance, Nora could see a tear sliding down her face.

"Yes," she said in a hoarse whisper.

"What are they?"

"Pictures of me at the hospital."

"Are there any marks on you in the photos?"

"Yes. There are bruises around my neck and on my arms."

Margaret took the photos back and handed them to the jury. Then she approached with a wadded-up piece of clothing.

"Do you recognize this?"

"Yes. It's the dress I was wearing."

"Do you notice anything unusual about it?"

"There is a blood stain here on the back. It looks as if someone has cut part of it away."

Margaret took the dress away and handed it to a juror.

She stood in the middle of the room for a moment and then she said, "Ms. Gray, is the man who raped you in this courtroom today?"

"Yes," Simone said.

"Can you identify him?"

Simone pointed at Quentin Johnson, her arm outstretched, her hand visibly trembling. "He is right there, in the white shirt and tie."

Margaret nodded solemnly.

"No further questions, Your Honor," Margaret said.

Bill Farrell asked permission, then stood. He went over the events of the evening again, taking out the map, going over the details.

Then, suddenly, he said, "Ms. Gray, are you married?"

"Objection, irrelevant," Margaret said.

"Sustained."

"All right. Were you alone during this visit?"

"I've said so, yes."

"You danced with Mr. Johnson."

"Yes."

"And you asked him to walk you home."

"He volunteered. I accepted."

"Going back, you did use the men's room at the club, Oz?"

"Yes, I did."

"And why didn't you use the women's room?"

"It was locked."

"Do you know why it was locked?"

"I presume because a woman was in there."

Low-level titters from the jury box.

"Isn't it true that you followed Mr. Johnson into the men's bathroom and seduced him?"

"No, it isn't."

"Isn't it true you had consensual sex there in the bathroom?"

"No, I did not."

"You stated that Mr. Johnson had vaginal and anal sex with you?"

"No," Simone said. "I stated that he raped me vaginally and anally."

"But you did say there was anal sex."

"Yes, against my consent."

"Are you aware that the doctor found no rectal tear?"

"Objection," Margaret said. "Ms. Gray is not a medical expert."

"Sustained."

Mr. Farrell rolled his eyes and regrouped. Finally he said,

"According to your testimony, Mr. Johnson had sex with you against the wall of St. Louis Cathedral."

"He raped me. In Pirates Alley. Whatever building is there."

"It is St. Louis Cathedral. It is a church, is it not?"

"I have never been inside there. I can't confirm that it is a church."

Mr. Farrell looked down at his notes. While he was looking, Simone said, "He would know that better than I would. And if it is a church, that just makes it more disgusting."

"Your Honor, I haven't asked a question."

"Please refrain from extraneous comment, Ms. Gray," the judge said.

Mr. Farrell said, "Did you scream, Ms. Gray, during this alleged conflict?"

"I couldn't, at first. He was choking me."

"Later, when he took his hands away?"

"I was afraid to scream."

"Why?"

"I feared for my life."

"Did he have a gun?"

Simone hesitated, then said, "I don't know."

"Excuse me?"

"I don't know."

"But you didn't see one."

"No."

"You didn't see a gun or a knife?"

Simone sighed and said, "I didn't see a penis either, until he forced it into me."

"Objection, Your Honor."

"Ms. Gray, please refrain from elaborating."

"As far as you were aware, he did not have a weapon."

"I had no way of knowing if he had one."

"But you did not see one."

"No, I didn't."

Mr. Farrell nodded, then said, "You had several drinks that night?"

"No. I had two or three before the rape, and many after."

"Were you drunk?"

"No, I wasn't. Not during the rape, anyway."

"Were you wearing a necklace that night?"

"Yes, I was wearing a sort of silver chain. It's in the photograph."

"And isn't it true that the marks on your neck were a result of a rash, an irritation caused by the necklace?"

Simone stared at him, her face turning red with anger. "Mr. Farrell, I am not in the habit of going to the emergency room, waiting for four hours, submitting to a pelvic exam, getting a half a dozen shots and a prescription for the AIDS cocktail simply because I have a rash on my neck."

Mr. Farrell looked at the judge. "I believe she has been admonished, Your Honor."

Judge LaSalle shrugged and said, "Sounded like a good answer to me."

Mr. Farrell stared at his notes a long time, then said, "So you write for a living?"

"Yes," she said.

"You're a journalist."

"Yes."

"And a journalist is always looking for a good story."

Simone read him right away. She said, "It's rare that a food review will include sexual assault or any other life-threatening event. Tends to put the public off."

"Your Honor . . ."

"Mr. Farrell, it was a preposterous question. The people should have objected. I will let the record reflect her answer."

Mr. Farrell remained still for a moment, then seemed to decide he should get out while he could. "No further questions," he said.

Nora and Poppy shared a look. That sealed the case, Nora was thinking, and Poppy seemed to agree. Simone stepped down from the witness box, glancing briefly at them as she walked out.

The judge called for another recess. Nora, Adam and Poppy stood and, without speaking, went into the hallway. Instead of finding Simone collapsed and broken, she was pacing the hallway, smiling at them, wiping at her eyes with a Kleenex.

"How was it?" she asked.

"Great," Nora said. "You did great."

"I'm so sorry," Adam repeated.

"Yeah," Poppy said.

"God, I feel so exhausted. But I'm going for a walk," she said. "Thanks for sticking it out."

And then she walked away. Nora turned to Adam and Poppy. Poppy had a serious look on her face.

"She danced with him," Poppy said. "And she asked him to walk her home."

"What difference does it make?" Nora demanded.

"It's just not what she told us."

"Maybe she was embarrassed."

"It's just different. That's all."

It wasn't long before a clerk came out and told them that the defense was about to put their witness on. They had only one witness—the defendant himself. They didn't want to miss his testimony.

Quentin Johnson was nervous on the stand. He looked so slight and ineffectual in the witness box. It was hard to believe he had ever hurt anyone. He had a little boy's face and a slight body, made to look even more innocent by his white shirt and tie. He told a similar tale of how they met in the club, but after the part about the fast dance, his tale began to conflict with hers. He said that he wanted to go to the bathroom, and she followed him. He went inside the men's bathroom, and while he was doing his business, she came inside the room, locked the door and said, "You're a fine-looking man." At which point she started to undress him, and they had sex there in the stall.

Later, they parted at the door of the club, on good terms. He didn't see her again until she accused him of rape.

Margaret stood up for cross-examination.

"So, if she came into the bathroom, how did it happen? Did she start to kiss you?"

"No," he said, as if the thought offended him.

"You started to kiss her?"

"No. Nobody kissed anybody."

"Well, how did the sex act occur?"

"It just did," he said.

"Did you take her panties down?"

"No."

"Did she take them down?"

"No."

"Then, I'm confused. How did it happen?"

"You tell me," he said, throwing his head back in a gesture of defiance.

"No, Mr. Johnson, I am the attorney. You tell me."

"Nobody pulled anybody's panties down. I just moved them to the side."

"And how did you have sex? From the front, from behind?"

"From behind. Her behind facing me."

"So you had sex in the stall, without pulling her panties down, her back to you."

"That's right."

"What happened when it was over?"

Quentin Johnson just looked at her. "Nothing, I guess."

"Did you talk?"

"No, we just walked out. And then she went outside and went home."

"So you want us to believe that this woman, who travels all over the world, who visits one strange city after another, taking care of herself, never encountering any violence . . . she just waltzes into a bathroom with you, has raw sex there in the stall, then walks away? That's what you want us to believe?"

"I don't want you to believe anything. That's what happened."

"How do you account for the bruises which were later photographed? And the hemorrhoids? The way she was physically violated?"

"I don't know."

"And you want us to believe that after leaving you, during her walk home, she was attacked by someone else? Someone else beat her up and left her bruised and bloodied?"

"I don't care what you believe. It wasn't me."

"No further questions, Your Honor."

Quentin Johnson stepped down, and Nora glanced at Poppy, noting the way she looked at him, as if she wanted to give him the benefit of the doubt. It made her furious, but she said nothing.

It was almost ten o'clock that evening when the attorneys and the judge started to try to determine whether to hear the closing arguments. All of them appeared exhausted, and said that though they wanted to see an end to it all, it would be nice to put the most important part of the trial off till the next day. Nora left the courtroom and found Simone sitting outside, drinking a Diet Pepsi and waiting for the next move.

"So Poppy's husband came. That's a big deal. I feel like a celebrity," she said.

"You're bound to win, Simone. This guy was such a loser."

"Well, you never know."

At this point, Margaret walked out, moving with her athletic gait, and said, "The judge is putting off closing arguments till tomorrow. I think that's a good thing. The jury is tired. Let's just go home and sleep it off."

"How does it look like it's going?" Simone asked.

Margaret gave her a noncommittal smile and said, "You never know about these things. It's best not to speculate. But don't worry, you did fine. It's now up to us, and the jury. It all comes down to how much they believed you."

Outside on the courthouse steps, they waited for a cab—Nora, Simone, Poppy and Adam. Simone smoked a cigarette and looked peaceful, as if she had completed a work of art.

"So was I believable?" she asked them.

"Of course you were," Nora said.

Adam smiled, and Poppy just stared off into the night.

# 11

When Nora came back to her room, the message light on her phone was not flashing. She sat down on the bed and stared at it, wondering what to make of it. He had said he would call. She called the operator to make sure that it was working, that she hadn't missed a message. The operator said no one had called. "Oh, good," Nora lied, not wanting to reveal her neediness to a stranger.

It was just as well. She was tired and wanted to go to sleep. She took a long bath, put on her nightgown and crawled into bed with a copy of *Cosmopolitan* magazine. She could hear in the distance the rumble of thunder. Another storm, she thought, to clear the air, cool things down for a little while. She was mildly disappointed that no one had wanted to go out on the town. She had thought Simone and Poppy and she might do a little drinking, might even laugh and celebrate how well the trial had gone. But Adam's arrival had thrown things out of kilter. And besides, Nora wasn't certain that Poppy was completely onboard with Simone's story. She could tell that Poppy seemed to be siding with the defendant, at least a little bit. Not that she doubted Simone had been raped. But she felt a little betrayed that certain details had been left out of Simone's original account. Nora admitted to herself that it had thrown her at first, too, but after sitting through the trial, she decided she didn't care. Even if the details leading up to the rape were spotty, the rape itself was consistent and believable. It didn't sound like a story anyone would concoct. Why would she have done that? Why would Simone have put herself through this ordeal if she hadn't been terribly violated? The man was a liar. His squirmy, fidgety posture on the stand convinced her of that. Nothing he said had sounded like the truth. But then, of course, it didn't matter what she thought. Only what the jury thought mattered, and they had remained inscrutable. They had sat there, staring at their laps or at the wall, refusing to show any emotion or even the slightest degree of interest. Maybe they had it in for Simone because she was beautiful, because she was from California and she had a good job. Maybe they thought that even if this local man, this member of their community, had raped her, she had asked for it. It was a crazy, backward way to think, but it was not unimaginable. Nora thought of her own daughter having to grow up in a world like that, where women were expected to behave or pay the consequences. It was a horrifying thought. She wanted to call home, but it was far too late. Suddenly, she missed her daughter and wanted to hold her, to cuddle the way they sometimes did late at night when Annette couldn't sleep. It was the only time Annette really wanted to be touched. She would curl up against her mother like a kitten, and they would watch some silly movie on TV, and soon Annette would be snoring, her body rising and falling in a peaceful rhythm against Nora's rib cage. She missed that. Michael never cuddled with her anymore. He was far too mature for that, too manly. Although as a child, he had been much more interested in physical contact than Annette was. As a baby, he always wanted to be held. Then one day, he just reached his limit. He did not want to be touched anymore. She supposed that reaction was normal, and she tried not to blame herself.

A terrible idea occurred to her. Could Michael be picking up on her distrust of men? Was that forcing him to move away from her? Worse, he might even understand the hostility she felt toward his father. Children could sense these things, all the magazines said. They noticed a change in energy, read between the lines, interpreted signals. As if the thought of raising her children weren't daunting enough . . . now she had to confront the possibility that they were clairvoyant?

She decided to reject that notion out of hand. Experts be damned. She never badmouthed Cliff, and that was difficult enough. Her thoughts, she hoped and prayed, were still her own.

Besides, she had had her fill of child experts long ago, when Michael was a baby. One paragraph in some sacred manual said that the parent should not make a face or react in any way to a smelly diaper, lest the child should get the sense that the parent was disapproving of his waste.

"Great," Cliff had said, when she read this aloud. "We're raising an entire generation of kids who literally think their shit doesn't stink."

And they'd laughed, tossing the book immediately into the trash can.

They *had* laughed, Nora recalled. She hadn't imagined it. It wasn't all a lie.

The Cosmo Quiz was "Can This Relationship Work?" It

was meant to be taken alongside a partner. You were supposed to determine whether or not you had enough similar
interests. The first question went like this:

Your ideal vacation would be:

A. A tropical place where you are required only to sit
   in the sun and order cocktails by the pool.

B. A European city, full of museums, fine restaurants
   and walks by the river in the moonlight.

C. Skiing in the Rockies, an outdoor Jacuzzi in the
   nude and a bottle of champagne by the bed.

D. Camping in Yosemite, beers on ice, franks on the
   fire.

Nora stared at the list for a long time and couldn't decide.
They all sounded good to her, and they all sounded equally
impossible. She tended to take these quizzes as if they were
real tests, as if there were a correct answer for which she
would be commended. And in that spirit, she knew she
should probably want to visit museums and take walks in the
moonlight. Those choices made her sound like a more substantial person.

She was about to circle the letter *b* when there was a knock
on the door. She sat up in bed, her heart hammering.

"Yes?" she called out from the bed.

"Are you in there? It's me, Leo."

She froze, not really knowing what to do. She wanted to
see him, but she was lying there in bed, in a thin white cotton
nightgown, devoid of any makeup, caught in the act of the
Cosmo Quiz. She knew she had to respond, but she didn't
know how.

"Yes, I'm in here. Give me a second."

"Hurry, please," he said. "It's starting to rain."

She put the magazine down, then pushed it under the bed. She got up and smoothed down her nightgown, ran her fingers through her hair and decided, the hell with it, he should accept her as she was, if he was going to accept her at all.

She opened the door, and the humidity of the night rushed in, along with the singing sound of fresh rain. Leo stood there, in jeans, a white T-shirt and a denim jacket. He looked beautiful. He wasn't as heavy as she remembered. She realized now that he was short and barrel-chested, not fat at all, just stout and well built. He had sleepy brown eyes and a welcoming smile.

"I guess I should have called," he said.

"Oh, yes, well . . ."

He stepped inside the room and shook the rain out of his hair.

"Did you get my message?"

"Earlier, yes," she said, "but we got back late and I didn't feel like going out."

"I waited at Harry's for a while."

"You could have called."

"I didn't have the number with me. I thought I'd take a chance."

"Well, come on in and get dry."

The room had a sitting area not far from the bed, a stiff-backed antique couch in front of an antique reproduction coffee table. He sat down and smiled at her, crossing his legs.

"You look nice like that," he said.

"I was in bed."

"You look good without makeup."

"Oh, well. You know what they say. Makeup has a way of making you look older."

"You look very young. And very pretty."

"Are you drunk?" she asked.

He laughed. "No. I only had a Diet Coke at Harry's. I was waiting to start drinking with you."

"Oh. Well, I was at the trial all day."

"How did it go?"

"It went pretty well. It was harrowing, but it was okay. Do you want something to drink?"

"Do you have anything?"

"Well, there's an honor bar right outside my door. How about some wine?"

"Sure."

She stepped out into the night. The rain was coming down harder now, and it pelted down on her hair and her nightgown, and she stepped in a couple of puddles. But the air was so hot it felt like a warm shower. She poured the drinks and when she came back, Leo was still smiling.

She handed him his glass of wine and he raised it, saying, "To New Orleans."

"Oh, I don't think I can drink to that."

He shrugged. "To us, then."

"Okay."

They clinked and sipped their wine. She sat in a chair across from him.

He said, "I guess you think I'm the moodiest person on earth."

"No, I don't think that. There are a lot of moody people."

"It's just that when I'm with my kid, sometimes I'm pretty focused on that. When I'm away from her, I can let other things in. I came close to losing her, and I try very hard to make sure that I'm a good father."

"How did you almost lose her?"

"By not being a good father, in the beginning. It's a long

story." He sipped his wine and smiled. "Now I'm on the verge of getting full custody. Her mother, who was so adamant about taking her away from me . . . well, now she's met another man, so she wants her free time. I just want Nicole to grow up feeling wanted and valued. It's tough."

"Yes, being a parent is hard," Nora said.

"Even harder when the parents hate each other."

"Oh, I don't know. My ex-husband and I dislike each other a lot. But we somehow keep it from the kids."

"How do you do that?"

"Well, he does it by being absent from their lives. And I make sure I never talk negatively about him, no matter how angry I am."

"You're a strong woman."

"No, I'm not. I'm very vindictive, but I've got time. I know that the kids will figure it out. It will have a stronger impact if they get there on their own."

He nodded, sipping his wine. "That's why you're the stronger sex."

She laughed. "Because we're mean?"

"No. Because you're patient."

Nora thought about that, wondering if she were really patient or just passive, relying on nature to take its course, relying on her children to develop insights, growing into a natural wisdom. But there was no guarantee that would happen. There was no real reason to think they would ever side with her. If she continued to protect Cliff, and he continued to feed the lie, there was every chance they would grow up siding with him, just because he could invent a more pleasant story. Or an easier one to swallow. It occurred to her that she should start telling them her side of things soon.

Thinking of it made her feel like Simone on the witness stand, trying to get an indifferent jury to believe that her story was more believable, even though it was far less pleasant. In the end, how did the truth get decided? If the jury turned against Simone, would that make her case any less valid? And if her kids didn't believe that their father had misbehaved, would that be some failure on her part? Maybe so, in both cases. Because, she supposed, the burden was on the teller to make the audience trust that the bad deed had mattered, had done enough damage to warrant the rage and the hurt it left in its wake. The goal was not to get them to believe. The goal was to get them to care.

Leo said, "So how is Poppy these days? Is she happy?"

Nora was caught off guard, and she stopped herself from answering the way she wanted to. Why should they be talking about Poppy? If he wanted to know how she was, he should go across the courtyard to her room and ask her.

But she censored this thought, and she said, "Well, she's as happy as anyone can be who is separated from her husband and attending her best friend's rape trial."

Leo laughed. "Poppy has a best friend?"

"What do you mean? She and Simone and I were very close."

"But Poppy never got close to anyone. I was the best candidate for that, and for a while we were almost joined at the hip. Her old man was determined to put a stop to it, though, and the thing I could never get over was that he damn near succeeded."

"But you didn't take the money."

"No. No, that wasn't what broke us up. It was far more complicated than that."

"Did you ever have any interest in seeing her again?"

He shrugged. "Out of curiosity, I guess. But I've known for a while that she was back in town, and I made no effort to see her. So I guess I'm not all that curious. Is she still pretty?"

"Yes, of course."

"She cared a lot about that, you know. She acted like she didn't, but whenever we were near a mirror, I was conscious of her stealing looks."

"That doesn't make her unique, as the gender goes."

"But she had this weird thing where she also despised her looks. Or despised the fact that she was judged on them. You know, she was this debutante, this queen-of-the-ball–type person. Her father forced her to go through with that kind of thing. That's why she . . ."

He stopped abruptly and stared at the floor.

"Why she what?" Nora asked.

He shook his head. Then he said, "It was why things ended badly between us. Finally she had to choose between my world and hers."

"You're saying she chose her father?"

"No, not at all. She totally rejected him. But then she seemed to set off on a journey, trying to find him again." He yawned, an act of exhaustion and frustration rather than boredom. "I don't really want to talk about her. Let's talk about you."

"There's nothing to say. I'm pretty ordinary."

"You don't look so ordinary to me."

She struggled to hide her smile. "Why did you want to see me again?"

"I enjoyed our talk," he said. "About ethics. You had some interesting points of view."

"I don't think I really got to say much. I'm not a terribly ethical person."

"Oh, really? How do you feel about the way your husband treated you? He left you for another woman, right?"

"Yes," she said, blushing.

"And what did you think of that?"

"I thought it was vile."

He nodded. "*Vile* is not a word that unethical people use."

"I am capable of passing judgment. That doesn't mean I'm ethical. Hitler did that."

The words were scarcely out of her mouth before she realized what his reply would be.

"But Hitler was an ethical person. At least, he would argue that he was. He had very strict standards, a rigid belief system. So there are those who would say that belief itself is the enemy of peace and well-being. Even the enemy of true morality, or Godliness. E. M. Forster said, 'I don't believe in belief.' I once assigned a midterm paper on that single sentence. Do you agree or disagree? Please discuss. C. G. Jung said, 'I don't believe in God. I know God.' Use the back of the paper if necessary."

"But what does that mean?" Nora asked, feeling lost. "You have to believe in things. You can't just know God. If people could know God, they would. That's the point of faith. You believe because you don't know."

"And if you want to put your trust in the great thinkers, let's take Einstein, who decided that the speed of light is the only constant, which must mean that the speed of light is the only truth. Ergo, the speed of light is God? Well, before you go hanging your hat on that idea, chew on this. Einstein, though a spiritual man, died in a state of despair because he felt that his life's work had denied the existence of God. All that time he was trying to prove God, and he disproved him instead. Disproved him in a literal sense, because his work led to the atom bomb. How do you like those apples? Great Man's Life Destroys World."

"But it didn't . . ."

"But it *could*. I mean, let's face it. You and I could sit here all night, think as hard as possible, phone all our friends, call in all our favors, and we still couldn't destroy the world. We couldn't even hurt it much."

"We couldn't save it, either."

"No," he said. "There's always a downside."

Leo grew quiet, staring at the ceiling as if he expected something to appear there.

"Another drink?" she finally asked.

"Of course."

Nora went out into the rain to refill their glasses. She was feeling a little drunk, but she didn't care. In fact, she grabbed the bottle of wine and took her time walking back, letting the rain wash over her.

Leo was still watching the ceiling. He barely moved as she handed him a glass.

"So," Nora said, "let's review. If we can't destroy the world, and we can't save it, the fact is, nothing that we do matters very much."

"Correct."

"And nothing that is done to us matters very much."

"Not in the Big Picture."

"So a rape trial is an insignificant thing."

Leo didn't answer.

"And the fact that my husband left me for a waitress . . . that's even less significant."

Leo said, "In a world where nothing matters, there's no such thing as degrees. You can't qualify insignificance."

"So my husband did nothing wrong. What the hell kind of ethics teacher are you, if you don't believe in right or wrong?"

At last, Leo sat up and turned to her, not the least bit drunk, and looking a little annoyed.

"I never said that, Nora. This is an ethical debate. It's the Socratic method, that's all. You take the opposing view and see where it leads. At the end of the day, you have to make personal choices about right and wrong. Is there a moral imperative? An absolute definition of these terms? Who the hell knows? If I knew, I wouldn't be driving a cab."

"I didn't mean to make you mad," Nora said, feeling small.

"But you *do* make me mad," he said. "You probably make a lot of people mad, with your desire to make things fit."

Nora's throat tightened and she thought she might cry. She wanted to please him, the way she once wanted to please her father, and later, Cliff. The way she wanted to please everyone she encountered. She thought back to the day of her arrival in New Orleans, when Poppy said that her tragic flaw was her sense of equation. And she realized that in her crazy way, Poppy was right. That Nora's obsession with fairness would be her downfall. If she wasn't careful, it could lead to madness.

"But I want him to be wrong," she said, hating the childlike tension in her voice.

"Who?"

"My husband," she said.

"Well, one way or another, we're always getting what we want. More often than not, that's the bad news."

A flash of light and a crash of thunder, one right after the other, made the room shake, and they stopped talking. Nora couldn't help thinking that the God neither of them claimed to believe in was commenting on their discussion. They listened to the rain, hammering like golf balls on a tin roof.

Nora leaned back in her chair, sipped her wine, then closed her eyes. When she opened them again, Leo was next to her, kneeling.

"I don't want to go home," he said.

"No, you shouldn't. You can sleep on the couch here. I

have to be in court tomorrow for the closing arguments. But you probably have to drive early, don't you?"

He touched her face with his fingertips. "That's not what I mean."

From out of nowhere, Nora was visited by a sense of ancient wisdom. She heard in herself a parent's voice, the kind of voice she had often longed for when dealing with her children, one she felt incapable of accessing on a day-to-day basis. When she opened her mouth, the voice came out, and she was impressed.

"I don't think that's a good idea, Leo," she said. "It would be really unwise for you to stay. I have to get up early, and so do you. Besides, we hardly know each other, and we're both friends with Poppy."

"I haven't spoken to Poppy in years. Twenty years, I think. I don't think she even counts as an ex-girlfriend anymore."

"Still, you see how it might be strange."

Leo smiled and rubbed his thumb across his lip. He studied her as he did this, as if he had her number and, with a little prompting, could tell her everything she ever wanted to know about herself. That frightened her, because she suspected he might have some disturbing insights, and she didn't want to hear them.

She straightened up in the chair and pulled her nightgown closer around her.

"Why did you want to see me again?" Leo asked.

"I told you. I wanted to thank you."

"Besides that. Why did you want to see me tonight?"

She thought about fabricating something that might make her seem more sophisticated or generous than she felt. But a strange impulse took over, and she wanted to tell him the truth. She had never really wanted to tell a man the truth before. It was something she had learned from her mother. *Always keep your secrets, never let them know what you're thinking, and, for God's sake, don't let them know that you want them.* Better yet, don't let yourself want them.

But hadn't her mother needed her father? Wasn't that why she stayed with him all those years, putting up with his tempers and his coldness and his endless, unrealistic demands on the family? They had to be perfect. They had to go to church and sit together. They had to smile, no matter how miserable they felt inside. When he came home from work, they had to be quiet, no matter how fiercely they had been arguing all day. Her mother could talk the buzzard off the back of a meat wagon, and Nora knew it took a monumental effort to stay quiet while he droned on about his dealings at work, and since it was abundantly clear that her parents did not love each other, need was the only thing she could think of that kept her mother in line. Boo had always encouraged Nora to do well in school. No, not *well*—better than everyone else. So she could go to college and get a degree, so she could make her own way in the world and not rely on a man. She had half accomplished that goal with Cliff. But now here she was, feeling uncomfortably close to needing Leo, for all the wrong reasons.

"I really think you should go, Leo."

"Well, I will if you want me to, but, like you said, that storm is pretty bad."

"I just think you should leave."

Leo nodded and he finally stood, still rubbing his thumb across his lip as he stared down at her.

"I think you're very confused," he said.

"Well, aren't you a master of interpretation? Everyone's confused, Leo. I don't get any special prizes for that."

He touched her wet hair. She felt angry, but before she could object, he pulled his hand away.

"I'll go now," Leo said. "Even though I think it would be a thrill to make love to you. I still remember how cute you looked the first night I saw you. Standing there talking to those criminals, being polite to them. I thought to myself, There is one innocent person left on earth. I have to get her into my cab."

Nora didn't smile. She thought it was cheap, the way he was trying to remind her that he had saved her. It had the potential to work, but the storm was heating up and she felt it was commenting on her circumstances. Like the weather in Shakespeare's *Julius Caesar,* foreshadowing the events. Or Jane Eyre and Mr. Rochester, the lightning striking the tree next to the place where they nearly committed adultery. Nora thought that it was probably a weakness, a failing of hers, that she tended to view her life through scenes from literature. How egotistical that was, how presumptuous to think that her existence mattered on such a scale.

There was another crack of lightning, a boom of thunder, and then the lights flickered and went out. Nora jumped, then sat perfectly still. She couldn't see anything, but she could feel Leo's presence.

"What was that?" Nora said stupidly.

"Probably hit a transformer. Happens a lot."

"Will you be able to get home?"

"Unless my car is on fire."

Nora remained seated, though she could feel Leo moving around the room. Any second she expected to feel him on her, his hands around her throat, his body pressing down on hers. She tried to think of what to do. Not hit him in the nuts; all the self-defense articles said not to do that. A man is programmed, instinctively, to protect that area. Go instead for the eyes or the throat. But she couldn't see anything. How could she fight back?

It didn't matter because she sensed that Leo was far away from her. She heard a door open and then felt a cool, damp burst of air.

"So, I'll see you," Leo said.

"You're going?"

"Yep."

"Well, we could talk later."

"Yes, we could."

She heard the door close again and she thought he had reconsidered. She waited for him to speak. But then she heard footsteps sloshing outside her window, and she knew he was gone. Even though it was what she wanted, it seemed odd that he had just left that way. Just good-bye, into the dark, rainy night. Sort of like her marriage. Cliff had left that way, in the middle of the night, and the next day, when she woke up alone, she knew she would be alone for a long time.

She felt her way into bed and lay there, staring into the darkness, fixing her eyes where she thought the ceiling should be. She dozed a little, and then the lights came back on, jarring her awake. She thought about turning them off, but it was pleasant, falling in and out of sleep this way, aware that life was going on somewhere. The storm was not a period at the end of the sentence. It was just a storm, like many she had lived through as a child in Virginia. She had been so afraid of them then. She would walk around the house, crying, and her mother would say, "If you were living right, you wouldn't be afraid."

That admonition would cause her to sit down on a step and think, *What does God know, exactly? What particular thing will I be killed for?* She was five at the time, but there were a lot of things, so many that she didn't know where to start. And then, she imagined, there were things she didn't even know she'd done.

But there was her little brother Pete, always Pete, lying in a heap on the floor, slowly dying from his head injury, while next door she slept with her blanket and sucked her thumb. She had heard the noise but she didn't want to know. So she had slept, and then he was dead. Was it her responsibility? Her parents never said so, but the doctor had asked her, "Didn't you hear anything?" Or maybe it wasn't a doctor. Maybe it was a policeman. Why would a policeman have been there? Whoever asked her, she just tucked her head and said no, nothing. It was, to her knowledge, her first outright lie.

Leo had said truth was the only important thing. But what could he know? How truthful was his life? He had taken money to stay away from Poppy. He denied it, but she believed Poppy more. Or she thought she believed Poppy. She thought she believed Simone, too, but there were all those details in the trial that didn't hang together. It was too much trouble, figuring out this life. It was too hard to live nobly. Was that even her goal? She had no idea what her goals were. She wanted to be good, in every respect, but what had goodness gotten her? She was a good friend to Simone, she hoped, but it left her lying awake, wondering about the details of the trial. She was a good friend to Poppy, even though she had almost slept with her former lover. She was a good wife to Cliff, though not good enough to keep him from leaving her. She was a good mother . . . well, was she really? No, of course not. She was hideous and lost, leaving her children with her crazy, sadistic mother so she could come down here and pretend to be a good friend. Oh, for God's sake, there was no predictable way to be good. Every action has an equal but opposite reaction, she recalled from chemistry class. And so, according to the laws of nature, there was no way to be perfectly good. Every instinct set off a chain reaction of consequences—some good, some bad, some neutral. The only way to avoid stirring up the universe was to do nothing.

The phone rang and she pounced on it, thinking it might be Leo. If he were calling to ask her forgiveness, she would forgive him. If he wanted to come back, she might consider letting him. At least she'd make another date with him. She wanted to hear his ideas again. She wanted to know how to live.

But it was Simone. Her voice sounded bright and cheerful.

"Good news!" Simone said. "The trial has been delayed."

"What? How?"

"Lightning struck a transformer near the courthouse. Whole place is blacked out so all trials have been canceled."

"But how can they know that? It's so early."

"It's nearly six A.M.," Simone said.

Nora felt shocked, wondering where she had lost the time. Had it gotten later than she imagined, talking to Leo? Or had she really fallen asleep and let half the night slip away?

"What does that mean?" Nora asked.

"It means we're all going to have breakfast at Croissant D'Or at eight o'clock. Meet us out front. Then maybe we'll do some sightseeing. It means we have a free day in New Orleans. Who knows, this could turn out to be a pleasure trip after all."

"But what about court?"

"They'll resume on Friday. Now get a little more sleep, and I'll see you out front at eight."

Nora hung up the phone and lay still, glancing around the room where only hours ago she and Leo had contemplated the meaning of the universe. She was surprised to realize she couldn't really recall his face. And none of the things he'd said stuck with her, only the vague, giddy feeling of lawlessness she had pondered while he dismantled the world as she understood it.

# 12

Outside the Collier House, the morning air was clear and virtuous, and New Orleans felt as if it had never had a bad intention. The streets smelled sweet, devoid of horse dung or alcohol or the stifling scent of overripe flowers and leaded fuel and crumbling paint. It smelled a little like Virginia, Nora thought, with its quaint magnolia blossoms and the dying influence of morning glories and air purged by the rain. It was deceiving, she knew. By lunchtime, all the old smells would be back, but she stood for a moment and sucked in the morning air, and tried to make it last in her lungs.

Across the street, the others waited. They looked like a cast of characters from some backwoods dinner theater, Nora thought, smiling at the notion, remembering all the bad dinner theater she had seen in Charlottesville. She and Cliff had attended a lot of them—she because she kept thinking she might actually encounter art or talent, and he because he thought he might see a place he wanted to buy and make over, eliminating the art and putting in its place a salad bar or a taco buffet. They never saw art, nor any restaurants worth preserving. Instead they saw only bored, restless housewives trying to act, and frustrated lawyers trying to write or direct, and disgruntled students from UVA doing all the mechanical work. Still, in those days she liked it, because it reminded her of when she wanted to write, when she thought she might do something more important with her life than be a business-man's wife, a mother to his children. She reprimanded herself for such a thought because, of course, it was noble to be a mother to Michael and Annette. It was a pleasure and a priv-ilege. Of course it was. Yes. She straightened out her navy skirt and pulled her white, sleeveless linen shell down as far as it would go, hoping to obscure her hips. She wasn't fat, but next to Simone and Poppy she felt curvaceous, which was the next worst thing.

Already Leo had left her consciousness. She hadn't slept with him, thank God, and she wondered just how stupid she would have felt if she were crawling out of her room, trying to disguise a look of deceit and self-interest. She had done the right thing. It always felt good to do the right thing. She re-membered this truth from when she was a child, on those oc-casions when, as a teenager, she actually gave in to attending church, and after it was over she felt pure and worthy of her parents' affection. They still bickered over Sunday dinner, and occasionally her father would say she had not sat up straight enough or sung a hymn loudly enough, but basically she had served her purpose. On the days when she claimed to be sick and stayed in bed and missed church, her father's eyes would fall on her like the dark soot of disappointment. Those were difficult days. She was glad they were gone. She had felt relieved when he died.

It was a difficult thought to have, as she crossed the street toward her friends. But there it was. It was true and undeniable. If anyone had asked what she was thinking, she would have said just that: "I felt relieved when my father died." When he died, he took with him all his unrealistic expectations, and those sour glances across a room, and that foreboding sense that she was bound to disappoint him. It was something she had felt for years, across the miles, and even beyond the grave.

Simone and Poppy both looked unaccountably happy, giggling as they looked at each other. And next to them stood Adam, just outside the circle, as if he didn't get the joke. He wasn't included. Nora wasn't sure what he was doing there.

"Can you imagine what a stroke of luck that was?" Simone said as Nora approached.

"I think it's a pain in the ass," Nora volunteered. "I'd think you'd want to get the thing over with."

Simone's smile faded a little, but she said, "Of course I do, but I appreciate the break. Tomorrow we hear the closing arguments and the verdict. Today we party."

Adam said, "Nora, I hope you have your hiking boots on. Poppy wants to take us on a trip."

"She doesn't need hiking boots. We're just going to St. Charles Avenue."

"But the bayou first," Simone insisted.

"Whatever you say," Poppy agreed.

They walked around the corner to Croissant D'Or, which was supposed to be a famous place, though Nora couldn't figure out why. It was just a bakery, and they all got croissants and coffee and sat at a table near the window.

They ate their food and sipped their coffee. Adam was very silent, and Poppy wouldn't meet his gaze. Nora thought he seemed nice and unthreatening. With his dark, curly hair and coffee-colored eyes and gentle smile, he seemed like someone worth paying attention to. But Poppy treated him as if he were part of the furniture. A couple of times he reached for her hand, touched it, and Poppy whipped it away, as if she had been burned.

All around them, young people sat scribbling furiously while they sipped their coffee. No one seemed concerned about the time, or how they were dressed.

"Wouldn't it be nice," Poppy said, "to be a student again, and to think all that crap you write in a journal makes a difference?"

"It's important to put down your thoughts," Adam said.

"Then, put them down," Poppy replied, not looking at him. "The rest of us aren't interested."

"Maybe they're writing great novels," Simone mused.

Poppy huffed and sipped her coffee.

"So we're going to the bayou. What's that like?" Nora asked.

"Exactly what you'd think," Poppy said. "A dense swamp forest, full of snakes and spiders and mosquitoes as big as your hand. If you're lucky you'll see an alligator. But mostly we're talking about creatures of the swamp. Snakes and rats. They have their own beauty, I guess, but I was never trained to see it."

"We don't have to go to the bayou," Adam said.

"But if we don't go there, what will we do?" Simone asked.

"We could go to my father's house," Poppy said.

"Where is that?"

"I told you, off St. Charles Avenue. It's on the market. But I still have the key, so we can get in and take a look."

"You're selling it?" Simone asked.

"Of course I'm selling it. You think I want to live in it?"

"I think I could give the bayou a miss," Nora said. She had no interest in seeing spiders as big as her hand. Alligators held no fascination for her either.

Her eyes quickly locked with Adam's, and he smiled.

They chewed on their croissants, and suddenly Poppy said, "Well, if everyone is ambivalent about the swamp, that settles it. Let's go to my house."

"Sounds good," Simone said.

Adam glanced up at them, then fixed his eyes on Poppy. "I'm not sure that's a great idea."

"Oh, Adam, you don't think anything is a great idea," Poppy sighed. "At least no idea of mine."

"You don't have great memories of that time in your life," Adam reminded her.

"Who has great memories? The past is like a virus you can't shake. But sometimes, the best thing to do is tackle it head-on."

"Hear! Hear!" Simone said.

"Poppy, we need to talk," Adam said in a low voice. Not in an effort to hide it, Nora thought, but more in an effort to make her realize how serious this all was.

"For God's sake, Adam, I'm tired of talking to you. I don't even know what you're doing here."

Adam tucked his chin and stared into his coffee cup. His disdain seemed to resemble patience. He was going to wait this out, Poppy's desire to move under her own steam. It was as if he knew she would tire herself out, and he would be there when she came crashing down. Nora thought she might be imagining all this. Or, even worse, hoping for it.

As she looked at him, she acknowledged something stirring in her like a crush. That was ridiculous. Just a few short hours ago, she had a crush on Leo. Now Adam? Was she suffering some kind of disease that made her desire any man whose attention was drawn to Poppy? Or was she just so lonely that she could become fixated on any reasonably handsome man?

She told herself she just wasn't used to being single. It was a fresh start, analyzing men in an entirely different fashion. Even in college she had not really looked at men that way. She had waited for them to notice her before she formed an opinion. It had never occurred to her that she could look first.

They walked out of Croissant D'Or, not really certain of what they were going to do. They stood on the sidewalk and discussed their options, the way Nora recalled discussing plans in college. They would leave one fraternity party on Rugby Road, and stand there discussing the next potential source of entertainment. There was always an argument, but it was discussed in a tone of laughter and with a lack of concern. Nora was always a follower; she went wherever the stronger members of the group suggested. She took this role again, while Simone and Poppy argued about going either out to the bayou or to visit Poppy's childhood home.

The heat was returning, and though it was barely nine o'-clock, the sun pressed down on them as if it were midday. Nora was sweating. She felt herself stealing glances at Adam, who listened to the debate with his eyes fastened to the ground.

Poppy said, "By the time we get to the bayou, it will be hot and humid and awful. We'll wish we'd stayed home. Trust me. I live here. I know."

"But I want Nora to see it," Simone insisted.

"Nora doesn't want to see it. Do you, Nora?"

She didn't really, though she suspected she should. It would be something to tell the kids about. Even Michael would be interested in alligators and oversized bugs.

Deciding to take a chance, Nora said, "Let's go to the bayou."

"Yes!" Simone declared. "And later, your house, Poppy, if you still want to go there."

They piled into the rented car, some stripped-down version of an American sedan. Nora sat in the back with Adam, while Simone and Poppy took the front seats. Simone steered the car out of the city, onto the highway, and as they drove along the deserted stretch of road, Nora stared out the window, immersed in thought. She thought of the way the weeping willows and other trees sagged, as though trying to touch the ground. The trees looked tired and defeated, the way she occasionally felt. She wondered if the city itself had worn out the environment. As the inhabitants gave up on the possibility of happiness and freedom, so did the trees give up on offering pleasure and respite. Why should they expend effort to relieve a collection of people who didn't value such relief?

The drive passed quickly. The radio was tuned to NPR, some pretentious talk show that Nora had trouble concentrating on. Simone and Poppy discussed the trial in vague terms. Adam shifted his gaze between his lap and the window next to him. Once or twice he glanced at Nora and smiled solicitously at her, as if she were his only friend in the world. Again, Nora tried to remind herself that this was probably wishful thinking.

They finally arrived at Jean Lafitte National Park. Nora wondered once again about the pirate, if everything in the state was named after him, and if so, why? Why was this place so proud of its history of outlaws? Virginia was another place altogether. It was proud of the number of presidents and statesmen and framers of the Constitution it had produced. Jean Lafitte would have gotten no press in Virginia.

As Poppy predicted, it was hideously hot as they got out of

the car and walked toward the pathway leading into the bayou. They moved without question, as if they were being led on a tour. A few seconds into the swamp, Nora was overcome with a sense of awe and disgust. The two sensations hit her at once. The swamp was indeed creepy. The narrow pathway could hardly protect them, it seemed, from the wildlife hiding and festering in the ancient plant life. It all looked so primitive—curling ferns, bigger than any she had seen, and drooping trees, and spider webs as elaborate as cities forming between them. Spiders were in them, too, as big as toads, and somehow less scary because of their obvious nature. Most garden-variety spiders were scary because they could sneak. These creatures couldn't sneak up on anyone. It seemed they would create footsteps if they allowed themselves to tread on the ground. All around their heads, large insects buzzed. Occasionally, a thing or two would scurry across the path. What at first appeared to be tendrils hanging from the trees turned out to be snakes. There was nothing to stop the snakes from attacking, from hurling themselves on the tourists as they passed. Nora was conscious of being still as she walked, not wanting to upset the wildlife, not wanting to draw attention to herself. Simone and Poppy showed no such fear. They just chatted as they walked. Looking at Adam, she could see that he shared her fear.

She said to him, "What's a nice doctor like you doing in a place like this?"

He grimaced, then smiled and said, "Chasing his wife."

"You came here to get her back?" Nora asked.

He shrugged. He stuffed his hands into the pockets of his khakis. He was wearing a blue button-down oxford cloth shirt and loafers. He looked impossibly clean.

"I know the marriage is over, but I still feel responsible. Poppy is not well, you know."

"What do you mean?"

"She's not well," he repeated.

"She's sick?"

"Yes."

"Is she dying?"

"I don't think so," he said.

"Nora," Simone suddenly hissed. "Look at this."

She felt paralyzed, wanting to demand more information from Adam, but knowing she couldn't reveal anything unusual to her friends.

Nora looked at the water as they approached the edge of the swamp. Simone was pointing to a log floating in it.

"What about it?"

"Watch."

Simone lobbed something into the water—a rock, or something hard. And suddenly the log moved. It raised its head. It had dead eyes and a mean mouth. Something about the creature seemed familiar.

Nora felt herself making eye contact with it. Her breath caught in her chest. She realized that the alligator reminded her of her mother. That made her smile, guiltily, and then she thought, no, not Boo so much as her entire childhood, her wounded past.

Poppy said, "That's what death looks like."

"Oh, really?" Simone asked, giggling.

"Of course. They are killing machines. Don't you remember *Peter Pan?*"

"That's a fairy tale," Simone argued.

"Yes, but what isn't?" Poppy challenged.

Nora felt connected to the alligator, obligated to it, and her heart did not slow down until he lowered his head and swam away, obviously disgusted by them, and annoyed at having been disturbed.

It was the mouth, Nora thought, that was so familiar. The way Boo's mouth would stretch to outlandish proportions when she yelled or expressed discontent or mimicked someone. How Nora hated it when she did that, particularly the mimicking. She would change her voice to a strange, visceral snarl, and repeat whatever silly or offending comment she had heard, usually coming from her husband. Nora remembered hating her in those moments, staring at her as if she were possessed by a demon.

*Oh, God,* Nora thought. *I hate my mother.*

Suddenly, she felt as if she had entered some level of hell. There was nothing around her but the ingredients of nightmares. Snakes, spiders, alligators, bugs. Annette used to have dreams like this, and Nora spent a lot of time convincing her that no such place existed. But here she was, in the grip of her daughter's dreams.

Was this why she had left her children with her mother and taken time off work and flown across the country? To walk down a path that made her skin crawl? To stare into the eyes of an ancient reptile? This wasn't her idea of a vacation. Yet as she looked around the bayou, she had to acknowledge that there was a strange, harsh beauty to the place. Perhaps she was confronting her own mortality here, and perhaps there was something liberating about that.

"Can we go back now?" Nora said.

"Yes," Adam agreed. "I feel like we've seen enough."

"You haven't even seen the horror show," Poppy assured them. "That comes next. This is civilization compared to where I come from."

On the walk back, Adam said, staring at his feet, "Now Poppy is going to show you where her own private hell began and ended."

"What do you know about her upbringing?" Nora asked.

"I know what Poppy wants me to know."

"And what is that?"

He shrugged and said, "It changes from week to week. I've told you, Poppy is not well."

Nora looked at him, and for the first time she realized he was talking about something else altogether. He was trying to tell her that Poppy was crazy. Well, of course she had become moderately crazy, with all this God talk. But Adam's need to prove and avenge her insanity seemed equally desperate.

It was so hard to tell anymore who was telling the truth and who was lying. Who was sane and who was crazy. Simone was raped, or maybe she wasn't. And Poppy was their friend, or maybe she never was. Nora walked along, her arms folded against her stomach, and she prayed a hypocritical prayer to a God she didn't believe in: *Just get me out of here and I will believe it all. And I will serve goodness. Just don't let me die here and I will prove myself worthy of surviving.*

Her shoes made a plodding sound on the dirt path. Bugs scurried and buzzed.

The four of them walked in a line, without speaking, like soldiers coming home from the war. Traumatized, reverent, hopeful. Afraid of what they might, or might not, find when they got home.

They didn't make it to Poppy's house. During the drive back to town, Simone began to cry. She did it silently, sucking in breaths, which could have been sighs or an attempt to suppress hiccups. It took Nora a long time to realize that she was actually choking back sobs. It was Adam who acknowledged it first.

"Are you okay?" he asked, leaning up from the backseat, putting his hand on her shoulder.

She flinched when he touched her, and he jerked his hand away, as if he had been burned.

Poppy was driving, both hands tight on the wheel, staring dead ahead. She didn't even glance in Simone's direction.

"No, I'm not," Simone said. "I feel like shit."

"Breathe through your nose," Adam said.

Simone actually laughed through her tears and said, "What?"

"It's Adam's cure for any ailment. That and 'Have a beer.' This is what all those years of medical school taught him," Poppy said.

"It keeps you from hyperventilating," Adam said wearily, as if he and his wife had had this argument many times before.

"I'm not hyperventilating. I'm just hyperupset." She paused for a second to give in to a sob. She wiped her eyes with the back of her hand. "Nothing is happening the way I wanted it to."

"What did you want to happen?" Poppy asked, but in a knowing tone, as if she already possessed the answer.

"I had this weird idea that we would all have fun, and I'd be able to forget everything. I mean, while we weren't at the trial. It would be like the old days."

"It is like the old days," Poppy said. "With the exception of Adam. We're all treating each other the way we used to."

"What do you mean?" Simone asked.

Poppy said, "You all think I'm crazy, and I think you're all just running from what scares you. Wait, I didn't mean it like that. I love you guys, and you are just the kind of friends I want. You help me get away from myself because you both have this way of getting the focus of attention."

"How did I do that?" Simone demanded. "By getting raped?"

"Well, yes, in a way."

"Are you saying I wanted to get raped?"

Poppy took a long time to answer. Finally she said, "I believc we are all where we are because of a series of choices we have made. Choices that either lead us to or away from God."

"I chose to get raped?"

"You chose the circumstances that led to that."

"Poppy, for God's sake," Adam said.

"What happened to you was horrible, should not have happened. But you did talk to the guy, and you did let yourself trust him . . ."

"Poppy, that's insane," Nora blurted out before she knew what hit her.

"See what I mean?"

"No, I want to hear this," Simone insisted.

"I don't think you do," Adam intervened.

"She knows what she wants, Adam," Poppy said. She signaled and carefully moved into another lane to pass a car. Her concentration was still perfectly intact, even as an argument as big as a hurricane was brewing inside the car. "Well, all I mean is this. If you chose to make yourself vulnerable, if you put yourself in harm's way, it was an important and necessary instinct. It was a lesson you had to teach yourself. You knew that you could not learn this lesson without submitting to an act of violence."

"Submitting?"

"And if you would only open your ears, you would hear God trying to tell you something."

"Oh, this is priceless. What is He, in all His wisdom, trying to say?"

"I don't know, Simone. This is your journey, not mine. But you are only hurting yourself by making yourself unavailable to hear it."

"I suppose God has an extra-special message for me, too," Nora said. "Making my husband leave me for a waitress. Was that some kind of divine telegram?"

"Everything is a divine telegram," Poppy said. "And God doesn't make anything happen. We make things happen. And He tries to explain to us what these lessons are for. That's all. Everything we need to know in life we already know. Everything we want, we have the means to achieve it. And the reason most of us don't is because we won't listen to Him. You have to be still to hear Him talking. He talks through us. In fact, it manifests itself in the sound of our voices. But we are constantly shutting ourselves down."

"How so?" Simone asked. She had stopped crying, and seemed more interested than angry.

Poppy said, "This is how it is. When you are confronted with a problem, and you solve it, you give yourself credit for creating the solution. But the solution already exists. It is an existing entity. To the degree that we can't or won't solve our problems, it's always because we can't be quiet or still long enough to see it or hear it. The solution has a life of its own. We don't create it. We simply find it."

"I see," Simone said. "So it's up to me to find the solution to my current problem. That is, if the jury does not convict Quentin Johnson, it's because I have not made it happen."

"There are two possibilities," Poppy said. "One is that you have not helped them see the solution. Because, for whatever reason, you don't want the solution badly enough. Maybe because you have not entirely represented the truth, so the experience is tainted and impure. The other possibility is that convicting this man is not the solution. The solution is somewhere else."

"Where might that be? Could you draw me a map, give a grid reference?"

"You already know where it is. You just have to listen."

"My God," Simone said, shaking her head. "You don't believe me."

"It doesn't matter what I believe," Poppy said.

"Of course it matters. How can I face tomorrow if my friends don't even believe my story? It matters more than anything."

"Why did you want an audience for this? Who are you trying to convince?"

"I was hoping for some support."

"But why? The truth, like the solution, has a life of its own. Having your friends here or not doesn't change that. For example, a child never throws a tantrum when he or she is alone. A tantrum needs an audience."

"How did you suddenly become an expert on children?" Adam asked.

"Because I was one."

"Well, maybe you shouldn't even show up tomorrow," Simone said.

Poppy sighed and said, "You haven't heard anything I've said."

"I want to go back to the hotel," Simone said.

"Of course you do," Poppy replied. "I knew you had no intention of going to my house."

"Oh, fuck it, let's go to your house, then. Is that what it's all about?"

"It doesn't matter. I'll go there alone. You wanted to take me on your journey. I wanted to take you on mine. But it doesn't matter. I'll take you back now. And Nora, where do you want to go? Back to your husband in Florida?"

Nora felt her cheeks turn hot. "Why are you attacking me?"

"It's just a question."

"Well, to follow your line of reasoning, it's an impossible question. You aren't actually capable of taking me back to my husband, are you?"

"That wasn't the question. I just asked where you wanted to go."

"I want to go back to the hotel, too."

"Okay. Consider it done."

Adam said, "You didn't ask me what I wanted."

"Let's hear it," Poppy said.

"I want to go back to New York, with you, and spend the rest of our lives there."

"Well, okay, then," Poppy said. "We all got our desires out in the open. Isn't that better than listening to the radio?"

Nora slumped in the backseat and watched the lack of scenery shoot past. She felt miserable. Her children were stranded with her mother, whom she hated, and she was stuck in a crazy kind of group therapy, with no leader, no answers, only troubling questions that made them all feel loose and twitchy and like they wanted to disappear.

Poppy dropped them off at the hotel. She wasn't going to stay, she said. She had someplace to be. Simone went straight to her room, and Nora and Adam stood in the courtyard, stranded, wondering what to do.

"Let's go for a walk," Nora suggested.

"But it's so hot," Adam said.

"It's good to sweat. In Victorian times, it was seen as a cure."

They walked around the Quarter, which was quiet and desolate in the midday heat. Adam's clothes were too heavy. His curly hair frizzed even more in the humidity. He kept taking off his glasses and wiping them on his shirt sleeve.

When they got to Jackson Square, they took a seat on one of the empty benches. The others were occupied by homeless people and street musicians. Nora thought she and Adam must look out of place, a couple of uptight tourists trying to appear relaxed. It was a stupid place to sit. The sun beat down, hard and heavy, and she felt even more exhausted than when they were walking. But they did nothing to rectify the situation.

"How did Poppy get so crazy?" Nora asked.

"Well, she's had a hard life," Adam said. "But, then, who hasn't? I don't mean to minimize it. Her father was a bastard, and he totally controlled and manipulated her. He was an alcoholic and he was abusive. I don't defend him in any way, and I applauded her efforts to just wipe her slate clean, put the past behind her. But about a year ago, she got into all this spiritualism. It kind of happened slowly. First she started working out at the gym, then she changed her diet, then she started doing yoga, and the next thing you know, she was right back in Christ's lap. I tried to go along with it. I tried to believe that it was okay for us to be different in that regard. I'm Jewish and not religious at all. But soon, she saw that as a flaw in me. She said that the Jews rejected Christ because they wanted a savior who would lead them into battle against the Romans. And when instead He asked them to turn the other cheek and forgive, they rejected Him. So she decided I came from a heritage of bloodletting and violence, and she couldn't live with that. I tried to reason with her. I said, 'So what if my ancestors, even my mother and father, believed that? I didn't. I have devoted my life to helping people.' She said that I have led people astray from listening to the inner voice, which is God. Or some such nonsense. And particularly because I'm a plastic surgeon. She says people are healed within, spiritually, and I am perpetuating the evil notion that healing their outsides, what they show to the world, will somehow make them whole. I don't think that at all. People come to me with problems, I fix them. That's how I see it."

"Okay, that's all pretty New Age and wacky, but it doesn't make her crazy. Why do you think she is crazy?"

Adam shifted uncomfortably in his seat and said, "A few months before she left me, she started to tell me a crazy story. She said her father was in cahoots with the devil. He had sold his soul, made a pact, or whatever. She was involved in that, she said. She didn't want to be, but he forced her. She said that he murdered someone in their home. A child. And he buried the child in their basement. He made her keep the secret, and she has kept it all these years, and now she wants to come clean, and clear her conscience. I am perfectly aware that her father was a bad man. But he was a judge, for God's sake. And if some child had been killed and buried in his basement, someone would have found out about it. I don't know why she fixated on this story. But the more I tried to reason with her, the more insistent she became. It was frightening to me, and then I finally told her that she had to drop this charade or risk losing me. She chose the charade."

Nora said, "And you're absolutely certain there's no validity to it?"

"No," he said, "of course I can't be certain. But what do you think?"

"I don't know," Nora said. "I wasn't there."

"But how about all that stuff she said to Simone? That was awful."

"I had the strange feeling that she wasn't really accusing. She was just raising possibilities."

"The woman was raped."

"She lied about some of the circumstances. She said so."

"Does it change the fact that she was raped?"

"No, of course not. But do Poppy's accusations change the fact that she was abused?"

"Look, I'm glad the judge is dead. But still . . ."

"The sun is very hot," Nora said. "Should we get out of it?"

"Yes, probably."

They started walking back to the hotel. Nora noticed a strange smile on Adam's lips. She questioned it, and he shrugged and said, "Oh, I was just thinking of how little this all matters in the scheme of things."

"What scheme is that?"

"The big one, where we're just two people from history who won't be here for very long. I have to give Poppy credit. She understands that part. The main thing about Poppy is that she is exhausting to live with. Because whether or not she is really in touch with the truth, she truly believes she is. And that is the scariest kind of person."

"It's easier to believe we have no control?"

Adam shrugged and stuffed his hands inside his pockets. "For evolutionary reasons, we choose the easiest path. The easiest path for Poppy is to believe in God. Okay, fine, I say, but you don't have to force that path on others."

Nora said, "What if Poppy is right?"

"You mean about God?"

Nora nodded, hoping he wouldn't think she was losing her mind.

"I don't think that matters. Poppy found what she needed to find in order to stay alive. We should all be so lucky."

Nora said nothing to this. After a moment, Adam said, "Why she needs other people to believe it is another question. That suggests doubt, doesn't it? I mean, if you're secure in your belief, it doesn't matter what other people think."

Nora had no answer ready for this. She stared at the ground, at the plastic cups and other festive debris collecting in the gutter, and finally she said, "I don't believe in belief."

She felt exposed, putting a thought into the air which didn't really belong to her, but one she had borrowed from Leo. An idea which, in fact, he had borrowed from someone else. But all ideas were borrowed, she realized. Centuries of

speculation, handed down, entrusted to those who were willing to speak them aloud. From Christ to Kierkegaard to Einstein, these ideas were never any stronger than the people
who chose to espouse them.

They moved through the haunted streets, still infected
with the laughter and the conversation of tourists who had
long since surrendered to the heat, imprinted by the crimes
that had occurred in ancient houses and dark alleys. The
ghosts of this city were real, Nora thought. Careless hurt,
misspent energy, fragmented ideas, abandoned beliefs, scat-
tered all around them, accumulating like trash. Or buried and
forgotten, like treasure.

# 13

There was another thunderstorm in the night, less severe, one that seemed to rattle in the distance like a truck on the highway. Nora found it vaguely soothing, and it kept her half-awake all night, a gentle reminder that her time here was passing, was almost over, and soon she would go back to her life, back to where she could figure things out. But she couldn't do it now, not in the middle of the night in New Orleans, with the conclusion of a trial awaiting her. It was pleasant, being freed of the obligation of having to figure things out. She felt justified in putting off all the major dilemmas of her life, like what to do about her errant husband, her psychotic mother, her estranged kids. At one point she actually thought about those invitations she was supposed to finish. They were still in her briefcase, untouched, and she knew she

was going to be in big trouble for neglecting them. They
were due in a week, and she would use every bit of that time
finishing them. She liked to finish early; it made her customers feel secure. But then she thought, *What difference
does it make?* If the calligraphy wasn't perfect, how would the
world be different? Who would really suffer? If these people
thought that the writing on the envelope was an important
part of the marriage process, was there really much hope for
them? Her job was fatuous and deceitful. She hated it. She
wanted to write books. Why was she wasting her life?

Nora eventually managed to push away these thoughts and
concentrate again on the trial. Her curiosity was piqued. She
felt she might learn something there, although in reality she
knew there was going to be no new information. She was going to sit and listen to the closing arguments, each side sum-
marizing the things they had already said. And then they
would wait for the verdict. That would be something like a
play-off game. She knew about play-off games, because
Michael dabbled in a number of different sports. He was not
terribly good, but he liked winning to an almost obsessive degree, and so she found herself hoping his hopes—harder than
he hoped them, probably—and she felt his disappointment
much more deeply than he ever could. There always was disappointment, too, as the teams Michael joined seemed to be
the weakest. He wasn't interested in basketball, though his
junior high had won the regional title. Football scared him,
and his school also made a decent showing there. He preferred soccer, where they were routinely humiliated, and tennis, where even though his teammates often won, Michael
usually struggled and floundered and lost, although sometimes he panted and prayed his way to a victory. Rooting for
Michael was always a matter of living on the absolute, exhausting edge of failure.

Had she been responsible for this? Had she raised someone who could not win, who did not embrace winning as a concept?

As disconcerting as that thought was, she was strangely at ease with it, and viewed it with the detached interest that Poppy seemed to view Simone's rape case with: no conclusions, just possibilities.

She woke up feeling refreshed. The air was sweet and cool, something she knew without stepping outside. She took a shower and washed and dried her hair. She put on an outfit she hadn't expected to wear in New Orleans—a white linen sundress and a coffee-colored sweater. She had brought it on the off chance that they would have an exciting night on the town and she would want to feel feminine and attractive. She liked the combination because it looked like a *caffè latte*. She knew she should probably dress in a more somber fashion, but why? If she had to sit through this harrowing event, she should at least like the way she looked.

But, then, she didn't think the last day of the trial would be harrowing. She thought it might be exciting. She was ashamed of that thought, but she entertained it anyway. She decided it would be her secret.

She had breakfast with her friends in the courtyard, and she noticed Adam staring at her and smiling at her. She wondered if he were trying to make a connection with her, because of the talk they had the day before. Or maybe he just liked the way she looked. She recognized a warm feeling toward him. He seemed to provide an anchor of logic and sanity to this whole affair. He didn't look at his wife much. Poppy was dressed in black, as usual, her hair neatly pushed back behind a hair band, every strand in place. Her makeup was carefully applied, making her look austere. The only hint of color on her was her lipstick, a deep Chianti shade. Nora wondered why the only part of her body Poppy was willing to draw attention to was her mouth.

Simone was wearing a navy pantsuit, sleek, like something an advertising executive might wear. She had her black hair pulled into a twist at the back of her head. She ate very little and smoked incessantly. Nora wanted to do or say something that might reassure her, but she had no idea what that might be, so she stayed silent, concentrating instead on her scone. They talked about the weather. They talked about where to eat dinner that night. They talked about the coffee, which was dark and rich and delicious. And then it was time to go.

They took a cab to the courthouse, and Margaret met them on the steps. She was wearing a gray suit, a skirt that hit above her knees, thick flesh-colored stockings and pumps. She dressed like someone who had no idea how women really dressed, as if it were all a foreign concept to her. Nora was conscious of Margaret looking at her clothes, as if she found them either appealing or frightening.

"Well, we're almost in the home stretch," Margaret said, as they followed her down the long hallway to the courtroom. "I have to tell you now that rape trials are the most unpredictable. I have no idea how it's going to go. I feel we have made our case, but it's up to the jury, and we can only pray that they haven't turned against us. Generally, juries want to convict. But in rape cases, there is a lot of gray area."

"If we lose, then it's over?" Simone asked.

"Well, yeah. But let's not think that way."

Poppy, Adam and Simone followed Margaret into the courtroom, but Nora found herself hesitating. She said, "I think I want to stay out in the hallway for a while."

"Sure," Margaret said. "We'll come get you for closing arguments."

When she went back into the open, empty hallway, Nora

felt nervous. She wasn't sure why she wanted to be alone. She knew she wanted to think, to take some deep breaths, to gather her strength. But why? Even Simone was ready to face the outcome of the trial. She decided not to question her hesitation. There was always a reason for things like this.

She sat on a bench in the hallway and stared at the marble floor. Soon, she imagined, she would be in a courtroom like this with her husband, getting a divorce. It was strange, she thought, the way so many important life decisions were handed on to a cast of strangers, a bunch of detached, uninterested people in a courtroom. What could a judge know about her circumstances? What could a jury understand about what happened to Simone? To really understand her plight, you had to know her, to know that she wouldn't put herself through this ordeal if it weren't necessary.

A person would have to be crazy to volunteer for this kind of attention.

Crazy. Like Poppy. Was she really crazy? And what was with the dead child story? Suddenly, with a jolt, she recalled Leo asking if Poppy had told her about the baby. "What baby?" she had asked, and immediately Leo acted as if he had misstated something.

While she was thinking about these things, a middle-aged black woman approached her and smiled. She was carrying a sleeping child, a little boy about four years old. She put the boy down carefully on the bench. He never stirred, just fell right into a sleeping position.

Nora smiled at her, and the woman smiled back.

The woman said, "Funny how when you a child, you can sleep anywhere."

"Yes, it's an enviable trait," Nora said.

"I used to be like that once."

"I think we all did."

"You got a cigarette?" the woman asked. She had a sweet, round face, and big, apologetic eyes.

Nora said, "No, I don't. But I don't think you can smoke in here anyway."

"Oh, that's right. They done all but stopped smoking everywhere."

"Yes, they have."

"What difference do it make if I want to smoke? Do the state of Louisiana have any cause to care about that?"

"It's a complicated question," Nora said, though she generally embraced the notion of banning cigarette smoking. It did seem fairly creepy, though, that people couldn't even smoke in bars anymore. Instead they all clumped together outside the front door of various establishments. The new laws had not changed habits; they had changed only the location of the habits.

"You in this trial?" the woman asked, nodding her head at the door of Section D, Judge Louis LaSalle's courtroom.

"I've seen some of it, yes."

The woman shook her head and said, "I don't know why this girl has it in her head to punish my Quentin. I ain't saying he hasn't seen his share of trouble. But to rape somebody, well. I raised him better than that."

"Oh," Nora said, suddenly feeling short of breath. In a heartbeat, she recognized this woman; she had been there all along, sitting behind them. She was Quentin's mother.

"I come to the jail on the night he was arrested, and he said to me, 'Mama, I swear, I did not do this thing.'"

"I see."

"He always told me the truth, always, his whole life."

"Well, maybe he doesn't understand . . ." Nora stopped, uncertain of how she wanted to complete that sentence. Maybe he didn't understand that forcing sex on a woman, even though she seemed eager and willing earlier, was still a bad thing.

The woman said, "That girl, she got the devil in her. I swear, I look at her and I see a meanness in her eyes. Like she want to do something bad to my boy. She knows him. She done talk to him, and then she turn around and say he raped her? What's that about? You don't want nothing to do with a man, you don't talk to him."

"Well, talking is one thing," Nora said, and found she was unable to finish the sentence.

"Maybe she flirted," the mother suggested. "And Quentin took it the wrong way. He always been a handsome boy, and he used to getting attention. She give him a signal, I reckon, then he took it wrong. That ain't rape. Least, it wasn't called that in my day."

The little boy stirred in his sleep. She reached over and touched his brow, and he settled down.

Nora said, "I think it's only fair to tell you, I'm friends with the woman who was raped."

"Yes, I know. I seen you sitting next to her. But, then, too, I looked in your eyes, and I knew you was good. I knew you were running things over in your mind."

"But I'm not. I believe my friend."

The black woman eyed her suspiciously and then asked, "How old are you?"

"Thirty-seven."

"Me, too. I had Quentin when I was fourteen. His daddy was no-count trash. But I still told myself, I'm going to raise this boy right. And I did. How he ended up in this place is a big mystery."

"Maybe he really did it."

"No, ma'am," the woman said, shaking her head. "You go through this life without knowing much, but one thing you do know is your child. Now, I know he capable of robbing some gas station for the money, but my Quentin never had to force no woman, white or black, to do anything."

Margaret appeared at the door of the courtroom and said, "Nora, we're ready to go."

Nora felt embarrassed. In fact, she felt caught, fraternizing with the enemy. The way Margaret was looking at her did nothing to dispel that fear.

Nora stood. She turned to the black woman and said, "Well, it's time."

"Yes, I guess so."

"We'll have all the answers soon," Nora said.

"Well," the woman said, standing, stretching, "we'll have some answers. We don't know if they are *the* answers. We won't ever know that."

Nora was happy to get away from her and into the courtroom, where her friends sat in the front row, waiting.

She slid into the booth next to Simone. No one looked at her. She thought of Quentin's mother, out there with the child, who had to be her grandchild. Or maybe not. She was so young. It was hard to imagine what she was going through. Quentin sat up straight and tall at his table, as if he expected to be treated with respect.

Next to her, Simone slumped in preparation. Next to her was Poppy, and on the other side of Poppy was Adam.

Margaret asked permission, then approached the jury. She made a cogent argument on her client's behalf. Simone had come to town on business, had trusted a stranger and was violently attacked by him. Why would her client lie? She had no reason to. They'd all seen the photos, the dress, the evidence. Why didn't Simone Gray scream? Because she couldn't. Because she knew she would be killed if she tried to ask for help. Nora let herself glance at Quentin while this argument evolved. He stared straight ahead, and smiled slightly, as if he were thinking of something else.

"You've heard the testimony of the doctor, the three police officers, the night clerk at the hotel. If you don't believe our story, if you believe theirs, then you have to believe that all these strangers have conspired against the defendant. These people who didn't know each other at all, for some reason they all got together and ganged up on this poor, innocent victim. Or you can decide that maybe the one person who isn't telling the truth is the defendant. The one who has the biggest reason to lie.

"Simone Gray was raped," Margaret said. "That is why she is here, that is why she has gone through the trauma of the charges and the trial, and this is why the jury must convict." The evidence, Margaret said, was overwhelming. For the sake of their own children, for the sake of New Orleans and a civilized way of life, they should convict.

"Ladies and gentlemen, I feel certain you will return a guilty verdict. Let this man know that he has not fooled you."

Quentin's lawyer then stepped up and made his argument, saying that Nora had had consensual sex with this man in the bathroom. That she had grown embarrassed by her impulse and decided to call it rape, even though it was just plain old consensual sex. Simone listened to all this, leaning forward, chin propped on a fist.

Simone had talked to him, Nora thought. Why? Why had she bothered? Was it really possible that she had given in to an impulse, then felt embarrassed by it?

Then again, if Simone had been embarrassed by her impulsive act, why would she have chosen to draw as much attention to herself as possible by contacting police officers, doctors and, eventually, the D.A.'s office? It seemed like a lot of work to justify an impulsive act.

Nora wasn't sure why she was running all this through the logic mill. It wasn't as if she doubted Simone. But the conversation with Quentin's mother had left her a little unsettled. She was a real person, afflicted with genuine concern and confusion. Nora wondered what it would feel like to have her own son accused of rape. Wouldn't she defend him in the same blind, supportive manner? Michael was capable of turning on her. In fact, he had done so. Yet she would never turn on him, she thought. Never desert him, never hesitate to support him. In this respect, parenthood seemed like an illogical imbalance.

The next thing she knew, the trial was over, and after being given some convoluted instructions, the twelve men and women of the jury filed out and the judge disappeared. She and Simone and Poppy sat still in their seats until Margaret approached them.

"Well, it's out of our hands now," Margaret said.

"What's going to happen?" Simone asked.

"Who knows? Like I said earlier, rape trials are impossible to predict. I think we made a good case, but you never know how these people are going to vote."

"Will we get a verdict tonight?" Simone asked.

"We might, or they might decide to break. Hard to tell. You guys hang around for a while."

"Can we go outside?" Simone asked. "I'm dying to smoke a cigarette."

"Yes, but don't go far."

The three of them walked down the empty hallway without speaking. They finally made their way out onto the front steps. They sat on the top step, and Simone took out a cigarette and smoked it slowly, staring at the street.

"I think you had a good trial," Poppy offered.

Simone looked at her. "What's a good trial?"

"Well, your lawyers presented the case well."

"They aren't my lawyers. They are D.A.'s. They represent the state. It's the state's case."

"Even so," Poppy said, "they did a good job."

Simone exhaled the smoke in Nora's direction and asked, "What do you think?"

Before she had time to think about it, Nora said, "Why did you talk to him at the club?"

Simone stared at her for a long time. She felt Poppy staring at her, too. Nora felt in danger, like the child who pointed out that the emperor was naked.

"What do you mean?"

"I mean, you did talk to him."

"I talked to him because he talked first and I didn't want to be rude."

"I remember you in college," Nora said. "You never cared about being rude. At parties, you'd get rid of guys in an instant."

"This isn't college."

"But still."

"Hell, Nora, I don't know why I talked to him. Maybe I was drunk."

"You said you weren't."

"Either way, did I deserve to get raped?"

"No, of course not."

"You danced with him," Poppy said.

"Yes, we danced. Dancing and talking is not equal to consensual sex. What is wrong with you two?"

"But why would you do it?" Nora persisted.

"Oh, for God's sake, Nora! Why would Cliff tell you he wasn't seeing anybody when he was fucking a path across the college campus—" She stopped herself, then said, "I mean, across Virginia."

"What do you mean by that?" Nora asked.

"Nothing," Simone said. She lit another cigarette and stared at the empty street.

*Cliff was cheating even then,* Nora thought. *How could I not know it? How could I have married a man who never really cared about my feelings? I deluded myself, that's how.* And that was how Simone did it. She trusted someone who wasn't worth trusting. Hadn't they all done that, to some degree or another?

They sat for a long time without speaking. Simone seemed to smoke several more cigarettes. Nora kept waiting for a good time to speak, but it never came.

Finally Margaret came out, looking tired and dejected.

"The jury wants to break," she said. "They will reach the verdict on Monday. Can you stay?"

Nora didn't say anything. She was still concentrating on Simone's words. Was Cliff cheating on her even then? If so, how was it that Simone knew and she never did? Why didn't her friends tell her that? If they had known, they let her walk right into an unhappy marriage. They had come to her wedding and danced and eaten rubber chicken and congratulated her, and no one had had the guts to tell her.

"I can't," Simone said. "I have to get back to work."

"I'll be here," Poppy said. "I live here."

"I wish you could stay, Simone," Margaret said. "I hate for you to leave, not knowing."

Simone lit another cigarette and said, "Oh, well, I feel like I know. I got a look at their faces during the closing arguments. Even if they think it happened, they believe I was asking for it."

"Oh, I don't know about that . . ." Margaret argued, half-heartedly.

"Or they think maybe it happened, but it didn't hurt me

that much. I mean, here I sit with all my well-dressed friends, no visible scars."

Margaret said, "Have a little more faith in the judicial system than that."

"Why?" Simone asked.

"Yes, why?" Poppy agreed. "My father was a judge, you know. I have a very good idea of how it works down here."

Margaret met Poppy's eyes, and there was something accusatory in them.

"Everybody remembers Judge Marchand," Margaret said, though she wasn't nearly old enough to have ever worked with him. "He was a legend."

"Yes," said Poppy. "He was."

Margaret sighed and stood, wiping off the back of her skirt like a tomboy. "Well, I guess we'll have to call you in Los Angeles," Margaret said.

Simone said, "Margaret, tell me what you really think."

Margaret looked at her, as if the question were completely inappropriate.

"About what?"

"The verdict."

Margaret said, "Simone, crazy as it sounds, rape convictions are next to impossible. It doesn't have much to do with you. He's local, you're not. He's black, you're white. You talked to him in a club. None of this is your fault. But jurors have their own set of beliefs."

"Just tell me," Simone insisted.

Margaret lit a cigarette, letting a pregnant moment pass.

She blew out the smoke and said, without much emotion, "Not guilty."

Simone nodded, her eyes on the ground.

"But you never know," Margaret said, as a parting gift before she walked away.

Nora put a hand on Simone's arm.

"She's just guessing, Simone."

"Not guilty," Simone repeated.

As if it were the final word.

They parted in front of the hotel. There was no mention of taking the evening a step further. No one even suggested having a drink on the patio. Nora suspected that once they all said good night, they would pursue their own interests. Poppy might get in her car and drive somewhere. Simone might take a drug or have a drink in her room and call someone on the phone. And Nora thought that, indeed, she might go out. Something about the French Quarter was tempting her. It was almost the end of her trip, and despite all the dramatic twists and turns, the visit to New Orleans had not fulfilled her expectations. She wanted to have an adventure. She wanted to feel different about herself. She longed to learn something.

Inside her room, she sat and stared at the walls, thinking of the noisy, exhilarating atmosphere of Bourbon Street. It felt dangerous, and unlike her. She wanted to be there. She realized, her heart thumping wildly, that she wanted to know what Simone had felt like that night. She wanted to walk those streets, go into the club, maybe even converse with a stranger. Up until the moment Simone was raped, the evening had sounded great, crazy with excitement and possibility. Couldn't she take that kind of chance? Nora wondered. Couldn't she get close to the edge like that, then pull back, just short of disaster?

*This is insane,* she thought, even as she prepared for the adventure. She put on a tight, black, sleeveless dress and a heavy pewter necklace, and then clipped on earrings that were bigger than those she normally wore. In fact, she seldom wore jewelry at all, as it made her feel like a fraud. For the same reason, she also rarely wore open-toe shoes. Her mother said that it was whorish. But tonight she wanted to feel a little whorish, so she slipped on some high-heeled sandals. Her toenails were painted a shameless red. She liked the way they looked.

Her heart was racing as she stared in the mirror, and she reminded herself that she did not have to go. This did not have to happen. The reflection before her looked unnatural. She felt like a transvestite. She was afraid of seeing someone she knew, afraid of letting her awful secret out. But what was her secret? Wasn't it just that she was really someone who never dressed like she intended to have a good time? That was her secret: She was frightened of the world, and she dressed in a frightened, apologetic way. As extreme as these clothes felt on her, she was certain that she wouldn't be looked at twice on Bourbon Street.

There was a knock on the door and she froze, feeling stranded in her game. She felt caught. Punished, as if the hand of God had intervened. Boo always promised that God would react this way. "Get too high on your pedestal, and He'll knock you down." She always believed that when she was young, but now she had another idea. She remembered how a friend in AA had once told her, "You're only as sick as your secrets." And now Nora had time to reflect on her secret. Her secret was that she didn't have one. And she desperately wanted to.

She threw her robe on over her clothes, kicked off her shoes and went to the door. Leo was there. He was clearly drunk. His eyes were glossy, his hair disheveled, and he held on to the doorway for support. Nora stared at him and wondered why she had ever, even for a second, entertained the notion of sleeping with him.

He said, "I didn't kill the baby. There's no baby."

"Excuse me?"

"I just talked to Poppy. She's decided not to sell the house after all. She wants to get a demolition crew in there and tear up the basement floor. She swears there is a baby buried there. But I had nothing to do with that. You have to believe me."

"Leo, you are talking nonsense," Nora said, though she was reminded of Adam's strange reference to a dead baby. Clearly something was going on, and she wanted to know what, but she felt like knowing it tomorrow. This kind of interruption was not welcomed.

Her mind disconnected from the present and she looked ahead, wondering just what it was she thought she would find out there in the French Quarter. Even if she connected with a stranger, did she think he would be the man of her dreams, the answer to all her problems? Could one man actually make her feel that her lost years with Cliff were not a waste of time? How much could one evening on the town really heal or protect her from her past?

Leo pushed his way into the room, looking like the wild-eyed Ancient Mariner, intent on telling her his story. Nora watched him as he paced, feeling a little bit superior to him because she wasn't drunk, even though her fancy clothes under her robe reminded her that she was just as irrational.

"It wasn't even our baby. It was his," Leo said.

"Whose?"

"Judge Marchand. Her father. See, some woman brought this baby to the house and left it, saying it was his. He was responsible for it. He told Poppy to take care of it. And she did for a while. We were together then, and she convinced me that it could be our baby. We could get married and raise it. I kept trying to say, 'Look, this is your father's responsibility.

It's wrong of him to pass it off onto you.' He was a powerful man. He wasn't about to admit to this illegitimate child. But he didn't know what to do."

"Are you sure you know what you're talking about? You seem a little disoriented, Leo. Maybe you should go home and sleep it off."

He barely acknowledged her words. He just kept talking, sweeping his hand through his thin, stringy hair.

"That's what the money was about. Judge Marchand tried to pay me to get rid of it. Not to kill it. Just take it somewhere and put it up for adoption. But I was all young and stubborn and full of myself. I said he had no right to put this off on Poppy and me. I refused his money. I had kind of bought into what Poppy said. I would have married her in a minute and raised that kid. I would have done anything she said. But he got to her. He told her she had a future. She couldn't throw it away on me. He convinced her. But in the meantime, the baby was there, and she didn't know what to do with it."

"So what are you telling me? He killed the baby?"

"No," Leo said, shaking his head. "Of course not. He just took it somewhere. Gave it away. It would have been easier if I had handled it for him, but I refused. So he took the baby away himself. But after the baby was gone, Poppy kind of went nuts. She missed it. She thought it belonged to us."

"And then what?"

Leo stood still, thinking, chewing on a nail. It was as if the story had suddenly broken down. He couldn't remember. Finally he looked at her.

"Poppy loved the baby. She was all alone in the world. She had always felt distanced from her old man. And why shouldn't she be? He was just a bastard. A corrupt man, in business with all the crooks in town. Poppy's mother had been dead for years. Suicide, you know. Her old man drove her to it."

"Or murder," Nora reminded him. "That seems to be a possibility."

"Either way," Leo said, "she was alone. And the baby gave her hope, somehow. Poppy expected me to defend her. All her life, she wanted someone to intervene and stand up for her. I thought I was doing that by refusing his bribe. But what happened was, the baby went away, and Poppy blamed me."

"Think carefully about what you are saying," Nora suggested. "You make Poppy seem crazy."

"She's not crazy. She's just lonely. I didn't come through for her. I have to bear the weight of that. But there's no dead baby. No one killed a baby. And there is nothing under the basement floor. You have to believe me."

"I believe you, Leo. But if there is nothing under the basement floor, there's no real harm in Poppy pulling it up, is there? Just to prove things once and for all."

"I just think it is a very destructive act," Leo said.

"Maybe so. But destructive acts are important, aren't they? Deconstruction has become an important movement in the world. In literature and politics and psychoanalysis. Why not deconstruct? Why not prove what isn't there? You can build on that foundation."

Leo stared at her for a long moment, then said, "What are you wearing?"

Nora felt cold. She shivered and pulled her robe around her. "What do you mean?"

"You're all dressed up under there. Are you going out?"

"I . . . I thought I might."

"You haven't learned your lesson, have you?"

"I'm not going to do anything dangerous."

Leo smirked and said, "No one sets out to do anything dangerous. We all operate under the illusion of control. You can't control this city. You can't control yourself in it. Why are you doing this?"

Nora took off the robe, dropping the pretense with a sense of power and autonomy.

"You know what, Leo? You don't get to come in here and tell me how to behave. No one gets to tell me how to behave. My husband tried. He projected his own lack of self-control onto me, until he dumped me for a waitress. All my life my mother has tried to tell me how to act. She shed her disappointment onto me, and she needed me to be just as unhappy. Even my children try. They want to manipulate me out of my own free will. But here's the horrible truth. We're all free to do what we want."

Leo shrugged. "Okay, so do it."

"Thanks for your permission. Now excuse me."

She attempted to brush past him. He grabbed her arm.

"She is going to take you out there tomorrow. But remember, there is no dead baby."

"So you've told me, over and over."

He stared at her and said, "Do you want me to walk with you?"

"No, I really don't. I want to be alone."

"Just remember, I tried to warn you."

"Leo, you are drunk. You should get in a cab and go home. And tomorrow you should spend a long time thinking about why you wanted to come here in the first place. I didn't encourage it."

"Wait a minute, you called me. Remember?"

"It was an impulsive move."

"The truth lies in impulse."

"Save it for your classes."

"My students don't believe me."

"Maybe," Nora said, "because you don't believe yourself."

She walked out of the hotel room, into the dark, humid night, in search of a life-altering experience. Or, at the very least, hoping to find a reason to stay awake.

# 14

Nora walked down Chartres Street to St. Ann, then up to Royal, then past Royal to Bourbon. As she neared Bourbon Street, she heard the din of celebration. There was always a party in New Orleans, it seemed. She wondered how Mardi Gras and Jazz Fest and other events managed to distinguish themselves. Partying seemed the natural state of things in the French Quarter.

It was getting close to eleven, and the streets were so crowded it was hard to walk. People moved in clusters, middle-aged men and women carrying plastic cups of lethal drinks (hurricanes, probably), laughing louder than they probably ever did at home, feeling liberated by the lack of rules, the permission to act up in public. These were probably accountants and lawyers and insurance salesmen, and they probably depended on their wild night in New Orleans to distinguish them, to reassure themselves that they did not have one foot in the grave. How sad it would be for all of them to return to normal life, Nora thought. How sad it would be for her. She didn't want to think about it. She didn't want to think about the stack of unfinished invitations in her briefcase. She didn't know what she was going to do about the fact that she had neglected her work. She hoped New Orleans would help her forget that fact. And once she purchased a beer and had several sips, still standing on the street, she ceased to care.

But she knew, of course, that it was all a sad illusion. As she glanced at the merrymakers around her, she realized they all had real lives to get back to, and it was a depressing fact that none of their lives back home were as good or as lively or as invigorating as these frantic moments of abandon on Bourbon Street. *What kind of life is this,* she wondered, *that we have to steal happiness from undisciplined moments in a strange city?*

Shouldn't it be the other way around, she wondered? Shouldn't our real lives be full of excitement and stimulation, and our vacation lives provide peace and quiet and dead calm? Things had gotten turned around, and she wasn't sure how. Hadn't she always meant to live an exciting life? How had she neglected that, as if it were no more important than a pedicure or hair streaks?

She thought about Leo and his strange and frantic story about the dead baby. She wished she had some such legacy, but she didn't. She had simply endured a painful existence with her cold and angry parents, and she had finally escaped, into a cold and distant marriage, and now she was stranded with her children, trying to figure out another way to be. She constantly felt it was her responsibility to come up with a meaning of life to pass on to her children. But they were nearly grown—at least Michael was, and Annette was trying hard to get there—and she had no valuable information to offer. Just get grown, try to stay alive and out of trouble, don't make waves, don't get noticed, don't feel miserable. What kind of advice was that?

She realized she could offer her children no more valuable information than she herself had achieved. If her life ended up sad and misguided and without definition, how could she promise them that their lives would be different? *They learn from you*, a voice in her head said. *They cannot conceive of anything more than you have experienced. One day they might move beyond you, but they will always blame you for not showing them the way.* She wanted to know the way, so that she could tell them. Would it help that she had attended this rape trial, that she had met such strange characters as Leo and Adam and Margaret and Quentin Johnson's mother? Would it ever matter that her best friends were Poppy and Simone? Would her children just consider her foolish because she put her faith in these friends? It was hard to say on this night, or on any other, but the beauty of being on vacation was that none of it could really matter. It was an escape from reality.

She walked down toward the end of Bourbon Street, until she finally got to the club called Oz, where Simone had encountered Quentin Johnson. The scene outside was noisy and boisterous. She tried to imagine what Simone had felt like, making her way inside. Did she hope to encounter Quentin? Or was she content to be alone? Did she feel relieved when she saw a welcoming face?

Nora made her way past the bouncer. He was a large black man who made a big deal out of checking her ID. Nora laughed, and when he noticed her age on the driver's license he pretended to be amazed. It was a cheap trick, but Nora appreciated it. She felt an adolescent need to say, "Look, I'm old and I have two children," but she somehow knew he was aware of her trek around the business of life and was making a game out of it all. Or maybe he was making fun of her. She felt old and out of place in her black sundress and big jewelry. The noise inside the club was deafening. There was the relentless beat of disco music, and the lights on the dance floor changed at a dizzying pace—from blue to green to yellow, then back to blue. Even if she had not seen the sign on the door (THIS IS A GAY CLUB, BE NICE OR LEAVE) she would have known where she was. True, there were several mixed couples dancing, but the club was really made up of gay couples. For a second, she wondered what her father might have thought. He had wanted her to be a teacher and stay close to home. Here she was, drinking a beer in a gay club in New Orleans. Life was a funny business.

She tried, as she had vowed to do, to think of how Simone must have felt here. How she must have felt when she turned to see a friendly face. It was easy to understand why she would have trusted him, would have followed him anywhere. It was not a scary place; all the patrons seemed to know each other. Nora felt safe, sipping her beer at the bar, but if someone had asked her to dance, she wasn't sure how she would have responded.

Suddenly someone touched her shoulder and she turned, ready to explain that she was a heterosexual woman who wanted to be left alone.

The man who touched her shoulder was Adam.

"What?" she said. She wasn't sure what else to say.

Adam smiled at her. "What are you doing here?"

"I wanted to go out."

"It's not safe," he told her.

"I'm not doing anything dangerous. I just wanted to go out on the town."

"Are you drunk?" he asked.

"No, of course not. This is my first beer."

"You look beautiful. You don't even look like yourself."

She smiled and looked away from him. She was reminded of mixers in college, where promising UVA men tried to talk her into going with them somewhere, relying on her knowledge that they were all invested in their futures and would never do anything to jeopardize that.

UVA was good in that way. No matter how much a man wanted her, he wanted his career, his future, more. He wasn't about to risk that. Nora wasn't sure what to think of men now that she had entered the later years and they had all distinguished themselves. She realized she was moving into a second phase of life, where men were willing to admit their initial mistakes, but were they willing to change their approach? It was hard to say.

Her daughter, Annette, had started to read Edgar Allan Poe recently, and Nora had attempted to fuel her interest by saying, "You know, he went to the same school that I did, until he got kicked out for gambling." And lately Annette had started to amend her interest by saying to others, "This guy would have gone to school with my mother if he weren't a gambler."

Adam said, "I couldn't sleep, and I wasn't sure what to do. I saw you leaving so I followed you. Is that a bad thing?"

"Not yet, I guess."

"Let's dance," Adam said.

"I don't feel like dancing."

"There's nothing else to do here," he argued.

"Okay, so let's do something else."

Adam thought about it and said, "Do you want to get something to eat?"

"I'm not really hungry."

"So just walk with me."

She walked with him to the Clover Grill, and he ate a hamburger while she smiled and watched him. She said, "Look, I've talked to Leo and some other people who know Poppy, and there is reason to think she is crazy."

Adam nodded and said, "There are people who tell me she is an ambulatory schizophrenic. There are others who say she is just bipolar. But the bottom line is that she is crazy. So I support that assessment."

"Do you love her?"

"Of course," Adam said, biting into his hamburger. He smiled as he wiped the residual grease from his lips. "I love her very much. I want to protect her. The world doesn't know how to protect crazy people."

Nora thought about that. She thought just the opposite was true. In fact, crazy people were the only ones who were protected. All those years, her mother walked around with one foot in reality, treating her children and her husband with cold, unapologetic cruelty. And everyone let her do it. Everyone kept her secret. She was crazy, so instead of attacking her, they attacked each other. Just as everyone was now doing with Poppy. Nora and Simone had somehow not connected with each other this week, during this whole ordeal, because they were too busy at first combating, and then protecting, Poppy's insanity. It completely held their attention. It controlled them. It controlled Leo, too, and now Adam. Nora remembered, from some movie she'd seen or book she'd read, that the devil got his power from the fact that no one believed he existed. And now she thought the same was true of insane people. They controlled the universe by denying that they were crazy, and engaging others in the struggle to prove or disprove it.

"You realize Poppy intends to go out to her house and tear up the basement floor tomorrow," Nora said.

Adam shrugged, sipping his coffee. "She's been threatening to do that for years."

"But she's really going to do it tomorrow."

"No, she's not. She'll drag us all out there and get hysterical, and we'll talk her out of it and do something else."

"Why would we talk her out of it?"

"Because it's insane."

"So what? How will we ever know how crazy Poppy is unless we allow her to show us?"

Adam wiped his mouth with a tattered napkin and thought. He seemed to like the idea, though it was clearly a completely new approach.

"All right, why not?"

Nora smiled, stealing a French fry from his plate. "Adam, you seem like an intelligent, sane person. Why do you spend your life chasing her around?"

"I don't know. Why did you want to go to a gay nightclub by yourself in New Orleans? None of us has any idea why we want what we want. Or the lengths we'll go to to get it. In fact, most of us are so scared of it, we never even ask the question. So we sit at home and watch TV. I think that's why I like you. At least you're looking. I'm looking, too, you know. I realize the answer is eventually going to be to leave her alone. But I have to get there myself. No one can tell me."

He was cute. He was like a lot of guys she remembered from UVA, though she was certain that must be a false memory. He was dark, ethnic-looking, clearly Jewish, with black curly hair, laced with gray, dark eyes, too close together, thick lashes, a permanent five o'clock shadow. He wore small, rectangular glasses that made him appear smart, and more stylish than he really was.

"Where'd you go to school?" she asked him.

"William and Mary," he said.

"Really?"

He nodded. "I'm from New York. But I was always attracted to the South."

"What did you think of it?"

"Scared the hell out of me."

"How about medical school?"

"Duke," he said.

"Jesus, you just didn't learn your lesson, did you?"

"I like to be scared."

"But you didn't settle down there."

"I don't like it *that* much."

"You obviously belong in New York."

"Obviously. I thought I could satisfy my desire for danger by marrying a Southerner. And so far I have."

"Why plastic surgery?"

"Reconstructive surgery, please."

"Okay."

"Because I don't like sick people. No one dies in my practice. Even people with melanoma, they usually live. And if they don't, it's some oncologist who has to deal with it. There are enough people around to deal with sickness. What I want to work with is dissatisfaction. Honest to God, people waste their lives worrying about their noses, their chins, their breasts. I can fix that and let them move on to other things."

"Poppy says you work with battered women."

At the mention of this, he seemed to clam up. He pushed his plate away and stared at the remains for a while.

"My old man was the sweetest guy. I never saw him lose his temper. Didn't hit his kids, didn't even yell at us. My mother was overpowering, nagging him and belittling him a lot for his lack of ambition. She projected all her needs onto me, of course. It's an old story."

He sighed, as if gathering strength for the next part.

"One day, when I was about eighteen, I got into a fight with my then girlfriend. Captain of the cheerleading team, beautiful, smart, headed for Ivy League. I like to call those kind of women the on-paper girls. They look good on paper, you know, what you want to bring home to Mother. Anyway, we were fighting, and before I knew what was happening, I hit her in the face and broke her nose."

Nora stared at him, unable to believe it. She thought he was making it up to impress or attract her, though that made very little sense.

"There she was," Adam said, "this perfect girl, this perfect face, and I changed it. Forever."

"What happened to you?" Nora asked.

"Afterwards? Nothing much. Her father said he wouldn't press charges if I would pay for a nose job. So I took my bar mitzvah money, which I'd invested in the stock market and made a bundle on, and I paid for her nose job. She got her breasts done at the same time. She came out better. Do you understand? She looked better after they got through with her, and she was happier. And I thought, my God, these men, they fixed the problem. They got me off the hook. I didn't have to live with that pain forever, and I gave them the credit. Right then, I decided it was what I wanted to do."

Nora liked the story, but it worried her a little, too. Was it good that he had faced down his demon so early in life, and his career was, in effect, a penance for that? Maybe all of a conscious life was spent in penance. And perhaps she had not sought her own. Being abandoned by Cliff had always felt like punishment, a judgment passed on her. Maybe it was. But suddenly, sitting in the Clover Grill in New Orleans, she understood why she felt so lost in his absence. She had refused to see her part in the breakup. It had to be there. No one was blameless. And she needed to figure out what her part was, and pay her penance.

*But penance need not be paid in suffering,* she thought, the idea occurring to her like a peaceful revelation. *It can be paid in forward motion. Correcting the mistake is a positive move, a nurturing move.* Unlike the fierce, angry religion she had been raised in, this new religion she was discovering was nurturing and hopeful. You get better by being better. Doing better. Forgiving yourself and moving on. Could she do that? Did she have the courage?

My God, she thought, Simone was raped, violated and nearly killed. And she, Nora, had wasted all this time on details, clamoring for the truth, struggling with her disbelief. She doubted because it was safer than believing. She had spent her life in the false safety of the middle ground. Was she brave enough to leave it?

The way her heart was speeding up, the way she suddenly felt giddy and drunk, told her that she was. She wanted to try. It was a lesson Simone had desperately been trying to teach them, but they had been too paralyzed by fear and dread to learn it. Simone had faced death and discovered the secret to life. And the secret to life was so simple and pure. The secret was simply this: You're alive. Do something.

"Are you okay?" Adam asked.

She looked at him and realized that quite some time might have passed while she was contemplating all this. She realized, too, that she was wearing a detached, mysterious smile, and that that might have frightened him.

"I'm fine," she said. "I'm really fine. I just feel like going home."

"Let me get the check."

"No, I mean home. Virginia. My children. My life."

"Oh. Well, you should probably wait until Sunday."

"I will. I just mean . . . the fact that I want to go home is a new thing. To be in my life. I don't think I've ever wanted to be home. I didn't know what it meant. I'm sorry, I don't mean to ramble."

"You're not rambling," he said. "I know just what you mean."

He paid the check and they walked to the hotel in silence. Nora had so many thoughts racing through her head, she couldn't process them all. At the same time, she managed to glance around her and really see things. She saw the old, uneven sidewalks, and the stagnant rain puddles, and the trash collecting in the gutter, and the horse manure in the street, and the lovely old buildings in crumbling pastel shades, and the black night sky, and the wilting trees, and the lights in the distance, across the river, and she was aware of Lake Pontchartrain behind her, and she was aware of the music sifting down the street, bending around the corners, the lost laughter and fractured conversation, and all the business of life, falling like an unexpected snow, a common and uneventful and purely miraculous gift from the sky.

# 15

The sun raced through the windows early, before seven, and Nora groaned and rolled over, pulling the sheet over her head. She had forgotten to draw the curtains. Now she was paying for it. So excited by her recent revelations, she had simply undressed and crawled into bed, hoping to ruminate further. Instead, she had fallen asleep almost instantly. She was paying the price. But she wanted to pay the price. She was surprised and pleased to discover that her epiphany was still strong and valid. She still understood and believed in all the conclusions she had drawn the night before. She lay awake, running them over in her head, expecting to deflate and devalue them, but she couldn't. She didn't want to. She remembered her days in college, when she would smoke pot at night, have some great awakening, only to find in the morning that it was silly and specious. But that didn't happen this morning. She still believed in the plan she had formulated: You're alive. Do something. The directive in life, the moral imperative (if there was one, and she wanted to believe there was), was so uncomplicated. It could be expressed in single words, not complete sentences. It sounded like this: Look. Listen. Choose. Act.

That was an easy enough course of action. She thought she could do it. She really thought she could survive.

So she sang in the shower and smiled while she brushed her teeth, and she thanked God, or some such Higher Power, for her children, and for her awareness, and for her chance to begin again. But the thing she did not count on while she prepared for her day was that there were people out there who were invested in her not moving on. Not discovering the meaning of life, not paying penance, not doing better. There were people who were invested in her staying exactly as she was.

The first such person was her mother, who called just as she was stepping out onto the patio to have breakfast.

"You need to come home," her mother said.

"Yes, Mother, I'm coming home on Sunday."

"No, I mean today. Your children are in trouble."

"What's wrong?" She felt dizzy again, and she thought, *No, of course you aren't going to get away with this. There is further punishment to be had.*

"Well, your daughter cried herself to sleep because she misses you so much, and your son claims you're the reason that the marriage broke up, which is why he wants to go live with his father."

Nora sighed. "These aren't problems, Mother. They are simply the truth. Annette misses me, which is normal, so she cries, which is also normal. Of course Michael blames me, be-

cause I am partly to blame, and I just haven't had the awareness to realize that, or to explain it to him."

"*You're* to blame? That man is a criminal. Have you forgotten he is wanted by the state of Virginia?"

*The hallowed state*, Nora thought, and smiled.

"Yes, but Mother, I chose him, and I elected to stay with
him, knowing all this. Why did I do that?"

"Because you don't know a fool when you see one, that's
why."

"But why don't I recognize a fool? Is that a lesson you forgot to teach me?"

"Oh, so now it's my fault?"

"It's everyone's fault. Human beings are faulty."

"I told you not to marry him."

"You wasted your breath. I needed to do it. And yes, I contributed because how could Cliff really respect someone who
would indulge his vices? Of course he loved me, because I
could not make him stay. I couldn't because I didn't care
enough. It's complicated, Mother."

"You talk like a train hit you," Boo said.

"I don't expect you to understand. I'll be home on Sunday,
as planned. I'll drive down and pick up the kids."

"You don't care that your daughter is weeping in misery?"

"Yes, I care, but it's an experience she needs to have."

"She needs to suffer?"

"She's going to suffer whether she needs it or not."

"I believe you are on drugs," Boo declared. "Has that Simone put you up to something? Has she gotten you on
drugs? I never trusted that girl."

"I know, Mother. You don't trust anyone. And neither
have I, for a long time. But I have decided to trust myself. I
know I'm going to do the right thing."

"You have lost your damned mind."

"If my mind was damned, it was worth losing."

"You're going crazy," Boo declared.

"No, Mother, I have been crazy. I think I am going sane. Sometimes it feels like the same thing."

"You make me tired," Boo said, and Nora suddenly remembered a bizarre statement her mother used to make whenever anyone frustrated her. She'd say, "You make my ass want to chew a tobacco."

She giggled, thinking of it.

Then she said, "Tell the kids I love them and I will see them on Sunday."

"You haven't heard a word I've said."

"Good-bye, Mother."

"Listen, sister, if you think you can get off that easy, you have another thing coming."

"Think, Mother," she said. Boo was always getting clichés wrong. "You have another *think* coming."

"If you had survived the death of a child, you wouldn't be so careless with your own."

Nora thought about letting that remark pass. Through the years, she had practiced that approach with Boo. But suddenly she didn't feel like doing that anymore. The remark was careless and cruel, and it fed the lie that Nora had lived for years.

"I did survive the death of a child. I survived Pete dying. And I always blamed myself, but it wasn't me. It was you."

She thought she heard her mother catch her breath, and she felt frightened by what she was saying, but with her new-found resolve, she could do nothing but keep going.

"I heard him fall out of the bed that night, but I was just a child. I assumed the grown-ups would have taken care of it. And I'm sure he cried, and I'm sure you heard it, but you ignored it. Because that is what you do when children cry. You get enraged, and you wait for it to go away, and if it doesn't, then you punish."

"I cannot believe you are speaking to me this way. He was my child . . ."

"Yes, I can imagine the guilt you must feel."

"You are going to hell, young sister," Boo said, and her voice was tight with anger.

"Maybe you just ignored Pete crying all night, or maybe you went in there and gave him a good spanking, and threw him back in his crib."

"Are you saying I killed my child?"

Nora sighed and prepared to reassure her mother, as was her old habit, and then she realized that she was saying it, did believe it, had always secretly believed it. It might not be true, but it had settled in her heart like an infection. And rather than face the possibility that her mother could do such a thing, she had taken on the blame herself. She would rather live with the guilt than the realization that her mother was probably a monster.

But it was consistent, wasn't it? She remembered, as a little girl, the times she would have an ear infection, and would try to stifle her cries because if her mother came to see about her, she would berate her or possibly spank her to make things worse. She would take her to the doctor only when things got so bad they couldn't be ignored. And any inconvenience at night was not to be tolerated. What was her father doing all this time? Ignoring them all, no doubt, the way he did, denying that he even belonged in this life.

She was about to accuse her mother, then realized that her children were still in her care and she couldn't afford to alienate her. Besides, she was tired of accusing.

"No, Mother, of course not. I'm just tired and under a lot of stress. Maybe I will try to come back early."

"That's more like it," Boo said, sniffing. She paused and made a choking sound. Nora could picture her manufacturing her tears. For some reason, Nora pictured her mother young again, as she was when Nora was a child, with her thick black hair and black eyes and beautiful olive-toned skin. She was smoking then, always, though Boo didn't smoke anymore. She saw her sitting at the kitchen table of the old house, where they lived when Nora was little, all dressed up for a day on the town, pacing in the kitchen as she talked on the wall phone. The telephone number was Hemlock 8071. This was in the days before prefixes were attached. They used code words. But Hemlock? Why would a whole town choose a poison to represent them? It was fitting, but scary, nonetheless.

"I'm sorry I said that about Pete," Nora repeated, though she had every intention of saying it again, when her children were back in her care.

"You should be."

"I'll work on getting an earlier flight. Just take good care of them. And whatever you're angry about, even if it involves me, don't take it out on them."

"I swear, you are plumb losing your mind."

Nora hung up and sat there breathing hard. She should definitely try to get an earlier flight. She had to get her children back. But it wasn't that easy. She had to answer to her friends. She had to make sure they were all right, too.

When she came out into the courtyard, she found all of them except Poppy sitting at a table, staring distractedly into their coffee or up at the trees. They looked as if they had received bad news, and Nora wondered if somehow a verdict could have been returned.

It took her a moment to realize that Leo was with them.

He lifted his coffee cup to his lips with a shaking hand. He did not look at her.

"Did someone die?" Nora asked.

Simone blew cigarette smoke at the clouds and said, "This is Poppy's friend, Leo. He's here to tell us that Poppy's gone crazy."

"Poppy's *been* crazy," Nora said.

"Yeah, but now she's really done it."

Nora looked at Adam, simply wanting to know the facts, but he seemed to think she was asking for an explanation. He only shrugged and stared at his lap.

"She called," Simone said, "a few minutes ago. She's out at her house. And if her story is to be believed, she has dug up her basement floor."

"And found a body," Leo said, finally letting his eyes meet Nora's.

"A body?" Nora asked, her heart speeding up. She looked at Leo and waited for him to go ahead and confess.

Leo read her expression and said, "Nora, there is no goddamned body. There is no dead baby. We've been over this."

"Well, we should go out there," Nora said. "We should find out what's happening."

"We were just waiting for you."

Simone drove, with very little urgency. Nora wanted to take control of the car. She felt panicked. In her imagination, she pictured Poppy down on her knees in the basement, clawing up the dirt with her bare, white hands. At the very least, she pictured her crying, hysterical, letting her paranoid fantasies get the better of her. Why was everyone else so unconcerned? Nora wondered, looking around her. Simone drove with one hand, the other massaging the back of her neck. Leo sat next to her, leaning over occasionally to change the radio station. In the back, next to her, Adam at least had the good sense to fidget. But he didn't make eye contact with Nora. He stared at the scenery and chewed a nail.

Finally Simone pulled up in front of a sprawling Creole mansion, with a wraparound porch, ornate wrought-iron balconies, gables, an enormous magnolia tree in the front yard and an even larger weeping willow beside it.

It was beautiful, but Nora had no trouble believing that the house had a few secrets.

They knocked on the door, but no one answered. Then Leo opened the door with a key. No one asked where he had gotten it. Nora assumed he had had it since high school.

"Poppy? Where are you, sweetie?" Simone called out.

Her flippant term of endearment made Nora feel annoyed.

"We should check upstairs," Adam said.

"No," Leo said. "Downstairs. That's where she thinks the body is."

The house had the curious quality of being crowded with furniture, yet feeling completely unlived in. Not as if its owners had abandoned it, but as if they had never really lived there. Like a museum house, like Monticello, where, try as she might, Nora never could picture Thomas Jefferson living. Couldn't picture it as anything but a place crowded with European tourists and American schoolkids on field trips.

The furniture was not unlike that style—Regency, or whatever the hell it was, with all those curled legs and fancy designs, dark wood, damask upholstery, floral prints, so vivid they were almost obscene, and lots of pewter everywhere. The main room was a double parlor, typical of the era. A writing desk sat at the window, facing out. Nora pictured the legendary Judge Marchand sitting at it, working, scheming.

Leo opened the door to the basement, and Adam preceded

him down the stairs. Nora and Simone hesitated, as if they didn't want to know.

Nora said, "How long have you known that Poppy was crazy?"

"Always," Simone said.

"So why did you ask her to come here this weekend?"

"Because," Simone said, "she was the only person I knew who had seen worse than a rape trial. I knew it wouldn't faze her. With you, I couldn't be sure."

They stood there for a moment, and Nora didn't know how to respond. She looked at the wooden stairs leading down into the basement, a bare bulb swaying overhead.

"Should we go see?" Nora asked.

"Yes. We should."

They walked down the wooden stairs, their footsteps echoing off the bare cinder-block walls. When they got to the bottom, Nora saw Leo and Adam standing next to a mound of dirt. A pick and a shovel were propped against the wall. Poppy was sitting in a chair across from them, legs crossed, hands in her lap. She was smiling.

Leo was holding something. A small, decomposed skull sat in his palm, no bigger than a potato.

"Oh, my God," Simone said.

Nora felt dizzy. She thought about throwing up, but it was a thought rather than a feeling. It was a notion, something it seemed like she should do, though her stomach was too cold and tight to feel anything like nausea.

"His name was Christopher," Poppy said.

Leo shook his head slowly, staring at the skull. "But it's impossible. He took the baby away. This can't be true. I went with him. We took it away."

"He was so little," Poppy said, "I could hold him in the crook of my arm. He liked it there."

Now a real sensation clouded Nora's head, and she thought she might faint. She couldn't imagine how she had gotten to this place, in some basement in New Orleans, with a man who had saved her from being mugged holding a baby's skull in the palm of his hand. How could this have happened? She had played her life out so carefully. Nothing had ever indicated she would end up in this place.

She saw Simone wipe away a tear. But Poppy showed no emotion, except for that strange, stalled smile.

"Oh, God," Simone said. "Poppy, this was real. All this time, it was real."

"What made you think it wasn't?" Poppy asked.

Adam took the skull from Leo and examined it, turning it over in his hands, inspecting it like the scientist that he was, looking for clues. No doubt he was trying to figure out how the baby had died, looking for some evidence of trauma. After a second, he put the skull down on the ground, then looked over into the hole that Poppy had dug. He scratched his chin, thinking.

Leo said, "Oh, God, Poppy, I don't know what to say. I had no idea. You have to believe me."

Adam walked over to Poppy and knelt down in front of her. She smiled at him and ran her fingers through his hair, as if the horror of it all was finally mitigated by the proof, and by the fact that her friends believed her.

Adam said, "Sweetheart, this is not a baby."

She blinked languidly at him. "What do you mean?"

"I mean, it's not a baby's skull. It's a small animal. Probably a cat. It looks like a cat. And those other bones, in the hole there . . . they look like animal bones."

She didn't stop smiling at him. She said, "No, dear, you're wrong. It's a little baby boy."

He shook his head and reached for her hand. The way he was kneeling there, it looked as if he were proposing to her. And he talked to her in the same sweet, solicitous tone.

"It's not a human skull," he said. "I promise you. I know what they look like. I've seen a lot of them."

She shook her head. "No, Adam. This is one time when you're wrong and I'm right."

Adam did not take his eyes away from her. She finally looked at the rest of them.

"You believe me now, don't you?"

Simone took a step forward to peer into the hole. Then she said, "You're sure it's not a baby's skull?"

Adam stood, went over and picked up the skull again. Tracing an index finger along its edge, he said, "Most of the jaw is gone, but you can see how it protruded. There's only enough room here for a tiny set of teeth. Look, at the top here? This is where the ears were. A human's ears are on the side, of course. It's clearly a cat's skull."

Poppy stood and walked over to him. She looked at the skull for a moment, then her face lit up and she said, "Oh, that must be Prissy!"

"Prissy?" Adam asked.

She nodded. "My favorite cat. She liked popcorn. She'd chase it around the floor and then she'd eat it. It was so funny to see. She was black and white. Daddy hated her."

"How did she die?"

"She died," Poppy said, "when I got a B in French. Was that it? No, that was Lucky. I think Prissy died when I got a B in algebra. Or maybe it was because I talked back. It's hard to remember."

"What do you mean?" Adam asked. "I'm trying to understand."

She leaned over the hole and made a gesture toward the rest of the bones. "There are a lot of cats in there, aren't there?"

"A lot of bones, yes," Adam said. "I can't swear they're all cats."

"They are. We never had dogs. But see, Daddy thought it was the best way to teach me a lesson. If I did anything to disappoint him, the punishment was I'd lose my pet. I knew that the stakes were high. I knew the consequences. That was what he told me. So, in essence, I was the one killing the pet. He didn't make me kill them, of course. He did it with a nylon. But I had to watch."

Simone looked at her, as if this fact were even more disturbing than the dead baby. "He killed your pets?" she asked.

Poppy shrugged. "If Daddy hadn't pushed me, I wouldn't have amounted to anything. He said women never amounted to anything without men pushing them. He pushed my mother. Pushed her too hard, I think, right down a flight of stairs. But he was trying to help, you know."

"Oh, God," Leo said.

"Don't act surprised, Leo. You knew him," Poppy snapped, her voice taking on a different tone.

"I knew he was hard on you. I didn't know he was a monster."

"Of course he was a monster. He killed everything that I loved. He wanted to break my spirit. My spirit would be the death of me, he claimed. And he knew how to succeed, because he ran the whole town. People came here all the time, with their offerings, and he did them favors. That was why he wanted you to get rid of the baby, Leo. If you had done that, you would have won my hand, wouldn't you?"

"I couldn't do it, Poppy. I didn't think it was my job . . ."

"So you let him kill the baby. Because that's what he did when I disappointed him. He killed whatever I loved."

"He didn't kill the baby," Leo kept insisting.

"Well, we'll see about that."

Poppy dropped to her knees and started digging in the hole again, using a gardening spade. Adam knelt beside her and tried to take the tool away from her.

"There's no baby here, Poppy."

"There has to be. There must be."

She kept digging, and finally Leo joined in the effort to stop her. But she wouldn't quit, so Simone and Nora pitched in, and finally they all managed to tear her away from the grisly pile of bones, the graveyard of her failures, living right below her all this time, all these years, haunting her every move.

They finally got Poppy upstairs, and she lay down in her old bed. The room still looked like a teenager's room, with white frilly curtains and a handmade quilt on the bed, framed photos of the prom and other high school memories on her dresser, a bulletin board with dried corsages tacked onto it. There was even a yellowed note saying, "Call Louise about graduation Barbeque." Nora had an eerie feeling as she stood in the corner of the room, watching the others tuck Poppy into her bed, as if they were transporting her back to a better time. It seemed to be like some kind of antiquated treatment for insanity, surrounding the patient with evidence of her more stable life, going back to the point where it all began to unravel and plugging the holes as they appeared.

Nora watched and thought, *I hope I never go crazy.*

She thought of her own mother's dalliance with mental illness and wondered if she were destined to repeat it. How could she ever hope to be better than the sum of her parts, which in her case wasn't a hell of a lot? But then she looked at Poppy, who was clearly raised by an evil man, and she was fighting his influence to the bitter end. In fact, it might have been in deference to this cause that she had surrendered her sanity. If that were the case, Nora had no choice but to respect her.

Leo sat next to Poppy once she was tucked comfortably in her bed, and he lovingly smoothed the hair out of her eyes.

"I wish we could see him, don't you?" Poppy said to him. "Our baby, I mean."

"It wasn't our baby, Poppy."

"How old would he be now? Would he be grown up?"

"Yes," Leo said. "He is grown up. He is nearly twenty, I imagine. Probably in college. He's fine, wherever he is."

"I wonder if he remembers me."

"I'm sure he does," Leo assured her.

Adam stood watching the two of them, knowing he didn't have a place there.

"Should we call somebody?" Simone asked.

"Who would we call?" Nora asked.

No one had an answer to that.

Finally it was decided that they would leave her there with Leo. He would spend the night there, and in the morning they would try to find a doctor.

Adam said, "I want to stay, too."

"No," Poppy said, looking at him with a clear expression, as if she suddenly understood everything. "I want you to go. You should be in New York."

"But you're my wife, Poppy . . ."

"Oh, but that was just a way to pass the time. I was putting it off. I was trying to keep it from happening."

Adam seemed confused, but Nora understood what she meant. She had seen this day coming, the final reckoning, the merging of all her tortured moments, coming together in a frenzied confrontation. It was a long-held appointment with the truth.

Adam gave in because he didn't know what else to do. Simone leaned over and gave Poppy a kiss on the cheek. Nora did the same. Poppy smiled, but her eyes were on Leo. She couldn't seem to think of anything else.

"Good-bye, Poppy," Simone said.

"Don't worry about anything," Poppy told her. "My father is a judge. It's all going to be fine."

"What do you mean?" Simone asked.

"I know how it works. I called the judge and I explained it to him. Daddy helped him get his start, you know. He owes Daddy a lot. He has to return the favor. There is a code of ethics here, you know. It's a strange one, but it exists. There are people you can appeal to."

Nora looked at Simone. She thought perhaps there might be a translation forthcoming, but Simone just shrugged and headed toward the door. Adam waited for a second, then followed.

The ride back to the hotel was eerie and silent. The car moved as if in slow motion past all the beautiful homes in the Garden District, past the streetcar line, past the universities, and finally into the Quarter, which gave off a pale yellow glow and a distant clamor of music and laughter, like a radio with a blanket thrown over it.

Suddenly Adam said, "Did you see how many bones there were in that hole?"

Simone shuddered. She said, "It seemed like a lot."

"At least a dozen," he said. "Could that man really have

killed a dozen cats? Could he really have strangled them, with his daughter watching?"

"I think he could have done anything," Simone said. "I think anything could happen here. The harder it is to imagine, the more likely the scenario."

Nora said, "That's probably true of any place."

"No, it's especially evil here."

Nora stared out the window. She thought it was especially evil everywhere.

# 16

Nora and Simone shared a cab to the airport the next day. They didn't talk much. They mentioned the weather and speculated on how long it would take them to reach their destinations. Simone's plane was leaving at ten A.M., and she had to change in Denver. Nora's plane left at noon and was a direct flight.

"Oh, God," Simone said. "I have to put on my wig and do a restaurant review tomorrow. No rest for the wicked."

Nora watched the scenery shoot past. Once they got out onto the highway, New Orleans began to look like any place. Interstates crisscrossing, intermittent stretches of green broken by occasional factories, junkyards, warehouses, chain stores. It made Nora feel as if she and her friends had all been part of some collective dream.

"I wonder what Adam is going to do," Nora said, surprised that she had given voice to that thought.

"Whatever Poppy wants him to do, I expect."

The airport was not crowded, and they both checked in with ease. Simone took time to make small talk with the sky-caps, and Nora watched her charm them, wondering how her friend could recover so quickly. She thought that Simone had been transformed by her tragedy, but it seemed she had not changed very much at all. Maybe that had always been wishful thinking on Nora's part. She remembered the equation that was used in creative writing class to describe the nature of storytelling. The main character starts at point A, encounters an obstacle, overcomes the obstacle to arrive at point B. At which point, the character changes, or does not change.

"People would rather die than change," her therapist used to tell her, back when Nora was hanging on to the hope that Cliff would see the error of his ways.

"But he did change," Nora argued, always resistant to her therapist's logic. "He changed his whole life to be with that woman."

Her therapist considered that for a moment, then said, "Then you might have to confront the possibility that what Cliff did actually took some courage."

Nora felt, for the first time, that she might be on the verge of understanding this concept. And that she might be on the verge of seeing her tragedy as something else—an opportunity, perhaps. A new lease on life. A reason to start over.

But if Simone did not want to change, that was certainly a valid option, wasn't it? There was something to be said for picking up where one left off, the odd comfort of the old familiar. The terrible reassurance of the devil you know.

Simone said, "This is one of the few airports where you can still smoke. Let's go to the bar."

They went to the bar and ordered Bloody Marys. Simone smoked, one cigarette after another, proudly and defiantly, as if she were the sole protector of a sacred American tradition. Nora said nothing and secretly wished that she wanted a cigarette. Simone's defiant nature, as usual, seemed so appealing.

Sitting at the smoke-filled bar, sipping her spicy red drink, Nora wondered if she could be having an epiphany. All her life, she had wanted one. People had them in literature all the time, and she had yet to give up on the idea that hers was a story worth telling. If Leo were here, he would tell her that this sudden awareness, this clarity of purpose, was something that was inside of her, not a vision that would be bestowed upon her by an indifferent Universe. Was it really that simple? Could she really be in charge of it all, down to the tiniest detail? And if she wanted to have an epiphany in the bar of the New Orleans airport, was there really nothing to stop her?

Suddenly Simone said, "Not guilty. How do you like that? All that time and effort, and the bastard is going to get off."

"We don't know that," Nora said.

"You heard Margaret."

"Well, it doesn't change anything. You were raped, regardless of what they say."

"Still, you expect closure," Simone said, savoring her cigarette, twirling it around in the ashtray. "Well, if nothing else, I guess it was a great chance for us to get together. We wouldn't have done it otherwise."

"Really? You think that?"

"Of course not, Nora. Why would we?"

"Because we're friends."

"Let me ask you something," Simone said. "Why is it that we can't support each other?"

"Who? Us?"

"Well, us, specifically. But women in general."

"I don't know what you mean."

"Don't you?" She stubbed out her cigarette and lit another one. "You know what men say about war? They say that when they are in the trenches, they don't think about defending their country or any sort of larger ideal. They are defending their buddies in the trenches next to them. This idea of personal loyalty is what makes war work. And I think the events of this week have proven why women don't make good soldiers."

Nora felt her back stiffen. The old familiar tightness in her throat returned, and she fought the impulse to cry.

"Well, I don't think that's true. And it's not fair," Nora said.

"Jesus Christ, that's my point. Only women care about what's fair. Men succumb to loyalty. Blind faith."

"Simone, honestly. I left my children with my mother to be here. That was a very big sacrifice."

"You had your doubts, though. And Poppy never really believed me."

Nora sighed. She felt exhausted, as if the whole ordeal had been some tiresome initiation.

"Oh, come on, what's the big deal about belief? We were there for you. I can't account for your expectations. No one can."

Simone shrugged, studying her cigarette as if it were her source of power, or her only friend.

Nora said, "Look, what happened to you was wrong. I'm sure of that. Nothing can change it. And probably no one will ever understand it."

"I guess no one can ever follow me to where I've been," Simone admitted.

"Would you want them to?" Nora asked.

"Of course I would. Nobody wants to fight their battles alone."

"But there's no other way," Nora said, with a confidence she did not realize she possessed.

Simone slid off her barstool and swayed on her feet for a moment.

"I'm going to make a phone call," she announced.

"Okay, I will, too."

They went to a bay of pay phones, all of which were empty. They were the only people in the airport without cell phones, it seemed. Pay phones were one of many concepts which would soon be rendered obsolete, like typewriters and record players, checkbooks and, eventually, cash. Nora's head was swimming from the Bloody Mary, and she thought, the world is changing faster than I can keep up with it. How can I have an epiphany at this pace?

Nora dialed the number of her mother's house. But Boo didn't answer. It was Michael who said hello.

"Hi, honey. It's Mom. I'm at the airport. I'll be home soon."

"Oh, good!" Michael said, not bothering to hide his excitement.

Nora thought she must have heard him wrong.

"Good?" she questioned.

"Yeah. We've missed you."

"We?"

"I mean, Annette has. Mom, when you get home, can I buy a Telecaster?"

"What's that?"

"An electric guitar. They're cheap, like four hundred dollars. The kid who lives next door to Grandma has one. It's so cool. You could take it out of my allowance."

"But four hundred dollars. That's a lot, Michael."

"You bought ice skates for Annette."

"We'll talk about it when I come home."

"It's an activity, you know? It's like, learning something. You were always bugging me to take piano lessons. So why is this different? You know, if I have an interest, like music, it reduces the chances of me getting involved with drugs."

Nora laughed. "Oh, yes. Rock musicians are famous for staying away from drugs."

"Come on. Really. I want to do this."

"What does your father say?"

"Forget that," Michael replied. "He's an asshole."

"Since when?"

"I called him to talk about moving in . . . or at least spending the summer with him. He says he's going to be very busy. He doesn't want me."

"Well, I'm sure he doesn't mean that."

"Yes, he does. And I'm thinking if I had a Telecaster, I could be happy living with you."

"Well, that's reassuring."

"Look, it isn't so bad living with you. I mean, I'd kind of miss Annette. She's a goofball, but she's okay. I pulled her tooth, did she tell you? It was really loose, and I tied a piece of dental floss around it."

"So you really don't want to live with your father?"

"No. It was just an idea. Hey, Grandma Boo is crazy. Did you know that? She made me get up in the middle of the night to clean the cat's litter box. Did she ever do that to you?"

"Oh, yes."

"So, can I get the Telecaster?"

"We'll talk about it."

Of course she would get him the Telecaster. She would get him a thousand guitars, she thought. She'd drive him to his lessons, and years from now, she'd sit in the front row at his concerts. She'd do anything for him.

"Did you have fun in New Orleans?" he asked.

"It was interesting," she admitted. "I went to the bayou. I saw an alligator."

"No shit!"

"Michael."

"You say shit."

"Yeah, but I'm the parent."

"Okay, well, I'll see you when you get here. Don't let the plane crash."

"I'll do my best."

She hung the phone up and stood there for a long moment, smiling at the ground.

Simone approached her, looking dazed, her eyes fixed on Nora's face but not really seeing it.

"You want to do this all over again?" she asked.

"This what?"

"I just talked to Margaret. The judge wants to declare a mistrial. Seems one of the jurors forgot to disclose the fact that he's distantly related to the defense counsel."

"You're kidding."

Simone shook her head.

"How did he find that out?" Nora asked.

"An anonymous tip. It checked out."

They looked at each other. Was it possible that Poppy had managed to intervene? And if so, did it even matter?

"Well, what does that mean?" Nora asked.

"Margaret said that they would pursue charges again, with my consent."

"And if you don't consent?"

"It goes away. Quentin Johnson walks, I go about my business."

"At least it would be over," Nora said.

Simone shook her head. "Not for me."

"You're willing to do this all again?"

Simone stared at the tiles on the floor for what seemed like an eternity. Then she looked up at her friend. "You have a daughter. What would you want?"

"I'd want him to go to jail. I'd want him to pay," Nora said. "But that's my tragic flaw."

Simone stared at the strangers moving past them, as if they might somehow provide the answer.

"Fuck it," she said. "Let's do it again."

"All right."

"Will you come back?"

"What do you think?"

Simone smiled and squeezed her friend's hand. "Okay. I need a cigarette."

They drank two more Bloody Marys, and then Simone's plane started boarding. They hugged at the gate, and Nora stood back and watched as her friend walked through the metal detector. Simone paused to chat with the security guards, and their laughter echoed down the corridor. Nora smiled. So much good will, purchased with charm. Simone was still looking for an ally in the eyes of a stranger. This was part of the lesson she had not learned. And maybe that wasn't a bad thing at all.

Nora glanced at her watch and saw that she still had more than an hour to kill before her own flight boarded. She wandered around the food court but decided she wasn't the least bit hungry. It occurred to her that she had not bought anything for the kids, and they would be expecting something, so she made her way over to the gift shop.

Suddenly she saw Adam at the counter, buying a newspaper and a bag of peanut M&Ms. He was counting coins out of the palm of his hand, carefully, like a child parting with his hard-earned allowance.

She stood still until his eyes met hers, and he smiled.